THE VENUS SHOE

by Carla Neggers
launches

AVON'S NEW VELVET GLOVE SERIES

"IT'S WHAT WE FEEL IS A NEW TREND IN ROMANTIC FICTION—ROMANTIC SUSPENSE. THE VENUS SHOE is fast-paced romantic suspense in the Mary Stewart tradition . . . A book you'll be afraid to put down."

Kathryn Falk,
Romantic Times

"With THE VENUS SHOE, Carla Neggers has successfully brought the romantic mystery form into the 1980s."

Vivien Lee Jennings,
Boy Meets Girl

"THE VELVET GLOVE SERIES WILL BECOME AN EXCITING ALTERNATIVE TO THE STRAIGHT ROMANCE. ALL OF THE SENSUALITY AND MAGNETISM OF ROMANCES IS THERE AND ALSO THE 'CLIFF-HANGING' TENSENESS OF GOOD SUSPENSE."

Affaire de Coeur

"Mrs. Neggers' THE VENUS SHOE has the wit and panache of Charlotte MacLeod and receives a solid five-star ranking."

Barbra Wren,
Barbra Critiques

"THE VENUS SHOE weaves together a riveting tale of an unsolved mystery, a dangerous man, and a beautiful woman. The survival of love holds the reader in as much suspense as the danger."

Terri Busch,
Heart Line

Other Books in the
Velvet Glove Series:

CAPTURED IMAGES *by Laurel Winslow*
LOVE'S SUSPECT *by Betty Henrichs*
DANGEROUS ENCHANTMENT *by Jean Hager*
THE WILDFIRE TRACE *by Cathy Gillen Thacker*
IN THE DEAD OF THE NIGHT *by Rachel Scott*
THE KNOTTED SKEIN *by Carla Neggers*
LIKE A LOVER *by Lynn Michaels*
THE HUNTED HEART *by Barbara Doyle*
FORBIDDEN DREAMS *by Jolene Prewit-Parker*
TENDER BETRAYAL *by Virginia Smiley*
FIRES AT MIDNIGHT *by Marie Flasschoen*

Avon Books are available at special quantity discounts for bulk purchases for sales promotions, premiums, fund raising or educational use. Special books, or book excerpts, can also be created to fit specific needs.

For details write or telephone the office of the Director of Special Markets, Avon Books, Dept. FP, 1790 Broadway, New York, New York 10019, 212-399-1357.

Velvet Glove 1

The Venus Shoe

Carla Neggers

AVON
PUBLISHERS OF BARD, CAMELOT, DISCUS AND FLARE BOOKS

THE VENUS SHOE is an original publication of Avon Books. This work has never before appeared in book form. This work is a novel. Any similarity to actual persons or events is purely coincidental.

AVON BOOKS
A division of
The Hearst Corporation
1790 Broadway
New York, New York 10019

Copyright © 1984 by Denise Marcil and Meredith Bernstein
Published by arrangement with Velvet Glove Inc.,
Library of Congress Catalog Card Number: 84-91076
ISBN: 0-380-87999-9

All rights reserved, which includes the right to reproduce this book or portions thereof in any form whatsoever except as provided by the U.S. Copyright Law. For information address Meredith Bernstein, Literary Agent, 33 Riverside Drive, New York, New York 10023 or Denise Marcil Literary Agency, 316 West 82nd Street, New York, New York 10024

First Avon Printing, July, 1984

AVON TRADEMARK REG. U. S. PAT. OFF. AND IN
OTHER COUNTRIES, MARCA REGISTRADA, HECHO EN
U. S. A.

Printed in the U. S. A.

WFH 10 9 8 7 6 5 4 3 2 1

For my parents, Leo and Florine Neggers

Chapter One

I DON'T know why, but I was surprised the island had changed so little in seven years. I expected the blueberry bushes would be gone, overrun by staghorn sumacs and choke cherries, and as dead as my girlhood. They were there still, and so were the sparrows and the clearing where my father and I would beach our canoe, and the cluster of rocks where I would play when I tired of picking blueberries.

It was only me, Artemis Pendleton, I thought wistfully, who had changed.

Then a song sparrow pranced and trilled in the brush, and suddenly I was a girl again. I could see my father in his work pants and undershirt, his bushy eyebrows drawn in a command for silence. We would stand still and listen to the sparrows. Later he would tell me their song was "Madge, Madge, put on your tea kettle," and I would be amazed. Every year we went blueberry picking, and he would tell me things and I would be amazed. Everything he said seemed so important. I knew about the sparrows, and I knew to pick some red, unripened blueberries because they had more pectin, and to use a three-pound coffee can as a container because it had a plastic top and wouldn't tip over easily.

I had never picked blueberries alone. I had never come to the island alone.

I closed my eyes and tried to shut out the trilling of the sparrows.

Madge, Madge, put on your tea kettle . . .

Father wasn't there, and I was alone. And yet I knew about the sparrows and the red blueberries and the coffee can. He had told me, I had been amazed, and I remembered.

I opened my eyes and, smiling, ducked under a sumac to a shoulder-high bush of wild blueberries. I had been right to come after all. It was a shame I hadn't come earlier: Blueberry season was almost over, and now there wouldn't be enough berries for jam.

Two hours later the coffee can I had borrowed from my landlady was almost full, and I was sweaty and scratched and as content as I had been in years. With a happy sigh I set across the tiny island—a matter of thirty yards—to the clearing, where I peeled off my shirt and bra, tossed them in the shade with my day pack, and climbed out onto a flat rock. The air was still and muggy. The lake was clear, inviting. I knelt, dipping my hands into the water, and splashed my breasts and stomach. I rose and started to remove my shorts so I could dive into the cool water, but I froze with my thumbs tucked in my waistband and managed to hold back a scream of shock.

Just below the rock, off to one side, lay a man's hand.

It was opened and relaxed, tanned, not particularly callused. The nails were blunt, the wrist thick, with coarse, light hairs that somehow reminded me of my half-naked state. A large boulder blocked any view of the rest of the body.

I took in shallow little gulps of air that wouldn't make much noise. Probably the man attached to the hand was asleep or unconscious—or dead. I didn't know which to hope for. Very carefully, my eyes never leaving the motionless hand, I tiptoed off the rock. A twig snapped under my bare feet. I stood very still, waiting for a reaction from the other side of the boulder. Nothing happened. The sparrows began trilling. I wanted to shush them as I grabbed my shirt.

I wondered if that was all there was: a man's hand.

I shuddered, and quickly, as if something horrible might happen if I took my eyes off the hand, slipped my shirt over my head. I didn't bother with the niceties of the bra.

I straightened my shoulders and took a deep breath. Why was I so afraid? The bogeyman, Father had always said, was only in my imagination. Being afraid of whatever was behind that boulder wasn't going to change it. I started to march toward it but then decided to tiptoe.

I crept to the top of the boulder with the somewhat vague idea that this would give me a definite advantage over whatever—or whomever—I would see on the other side. I lay down on my stomach and peered down.

He lay in the shade of the gray birches.

At first I thought he *was* dead, but then I heard his steady breathing. He was merely asleep. He was no boy or scrawny college kid. His long, muscular legs seemed to go on forever. His chest under the black, clinging, collarless shirt was broad, and I silently took in the obvious strength of his relaxed, outstretched arm.

Yet he seemed vulnerable snuggled up against the lichen-covered rock. Now that I could see what was attached to that outstretched arm I was strangely unafraid. His face was tilted three-quarters up at me. I didn't recognize him, but still he stirred something in me. His jaw was very square, his nose straight, his mouth firm, even in sleep. His skin was pale beneath his light tan, and I guessed he had missed no more than this morning's shave. His tawny hair was tousled and unruly.

He looked very tired, as if he could sleep for hours. I crept down off the boulder and went around and knelt beside him. It seemed the logical thing to do. Now I could see that his jeans and shirt were still damp, his hair wet on the ends, his feet bare.

I made a move to wake him so I could find out who he was and if he was all right.

No. We were on an island in the private lake of a private estate. I knew everyone who worked and lived there. He was not one of them. I frowned.

He could be a guest at Rosewood, I reasoned. It wasn't likely, but it was possible.

My fingers curled around a rock not much bigger than my fist—just in case. With my other hand, I tapped the man gently on the shoulder. "Hello, are you all right?"

He grimaced in his sleep.

I should creep away in my canoe and pretend I never saw him, I thought. I tried again, more loudly. "Hello, sir, are you all right? I don't mean to disturb you, but—"

He swore and bolted up, suddenly wide-eyed and angry

and very alert. I was ready to make my escape—or at least try. But then he saw me and the unfriendliness left his eyes. He even seemed amused. I didn't know what he expected, but it wasn't a thin blond with blueberry stains on her shirt.

"Well, well," he said, "and I thought mermaids didn't exist. I see I was wrong."

I tried not to be too obvious about the rock. "My name is Artemis Pendleton," I said very politely. "I found you here, and I thought you might be hurt. I'm sorry I woke you."

He leaned against the boulder and narrowed his eyes as he ran them over me. Whatever had stirred in me earlier stirred again. I sat very still and wished I had bothered about the bra after all. I could feel my breasts unrestrained beneath the fine cotton of my sleeveless shirt and knew my nipples were outlined against the fabric. My blond hair trailed down my back in an untidy braid, and wispy curls stuck to my sweaty forehead. My blue jogging shorts were well suited to blueberry picking, but a bit baggy. I was not, I thought wryly, at my gorgeous best.

He sighed irritably, as if I had told him something he didn't particularly want to hear. Every feature—the thick eyebrows, the gray eyes, the straight, arrogant nose, the determined mouth—was hardened into aggravated alertness. I chewed unmercifully on my lower lip. What had I done? What had I said?

"Four goddamned islands in this goddamn lake, and you pick the one I'm on." He sighed again. "Jesus Christ."

So much for being a mermaid, I thought. My hand tightened around the rock. "Not intentionally, I assure you," I said in a voice steady with rectitude. "Who are you?"

His eyes flickered over me again, and he exhaled, more frustrated, I thought, than angry. "The name's Todd."

"First or last?"

"First." Deep lines cut into his forehead with his frown. "So what are you doing here?"

I decided not to push for a last name. "I was picking blueberries. I've finished—"

"Blueberries? Here?"

I nodded, not vigorously.

"Jesus Christ." He shook his head wearily, as if he

couldn't believe my answer. His eyes rested on me again. I licked my lips, trying to look confident and cool despite the perspiration glistening on my forehead and the flutter of uneasiness in the pit of my stomach. "So what do people call you?" he went on. "Artie or Missy or—"

"Artemis."

His eyes held me. They were darker than the rock behind him, a darker gray than I had ever seen in eyes. I tried to make out blues or greens in them, but there was only that hard slate gray. Now that he was awake, he seemed anything but vulnerable. I knelt uncomfortably with my hand still on the rock.

"You work for the Harrisons." It was not a question. His voice was quiet but deep and almost matter-of-fact. He sat in a half-cross-legged position, his damp jeans stretched taut over his thighs. I nodded absently, wondering how he knew. Perhaps he *was* a guest at Rosewood.

"Are you loyal?" he asked.

"Not particularly. I've only been here three months. Why?"

"Because I'm trespassing on Harrison property." He almost smiled, but his tone didn't change: still quiet, deep, matter-of-fact. "I'd rather not have to go through a long and embarrassing explanation of why I'm here."

I didn't think much would embarrass this thoroughly competent-looking stranger. "Oh."

"I suppose you want to hear it."

"No, not really."

He looked at me sharply. "What's that supposed to mean?"

I scowled, suddenly indignant.

"It means trespassers are not uncommon here. It means I'm tired, I'm hot, and I don't care who you are or what you are. I was just making sure you were all right."

I shut my mouth and regretted my outburst immediately. I *was* tired and hot, but I did care who and what he was. I watched his eyes travel over me again—suspicious, probing. Perhaps he was wishing I'd been a mermaid after all. I didn't know, but, despite my growing uneasiness, I was determined not to flinch under his scrutiny. He was nothing more than a common trespasser. A poacher, perhaps. Let him look! But my lips were dry, my throat tight, and I wondered why I'd been fool enough to have wakened this man.

At least the spirit of my father was all around me, and I knew if it came to that, I'd go down fighting. . . .

Then, impossibly, he grinned. A dimple appeared unexpectedly in his left cheek. "Blunt, aren't you, Artie? Sorry I scared you."

"You didn't," I said, only half lying.

The grin vanished and with it the dimple. He grasped the trunk of a birch with one hand and pulled himself to his feet. He looked down at me with a hint of amusement in his eyes. "Then why don't you put down your rock?"

"My rock? Oh. I didn't realize I still had hold of it." There was nothing to do but drop it and stand up beside him. It wouldn't do me any good, anyway. Todd—whoever he was—looked tough and more than capable of handling a woman who came up to his shoulders. Physically, at least. I still had my wits, and they had daunted more than one man in the past. I smiled. "I guess I'll be seeing you, then."

"No—" he said abruptly, stopping me as I started past him. He smiled quickly, the disarming dimple returning. "I was hoping you wouldn't mind giving me a ride somewhere. I don't think I'm up to another swim."

I tried not to look too taken aback. Of *course* he had swum here. His clothes were still damp. Oh, God, why hadn't I left him sleeping?

"My boat capsized and I couldn't right it—"

"Okay, okay." I hoped my impatience disguised my nervousness. What choice did I have? "My canoe's over here."

I started past him again, but this time I stopped on my own; only briefly, just long enough to notice that his left hand was wrapped in a wet, bloody handkerchief. I gave him a tight smile and went on.

He grabbed my shoulder with his good hand. His grip was firm but not harsh, and in spite of my uneasiness, that indefinable something stirred in me again. Unbidden, my eyes wandered over his face and saw there a refinement, an intelligence, I hadn't noticed before. Here was his chance to pitch me into the lake and take off with my canoe. Instead he stood there, and I couldn't help but react to the pressure of his hand on my shoulder, the intensity of his gray eyes searching my face.

"I snagged my hand on the boat motor," he said. "It's nothing. I'm not going to hurt you, Artie."

"I should hope not."

I wished my words sounded more indignant, but he let me go and I led him around to the clearing where I had beached the canoe. I knew at least part of what he said was a lie. How could he capsize a motorboat on a still, muggy day like this? And if by some freak chance he had, where was it now? Why hadn't I seen it on my way over? And why, if he was a trespasser who didn't want to make a long and embarrassing explanation to the Harrisons, would he cruise about their lake in a motorboat?

The lie itself was unimportant, at least to me, at least at the moment. What was important was the rest of what he had said. I knew then that this tall stranger wasn't going to hurt me.

He regarded the canoe with disrespect. It was twelve feet long, of battered wood and peeling red paint, and looked its two decades. "Rather a relic, isn't it? Yours?"

"No," I replied, hesitant.

One side of his mouth twisted upward, suspiciously. "I thought you said you weren't chummy with the Harrisons."

"I'm not," I said.

"This is their canoe, isn't it?"

"Yes. I borrowed it."

"With or without their permission?"

What difference did it make? Who was he to ask all these questions? *I* had a hundred questions I wanted to ask him—about who he was and what he was doing on my father's tiny blueberry island. But I said, "Without."

He grinned, and with the reappearance of his dimple and good cheer, I again felt strangely drawn to this unknown man. Todd with the bloody hand. He was good-looking, into his thirties, I guessed, but those were just simple facts. There was something else. Something fundamental . . . slowly, unwillingly, I admitted that I was very attracted to him. He had a physical presence I couldn't ignore. I couldn't shake the feel of his fingers on my shoulder, or the way his eyes had held me.

This had never happened to me before . . . never.

"A woman after my own heart," he said. "Shall we be off?"

After an awkward and obviously painful boarding of the canoe, Todd looked at me wanly and said he didn't know a damned thing about canoes, but if I told him how to paddle he would do his best. So, I thought, he *couldn't* have stolen my canoe, even if he'd wanted to.

"Don't bother," I said. "I can manage alone."

"I should have known," he muttered.

I laughed, but then I noticed his enigmatic look and was quiet. He seemed transfixed. Was it because I had laughed? "There's food in the pack," I said, changing the subject.

He eagerly pulled out the French bread, Havarti cheese, cucumber, and tomato I had packed earlier and discreetly ignored the bra I had shoved in with them before climbing into the canoe. I had figured there was no point in leaving behind a perfectly good bra, but now I was embarrassed. Pointlessly, it seemed. Todd was giving my lunch a disgusted look. "A feast only in the eyes of the starved," he said. "Care for any?"

"I could use a sip of the iced tea."

"What—oh, here it is. You do look a bit fried. Really, if you just show me how to hold one of those oars—"

"They're paddles, and you would only make it more difficult, especially with that hand." I drank from the thermos and handed it back to him. "Where do you want me to take you?"

He pointed to an inlet about two hundred yards west of the island. "That grove of pines over there will do."

I didn't think it necessary to point out that there was no need to worry, that the largest island, a tangle of dwarfed evergreens and thickets, obstructed a view of us from Rosewood's main grounds along the southern shore. Nor, I was sure, did I have to tell him that on a hot Sunday afternoon, no one was likely to be about anywhere along the rest of the lake's shoreline, which was mostly woods and a few neglected fields.

Todd held up a tomato, the reddest and plumpest from my landlady's garden. "How do you propose I eat this?"

"Like an apple."

"And this?" He held up the whole, unpeeled cucumber, also courtesy of Mrs. Martin. "Like celery, I suppose? Well, my dear girl, if I have cramps tonight, I shall know whom to blame. Do you always eat like this?"

"I like fresh vegetables."

"One would hope," Todd muttered, and bit into the tomato. Juice squirted over his hand. He frowned. "Tell me, what do you do at Rosewood?"

"I'm a gardener."

He was silent.

"I have a degree in plant science," I added.

"Do you?" He wasn't impressed. "From where?"

"The University of Massachusetts."

"How did you end up working for Richard Harrison?"

To answer truthfully would probably have taken hours, and even then I wasn't sure I would have arrived at the real reason I was working for Richard Winthrop Harrison, millionaire, gentleman farmer, owner of the thousand acres in upstate New York that were Rosewood. I wasn't sure I knew myself, so I said, "I applied for the job."

"Oh. But you're from Massachusetts?"

"Not originally," I said, careful to keep my voice even. "I grew up here—in Saratoga, I mean."

"What, are your folks divorced or something?"

"No."

"You aren't living with them, I take it."

We were just passing the time, I told myself. Idle chitchat. I said again, "No."

"Where do you live?"

"In Saratoga."

Satisfied, he finished off the tomato and started on the cucumber. "How do you like working at Rosewood?"

"It has its moments."

"I don't know, gardening sounds a bit tedious for a pretty girl. You must love your flowers."

He was trying to goad me now. I could see the twinkle in his eyes. It made me want to laugh, but I held back. "Actually, I intend to specialize in plant pathology when I get my master's."

"Aha! Now I see the light. You're saving your nickels and dimes to send yourself to graduate school. I suppose you're the kind of person parents tell their kids to be more like. Can't your folks help you out?"

"You seem to be very interested in my parents," I said

hotly. "If it's any of your business—and it isn't—they're dead."

I hoped my bluntness would embarrass Todd into silence, but it didn't. "Victory in the face of adversity," he said. "I suppose you graduated magna cum laude."

"Summa," I corrected with a snarl and knew I was overreacting, but I was hot and tired, and the memory of my parents was keen, a freshly opened wound. He couldn't know that.

"Well, then, I should think several dozen universities would offer you scholarships."

I sighed wearily. "It's just not that simple."

But it was. I had worked in the field for three years after graduation, and when I finally had applied to graduate school, universities were falling all over themselves to help me out. Six had offered me full financial aid packages. I had expected to choose one and enroll this September, but here it was, the first week in August, and I was . . . in a canoe with a man with a bloody hand who asked too many questions and was far too physically appealing—far too masculine—for my comfort. I wanted to be rid of him, and quickly.

But that, too, was another lie: I wanted to know all about this Todd, who he was, why he'd come to Rosewood, what had really happened to his hand. Beyond that, I wanted to know what it was about him that so intrigued me and made me so aware, even as I paddled along in the lake, of my own basic physical response to him. I had never been touched so immediately and so deeply by a man.

He, however, was still asking questions. "Are you naturally brilliant or just an over-achiever?"

He was half teasing, but I decided to answer him seriously. "I enjoy my work."

"But of course," he said mockingly. "I should have known you were one of those virtuous little students who accentuates everyone else's inadequacies with displays of calluses and tribulations overcome. The geniuses who float through life by virtue of their chromosomes are much easier to tolerate. I suppose your foremost obstacle is poverty. When did your folks die?"

Back to them again. "Seven years ago. In a car crash."

"That is tragic." He sounded as if he meant it. "What were you, twenty, twenty-one?"

"About." I had been two months shy of my eighteenth birthday, but why tell him that? "I moved in with my grandparents in Hadley. That's how I established my Massachusetts residency to attend the university."

"Your parents died here in Saratoga?"

I nodded. May twenty-fourth, eleven in the morning, and not just here in Saratoga.

Here. Here at Rosewood.

"Excuse me," I said. "What were you saying?"

"I was asking what made you come back up here."

"I told you: my job."

"I know, but why did you apply for it?"

His questions, I thought, were far more intentional than I had assumed. And he was nowhere near as disinterested in my answers. Or was it the heat playing on my overactive imagination? Father had always said an active imagination is a good thing: It keeps a worker from getting bored. Father. He and Mother—their memory—had brought me back to Rosewood. But I said, "Because there was an opening on Rosewood's staff, I have a degree in plant science, and I needed the work."

He grinned and mimicked me. "If it's any of my business." He rinsed his hand in the lake water; the other lay limp in his lap. "You know, you make a far better virgin moon goddess than a gardener."

Artemis, the Arcadian moon goddess. When I was little I thought Artemis was just the name of my dead aunt and me, but then I learned about the mythological origins of my name. Now I'm easily mesmerized by full moons, especially when I'm sipping Jack Daniel's, straight with no ice. There had been a full moon last night and a glass of Jack Daniel's at my side as I sat out in my landlady's backyard. Together they had made up my mind to come to the island this morning, but I knew I had made up my mind a long time ago, perhaps, even, when I had said I'd left Rosewood for good seven years ago.

Somehow I wasn't surprised Todd was familiar with the goddess Artemis.

"Don't forget," I said distantly, "Artemis was also goddess of the hunt."

"Oh, I know. Quite a vicious beauty, wasn't she?" He seemed amused. "You must know the story of Actaeon, the poor boy who chanced upon the goddess bathing. I believe she turned him into a stag and he was killed by his own dogs. How does the saying go?" He leaned toward me, his voice lowering, "There is none who has lifted the veil of Artemis and lived to tell it?"

I concentrated on paddling and licked my lips. "You're up on your Greek myths."

"Does that make you nervous?"

He seemed pleased with the idea, which both irritated me and gave me courage. He may not be an *ordinary* trespasser, I told myself, but he had an injured hand and didn't know how to paddle a canoe—not that he couldn't manage if push came to shove. Nevertheless, I was in control of the situation as much as he was. Besides, he didn't even have the foggiest notion how physically attractive I found him. And I was not about to tell him.

I smiled noncommittally. We had come to the pine grove. I maneuvered the canoe through the shallow water of the inlet and grabbed hold of a jagged rock that protruded a few inches out of the water.

"Can you wade the rest of the way?" I asked.

"I think so."

I hung onto the rock while Todd climbed out. He nearly tipped us over before clearing his long legs. He splashed into the thigh-deep water. Fresh blood oozed from his makeshift bandage, but he smiled. "Thanks for the ride."

"Sure."

"I'm an innocent trespasser, Artie. I know it must not look that way, but I am. I'd really appreciate it if you didn't mention me to anyone, but especially not to the Harrisons."

"All right. R. W.'s death on trespassers, you know. I'll keep your secret for you. You're a figment of my rabid imagination."

"Thanks, Artie." He patted my shoulder once, and I thought he would leave it at that, but he didn't. He leaned toward me and let his lips graze mine. "You're an interesting woman, Artie Pendleton," he said softly into my mouth.

I didn't think I responded—not outwardly, at least. He

remained very close and looked into my eyes as if searching for something, waiting. "I'm not afraid of you, you know," I said, my voice a breathy whisper.

"Good."

Slowly, boldly, his hand slipped down my shoulder and touched my breast. Impossibly, the nipple responded to his light, almost tentative touch and stood out against the dampened fabric of my shirt.

"Perhaps if we'd met under different circumstances—"

"Perhaps," he replied with a small smile.

He put his hand on my shoulder again and kissed me. His lips played against mine with such insistent gentleness that my body was left with no choice but to respond. My grip loosened on my paddle, and my free hand touched his elbow, very lightly. With no effort at all, this stranger was bringing forth responses from within me that I had long learned to control and repress at will.

At last he pulled away, reluctantly, I thought. I grabbed hold of the paddle with both hands, tightly, and told myself perhaps I should be glad he was going.

"Thanks, Artie," he said.

There was a huskiness to his voice, and suddenly I knew that he, too, was having difficulty controlling and repressing his physical responses. The attraction between us was something neither of us understood, but it was there, immediate and undeniable.

"You'll be all right?" I asked.

"I plan to be."

"Oh, mind the dogs. Dobermans. They patrol the grounds."

He gave me a strange look, then said dryly, "Yes, I know."

His hand. Of course: the dogs. Todd, whoever he was, had had a run-in with Mr. Harrison's Dobermans. I watched him wade to shore where he climbed onto the shaded, needle-covered bank. He gave me a curt wave, seemed to hesitate, then disappeared behind a thick, knotted pine. I thought I heard the crunch of a twig. Then all was silent.

A figment of my rabid imagination.

I turned the canoe around and paddled slowly out of the inlet.

Chapter Two

I WENT back to the island, stripped, and jumped into the water. I was hot and hungry and not entirely convinced I *hadn't* simply imagined the tall stranger with the bloody hand. Perhaps the effects of the moon and the Jack Daniel's still lingered, or perhaps coming to the island again, feeling the presence of my father, had prompted an illusion. A fantasy.

But why did my body still tingle with the memory of his kiss, his touch?

I dove deep and tried to wash away the feel of him but did not succeed. I couldn't respond so wholly to someone I'd conjured up. And, of course, there were the little pile of plastic bags and the empty thermos, all that remained of my lunch, to confirm his existence for me.

I decided he was what he said he was: an innocent trespasser who wanted to avoid making a lengthy and embarrassing explanation to the owner of Rosewood. I didn't blame him. Probably he had been camping, or fishing, or hunting . . .

And the bloody hand, the wet clothes—how did I explain them? Obviously he'd had a confrontation with the Dobermans, but why had he fabricated the story about the boat?

I didn't know. So I dismissed my questions as curiosities that might have come out in the explanation I had told Todd I didn't want to hear.

Besides, poachers and thieves don't quote Ovid.

But neither, I thought unhappily, do innocent trespassers.

I crawled onto Todd's boulder and lay on it like a lizard, letting the sun warm, dry, and relax my body. He could have plundered all of Rosewood and I doubt I would have moved.

At length, I jumped down and dropped onto the tufts of field grass still matted down from Todd's weight. The shade had shifted, exposing his cozy niche to the driving afternoon sun. At least, I thought, I had found him when I did. I felt the blood rush to my face when I imagined myself climbing down from the rock stark naked and planting my feet on a sleeping man.

I shuddered and ducked behind the boulder. Was he watching me, even now?

Then something caught my eye. A black object, perhaps a wallet or a shoe, lying in the dry yellow grass under a huckleberry bush.

It was a gun.

Not a hunter's rifle but an ugly little automatic with a short barrel and a bumpy handle. I picked it up. I had never touched a gun before. It didn't make me feel powerful.

It made me feel very, very nervous.

An innocent trespasser, my ass! How could I have been so susceptible to his charm? He owned a gun. I was disgusted with myself . . . and coming down with the creeps.

I quickly put the gun back where I found it. Todd would never know I had seen it. He—

No, that wouldn't do. I couldn't just leave it for him. Suppose he used it to kill someone? Just because I had let him kiss me—and kissed him back—didn't mean he was harmless. It didn't, in fact, mean anything except that he was damned good-looking and I knew it.

There was only one solution: Get rid of the gun. Toss it into the lake.

But that wouldn't do, either. The gun was evidence—of what, I didn't care to speculate. There would be fingerprints, registration numbers that could be traced. . . . He might as well have left behind his name and address. I had to keep it.

And when he came back and found it gone, he would know exactly who had it: Artemis Pendleton, the gardener.

Still, there was no choice. With two fingers, I picked it up at the very end of the bumpy handle. No doubt I had already muddled Todd's fingerprints with my own. I carried it gingerly to the canoe and laid it in my day pack.

Then I got dressed and headed back.

I half expected the strange man with the bloody hand to be waiting for me at my apartment. But he wasn't. Of course, I thought, he would wait until dark to go back for his gun, and then when he didn't find it, he would come after me.

No, he would hightail it out of Saratoga and never mind the damned gun. Indeed, if I were he, I wouldn't even go back for it. I would take me and my bloody hand as far from Rosewood as I could get and figure this Pendleton character had gone on home, had some lunch, and forgotten all about me.

Ha!

I locked my door and dropped my stack of Sunday newspapers on the floor. Then I made a pot of tea and a batch of blueberry muffins and settled down for an afternoon of research.

Afternoon waned into evening, and I still hadn't found any article—not even the tiniest item of news—that pointed to a man with a bloody hand and a gun who quoted Ovid. I laughed. The man quoted Ovid, not the gun.

Ridiculous. I got the gun out of my day pack with a linen napkin and laid it on my closet shelf under a straw hat with silk daisies stuck to a green ribbon that I had worn in a wedding party two years ago.

Then I froze up half the blueberries, stuck the rest in the refrigerator, and did *The New York Times* crossword puzzle.

Whoever Todd was, he was gone and wouldn't be back for me or his gun. My adventure was over.

I thought I might have found all of Rosewood dead the next morning, but instead I learned not of dead Harrisons, but of dead Doberman pinschers. One dead Doberman, actually. A second had been wounded—knocked on the head—and a third shut up in an abandoned cabin.

Adelia Harrison told me about the grisly scene in a ten o'clock meeting in her bright, country-decorated sitting room. Jeffrey Chapman, the head gardener, was there, and since I'd been inside the Rosewood mansion exactly twice

The Venus Shoe

during my three months as gardener, I sensed I was in trouble.

"You wouldn't happen to know anything about it, would you, Artemis?" Adelia asked, giving me one of her patricianlike smiles.

I smiled back. So she knew about my blueberry picking. It was my second meeting with the mistress of Rosewood since my parents' funeral. The first had been accidental, one afternoon late in May. She had stumbled on me in the rose garden, and I think I somehow shocked her. She mumbled, "Why, you look—you look . . ." Then she left quickly. I wanted to ask, I look what? Well adjusted? Normal? Happy? Content? Seven years was a long time, long enough, at least, to recover. But, I thought, not long enough to forget.

"I don't, no," I said innocently. "It sounds like the work of a trespasser." A tall trespasser with a wan grin and an incongruous dimple in his cheek, a man who had kissed me and quoted Ovid . . . a man whose gun was under my straw hat, and a man I couldn't seem to get off my mind.

"Undoubtedly, but we thought perhaps you'd seen some sign of him or her—or them. You *were* out on the lake yesterday, weren't you?"

Adelia didn't look like she wanted to chew me up and spit me out. She simply looked like she wanted an answer to her question. Maybe she thought I had done the damage to the Doberman pinschers, but I didn't think so. I watched her as she watched me. She wore a pink-flowered sun dress, and her flawless face was so perfectly made up she looked closer to forty than the fifty she was, but not the thirty I suspected she would have liked to be. It was getting difficult to hide the fine lines at the corners of her dark brown eyes. She patted her short brunette curls. She was Richard Harrison's second wife and seemed bizarrely artificial to me. I stood there, not trying to figure a way out of my predicament, but trying to figure out if she were real.

"You were seen, Artemis," Jeffrey Chapman said frigidly.

Jeff was Adelia's handpicked successor to my father and, in my opinion, a prig. We didn't get along. He didn't like it that I had written to Richard Harrison asking for a job at Rosewood and that he'd given me one without consulting his head gardener. I suspected Adelia didn't like it, either. The Pendletons were all better off forgotten. I didn't blame anyone at Rosewood for my parents' deaths, but they all knew it had been their driveway and its vicious curves that had killed them.

And I didn't blame Jeff for resenting me. Martin Pendleton was a hard act to follow, but he had managed to avoid the inevitable comparisons simply by being so incredibly opposite my father. Instead of stocky, muscular, blond, habitually dressed in work pants and T-shirts, Jeff was tall, lean, and wiry, with dark hair, a long, thin face, and a surprisingly thick mustache. I had never seen him in anything but three-piece suits. He had degrees in plant science and landscape design and never but never got his fingernails dirty. What he *couldn't* avoid was the fact that the grounds at Rosewood were largely my father's creation, from planning to planting, without benefit of a degree or even much of a staff.

Then along came Marty's daughter. Bad enough I had a degree and old Marty's disposition, but to have R. W.'s backing as well didn't endear me to Rosewood's Jeffrey Chapman.

"Oh, well," I said, shrugging, "what can I say? I took a canoe out to one of the islands and went blueberry picking. It was just something I had to get out of my system. My father and I used to go there often when I was young. You don't mind, do you?"

Adelia beamed at my deferential tone. "Why, of course not, Artemis! No, no, we were just wondering if perhaps you had seen anything or anyone suspicious. The attack on the dogs was quite brutal."

I recalled my stranger's bloody hand and suspected the attack on him was considerably more brutal. "How was the one killed?"

"Hit on the head," Jeffrey replied, "with a rock, apparently."

So—possibly—Todd had had a second confrontation with the dogs, *after* I'd dropped him off at the pine grove. He had had to clobber the Doberman with a rock because I was back on the island discovering his gun.

The Venus Shoe

Which meant he probably had missed it . . . and knew exactly when and where it had disappeared.

"How ghastly," I said.

Adelia leaned forward and centered a vase of fresh roses on an antique pine table. "Indeed. Those weren't attack dogs, but I've always told Richard something like this could happen. They won't be replaced. I don't like the idea of Doberman pinschers—no matter how tame—patrolling our grounds. One never knows when they might turn wild, and certainly an ordinary trespasser wouldn't know the difference."

I was relatively certain *my* ordinary trespasser would argue that the three Dobermans were indeed attack dogs. There wasn't one good reason not to tell Adelia Harrison and Jeffrey Chapman about him and his gun, except that I had promised not to. . . .

I had never been afraid of him, but, rather, drawn, intrigued, stirred. For reasons I had not yet been able to pinpoint, never mind understand, I wanted to see Todd again, which meant I couldn't nail him for defending himself against the Dobermans.

"I wish I could help you," I said lamely.

"No matter." Adelia held one hand up and wriggled her fingers, dismissing the subject. "I also asked you and Jeffrey here for another reason, Artemis. I know you're both very busy getting the grounds in shape for Labor Day weekend—we expect two hundred fifty people this year, did I tell you? I do hope we'll have good weather!"

"Oh, we will," Jeff assured her, on what authority I didn't know.

I began to breathe more easily.

"Well, no matter what, it will be a memorable party. Richard has hired the best caterers in New York and a jazz band and—well, that's not why I asked you here, to discuss the Labor Day weekend!"

She pushed herself straight up on the couch. I listened in disbelief. The incisive tone of a moment ago was gone. Adelia Harrison was once again playing the beautiful hostess of Rosewood, the society woman, the millionairess. And she was *chirping!* All I could think of was Tweety Bird. How could anyone who chirped be real, for God's sake? But suddenly I felt sorry for her: Did she think because she was rich and beautiful she had to play dumb to get along with people? Or maybe I just wasn't used to being around shallow, wealthy women and should quit looking for depth where obviously there was none. According to house gossip, Adelia Harrison not only chirped, she bitched. Frequently.

"We have a problem to solve," she went on. "I took my coffee into the conservatory yesterday morning and was horrified at the condition of the plants there. Just awful! I know that's not your fault, Jeffrey, of course. I discovered that an eighteen-year-old part-time summer employee has been in charge of their care. She doesn't know a thing about plants! I spoke to Richard about it, and he agrees that the indoor plants ought to be as stunning as those on the grounds."

"Of course," Jeffrey said heartily. "I'll get someone in here at once."

"Oh, but I don't want one of your big, clumsy field hands, Jeffrey. I want Artemis."

I had seen it coming. So, obviously, had Jeffrey. There was no use arguing. Adelia had made up her mind—and R. W.'s, too—that I would be the one to resurrect her conservatory. I would also be obliged to wear servants' whites instead of my usual shorts and top. That brought a gleam of satisfaction to Jeffrey's eyes.

He put me to work plucking wilted marigold blossoms for the rest of the afternoon. I would start in the conservatory the following morning.

I considered writing to all six graduate schools that had accepted me and begging them to let me enroll this September. I had accomplished all I had hoped to by coming to Rosewood.

No, I thought, I hadn't.

There was still the matter of my not exactly ordinary trespasser. Something in the story about the Doberman pinschers had struck a nerve. As I pinched off marigold blossoms with my fingers, my mind wandered. I couldn't quite pinpoint what it was that bothered me. Not the inference that there had been more than one trespasser. Jeff and Adelia hadn't seen Todd. I was fairly certain he could single-handedly kill one Doberman, wound another, and shut up a third. . . .

And then it had hit me: The third Doberman pinscher had been shut up in an abandoned cabin on the lake.

Before he married, my father had lived in a cabin, now abandoned, that overlooked the lake on the northwest shore.

It stood next to the pine grove where I had left Todd.

Chapter Three

Two weeks later Todd still hadn't come for his gun. I went out to the cabin once, but there was nothing that suggested more than a chance confrontation with three Doberman pinschers. The cabin had been used by trespassers before; why not now? Todd must have slept there, and in the morning the dogs had found him. He escaped by jumping into the lake and swimming to the island. There was a high ledge in front of the cabin. The Dobermans wouldn't have followed him off it into the water. But when he returned, they were there waiting for him.

I enjoyed the melodrama for a while. Every morning when I left for work, I would leave a little piece of paper in my door. It was always there when I returned in the evening, but, even so, I would make a stealthy entrance into my apartment. I would open the door gently and stand there, mop in hand, breath held, waiting for any intruder to betray himself. Once I thought I had something, but it was only my cat Ralph jumping off the refrigerator. I went after him with the mop, anyway, but he dodged and instead I hit my Madagascar periwinkle.

After that, I didn't bother with stealthy entrances.

In the end, I concluded that Todd was neither a thief nor a murderer—nor anything but a harmless, though *not* ordinary, trespasser. To be honest with myself, I was also forced to conclude that despite the kiss and all that he had stirred up inside me, Todd wasn't about to risk having to explain himself to the Harrisons, or to me, simply to see me again. We had been there together on that island and in the canoe, and he had simply taken advantage of the opportunity by kissing me. It was a blow to my ego—or, at least, I tried to pass it off as such. But that wasn't easy. The regret that we would never see each other again was too real, the loneliness that crept up on me at night too palpable. I missed Todd, although I didn't even know him. It was a strange feeling, frightening, but not one I could ignore.

Nor could I continue to ignore his gun. It still lay under my straw hat. I would have to get rid of it. By now I was sure it could never be traced to Todd. No doubt it was devoid of any fingerprints but my own, and illegal for me to keep under a straw hat in my closet.

But what to do with it? I couldn't just dump it in the trash. It was a gun, not some inoffensive hunk of garbage. I certainly couldn't bring it to the police to dispose of. What would they say when I told them how I'd come across it? *And why did you keep it so long, Miss Pendleton?*

"Toss it in the lake," I muttered to myself. "That's what I should have done in the first place."

I was sitting at the end of the dock in front of the boat house with my feet in the water. It wasn't quite nine o'clock. I had ridden my bicycle to work, as I usually did on Saturday, but this morning, instead of stopping for tea and croissants at a bakery I couldn't afford, I'd come straight to Rosewood and down to the lake to contemplate my problem with the gun.

A gruff voice erupted behind me. "You talking to yourself, Missy?"

I looked up at Bud McCarty. He was the commandant of the boat house, sixty-nine, tall, heavyset, and looked as Scottish as his name would suggest. He had been my father's best friend. He was also the only person in the world who could ever get away with calling me anything but Artemis.

I smiled. "A habit of long standing."

Bud frowned, as I expected him to. "You should have someone besides yourself to talk to."

"I have Ralph. Now don't get excited, Bud. He's only a cat."

I should have known better than to get flippant with Bud. He would do anything for me—except sanction my return to Saratoga.

"You have no business being here!" His face turned red,

and he shook a thick finger at me. "Rosewood is no place for you."

"Oh, Bud—" We'd been through this before.

"Why did you come back here, eh? Why? Nobody wants you here. You remind everybody of things better off forgotten. You should be with your grandparents."

"What makes you so sure they want me?"

"They do."

He said it emphatically, as though anything to the contrary would totally upset the cosmos. He was right. They did want me. They had opposed my decision to take a job at Rosewood. They couldn't understand why I didn't just live with them on their dairy farm in Hadley and commute to UMass, or why I didn't just go on and marry the blasted conifer pathologist I had been working for and be done with it.

"I know, Bud," I said in my best appeasing tone. "And I'm enrolling in graduate school this January, though I doubt I'll last here that long. I think I'll throw a screaming fit if I hear Emily and Marie Harrison discuss the eligible men coming Labor Day one more time."

A mischievous grin lightened Bud's face. "You should go on and find yourself an eligible man, Missy. It would be good for you."

I thought of the conifer pathologist, thirty-five, divorced, demanding more than a research assistant. I had turned him down, and he had fired me.

"I'm not so sure," I told Bud. Then I, too, grinned. "I don't think I'll ever get married. I'll live alone with my plants and Ralph and—"

"Oh, go on with you, Missy. You'll only need the right man to ask."

"I've been asked four times already."

"Liar. Besides, they weren't *right*."

"All right, three. One was serious, more or less. But—I guess I'm just too smart for men, Bud."

"You have too good an opinion of yourself, Missy. Now go on up and get to work. It'll be nine o'clock."

I gave the grizzled old cuss a kiss on the cheek and followed his advice. About getting to work, that is. Not about finding a man.

Even after two weeks, all too frequently my mind refused to acknowledge the questions with which my Ovid-quoting stranger had left me and drifted instead toward him, his grin, his thrilling touch. In our brief encounter, we had shared at least the possibilities of love and passion, fulfillment and commitment. Maybe it was just the perversity of fate that they were all that I had left of that hot day: possibilities. But somehow, despite my certainty that he would never return, I knew I wouldn't be too smart for Todd. After all, I had *been* myself—and he had kissed me.

I was trying desperately to convince a fatshedera it was alive when Emily and Marie Harrison wandered into the conservatory for brunch. I was hoping they would wander themselves right on out to the terrace, but they settled down at the white round table just a few yards from where I sat on the floor. I pretended not to see them.

Then Emily's tanned kneecaps were under my nose. I had to look up. She waved her coral nails at me. "Good morning, Artemis."

I nodded and plucked a dead leaf off the fatshedera.

"Would you care to have a cup of coffee with us?"

That was a first. Emily and Marie were Adelia's daughters, adopted by R. W. when he married their mother twelve years ago, and as suspicious of the common classes as I was of the wealthy classes. They were also as superficial as their mother: They chirped.

"Thank you," I said, wondering if I had misjudged Emily, the prettier and more sophisticated of the two sisters. "But I don't drink coffee."

She fiddled with the diamond on her necklace, which I thought looked gauche with her tennis dress. But that's my opinion, and my opinion didn't matter at all to Emily Harrison, which was a point in her favor. After two weeks indoors, I had figured out that everyone's opinion mattered to Adelia. She wanted to be worshipped by all—even the angora cats and old Marty's daughter. Emily didn't give a fig who adored her, or who hated her.

She laughed. "Suit yourself."

She started to bob back to the table but turned to me one more time. "You know," she said, "you really have turned this horror into quite a paradise. What's your secret?"

I smiled. "I know a dead plant when I see one."

Marie giggled from the table. She had her sister's long face, but not her thick, walnut hair. Marie's was a lifeless brown, for which she compensated with exotic styling. She was twenty-four, educated at Sweet Briar, and on the prowl for a husband, which I thought was passé for a woman of the eighties, but apparently not. Emily, two years older, had already had a stab at one husband, but she divorced him a year ago and now, according to house gossip, was working on a second in the form of a publisher from Boston.

"You mean all you've done is throw out the dead plants?" Marie said.

I said yes because it was easier than explaining which plants had died and why, which plants I had pruned and why, and which plants I had moved and why. The process had been fairly straightforward, and the results were obvious. The conservatory was transformed. It was a large room that jutted off the main body of the house and received east and west sunlight from floor-to-ceiling windows on three sides. The short south side faced an expanse of lawn and the brick path that led to the rose garden and, farther down the long slope, the lake. The long west wall overlooked the front lawns, and the long east wall opened onto the big stone terrace.

I went back to my fatshedera, and listened, one more time, to Emily and Marie chatter about the upcoming Labor Day bash, just one breathless week away. I had already heard all about the musicians and the skiers and the executives and the tennis star and the actors and the architects. . . .

I decided the fatshedera needed special attention in my workroom off the kitchen. Emily and Marie were too busy discussing the attributes of a certain television journalist to notice me leave.

Nancy Lerner nearly knocked me over on my way down the hall. She was the pudgy, freckle-faced Skidmore freshman responsible for the premature demise of two dozen of the conservatory plants, but she was also the nicest and smartest person I had met since coming to Rosewood. She caught the fatshedera on its way to the floor and, blushing, handed it to me.

The Venus Shoe

"I'm such a clod with plants," she admitted. "How's it going?"

"Fine, how are you surviving? I thought I saw you polishing silver earlier—"

"Three tons of it, I swear!" Nancy moved closer to me, conspiratorially; she adored Rosewood gossip. "Did you know Emily's broken off with her boyfriend?"

"The publisher?" I wasn't interested. "Well, she'll find someone else."

"I kind of feel sorry for her—"

I laughed. "You've been listening to Nora too much. She lives and dies on Emily and Marie," I said. Nora was the head housekeeper, a contemporary of Bud's, and about as pleased with my appearance at Rosewood as he was. "I assure you, Emily Harrison is a survivor."

Nancy was not convinced, but I knew my opinion mattered to her. I remembered being eighteen and thinking anyone twenty-five had to be worldly.

"Listen," she said, "a couple of friends and I are getting together in town tonight for a few drinks. You can join us if you want."

I was thinking of a gracious way to say no when I remembered Bud's lecture. Perhaps I did need someone to talk to. Sitting home alone one more night thinking about Todd and what to do about his gun wasn't going to do me any good. I was getting into a rut, and I was lonely.

"Thank you. I think I will."

She couldn't hide her surprise as she gave me the details. I wondered if I was that much of a snob, dismissed the thought, and went off with my fatshedera.

Saratoga Springs is the biggest town in one of the fastest growing counties—one of the few growing counties—in the Northeast. It used to be the watering hole for the country's wealthy and controversial, but the Gilded Age is over, casino gambling outlawed, and almost all the huge, sprawling hotels razed. Perhaps Saratoga could have become a quiet, unremarkable town in upstate New York, but that wasn't in its nature. Instead, it built the Saratoga Performing Arts Center, summer home of the New York City Ballet and the Philadelphia Orchestra and coveted amphitheatre for popular entertainers, and continued to capitalize on its location at the foothills of the Adirondacks to lure people from the cities.

And, of course, with the track still in town, Saratoga could never be quiet and unremarkable, at least not during August. Every summer since 1863, thoroughbred racing has come to Saratoga Springs, attracting thousands.

My first weeks back in town, I had prowled through all the new boutiques that accommodated tourists and the growing number of year-round residents. I peered into the elegant and trendy restaurants and admired the houses up and down the side streets, which were being renovated or had been renovated in my seven-year absence. It was all so very "cachet" now.

I arrived at the crowded tavern just off Broadway at nine instead of eight-thirty. Nancy and her four friends—Karen, Terry, Peter, and George—were already gathered around fake Victorian tables drinking exotic drinks. They all seemed so young.

After being introduced, I said a general hello, sat down, blew out the candle under my chin, and ordered Jack Daniel's, no water, no ice. Five sets of eyes widened. I wondered what Nancy Lerner had been telling her friends about me.

"Artemis, I thought you didn't drink!" she said.

"I don't, usually," I replied, not wanting to undermine Nancy's position as authoritative informer. "I have a weakness for Jack Daniel's."

I changed the subject and started a discussion of summer jobs. It made me feel like an undergraduate again. George was working for a local builder, and I listened carefully to his description of the renovations he was doing on a Victorian mansion on Circular Street. He was twenty-one, an economics major at Dartmouth, and the oldest of the five. I had a feeling Nancy had picked him for me.

The waitress delivered my Jack Daniel's and handed me a folded cocktail napkin. "Some guy over in the corner asked me to give this to you. Do you mind?"

"No, of course not."

I opened it up, six sets of eyes watching, and instantly went pale at the neat printing: "Artie: I'm in town. We need to talk. Come to my table or meet me outside. Alone. I don't want your friends to see me. Todd."

"Artemis, what is it?" Nancy asked.

The waitress was hovering. "I guess I should have told the guy to stuff it, but I'm a sucker for a handsome face," she said. "What do you want to do?"

"Leave," I mumbled, clutching the note.

"I can make sure you get out all right," George offered.

I regarded George's stocky build, but knew it was no use. He was more of a match for Todd than I was, but not enough of one. And I didn't want to involve him. All the romantic possibilities I had had about Todd vanished in the face of reality. I remembered all too clearly that he carried a gun. I shook my head, trying to think.

Nancy suggested we all go somewhere else, but again I shook my head. Leaving as a group would only make it easy for Todd to follow us.

The waitress took charge. "All right, look. You slip out the front and I'll run interference for you, okay?" She grinned. "I'm great at spilling drinks on people."

She scooped up my Jack Daniel's and was off. I left her a big tip, smiled as best as I could at my curious friends, and sneaked through the crowd.

Chapter Four

A BREEZE stirred the warm evening air. I started off at a brisk walk and forced myself not to break into a run. My Ovid-quoting stranger was back in town. Todd. The man with the wan smile, the dimple, the bloody hand. The owner of the gun under my straw hat. I supposed he would want it back, provided, of course, he knew I had it.

I tucked a strand of loose hair behind my ear as I crossed the narrow side street, lined with big old Victorian houses, and started down another, just as narrow and poorly lit. I paid no attention to the footsteps that were behind me, until, of course, they were beside me. Then I looked up.

Todd grinned and took me by the elbow. "Hello, Artie."

The dimple was there still, but I refused to be charmed. Neither it nor the firm yet gentle hold he had on me would make me forget my terror when I had found his gun. This was a man who had fought off three Doberman pinschers. I wouldn't forget anything I had discovered about him. But, wisely, neither would I show him what I knew. I smiled witheringly. "Hello, Todd, or whoever you are."

"I'd like to have a word with you, if you don't mind."

"Would it make a difference?"

He wasn't smiling now. "Not this time, no. We could have talked inside, Artie. It was your choice to leave. I saw your waitress coming at me and beat a path out the back."

I shrugged, as if it were all the same to me, which it wasn't. But as far as he was concerned, I thought he was only a harmless trespasser. A figment of my rabid imagination. I tried very hard not to remember how we had kissed: Let him think that sort of thing happened to me regularly.

"I didn't like your tactics," I said nervelessly.

His left hand remained tightly clamped on my elbow. I now could see that the Dobermans had torn the skin from his knuckles up past his wrist, but, except for a few scabs, the wound had healed. I wondered what he would do if I screamed. I wasn't particularly anxious to find out. He was taller, more muscular, and altogether more threatening than I remembered. His face was shaved, his hair combed but still unruly, his fine cotton pullover and well-cut pants neat and dry. He looked as though he belonged on Emily and Marie Harrison's list of eligibles. I had liked him better as a competent-looking but innocent trespasser who needed a shave.

And happened to carry a gun. I couldn't show him I knew about it, but I had to remember it!

The Todd I had missed and daydreamed about must have been the figment of my imagination, I thought, not this man. This man was real—scarred, threatening, perhaps even armed.

My stomach quivered with uneasiness, and I wished I'd drunk my bourbon before I'd sneaked out, but I said without fear, "Why do you want to talk to me?"

"Because I owe you an explanation. It's all right, Artie. Relax, will you? My car's over here."

He guided me to a dark gray Alfa Romeo just up the street. Maybe he wasn't dangerous, but he was definitely not a hapless trespasser. Then who? He opened the door on the passenger side and didn't let go of my elbow until I was sitting down and he had given me a look of warning. Then he shut the door and went around to the driver's side.

I considered bolting, but only for a moment. I couldn't outrun him or his Alfa Romeo, so why arouse his suspicions by trying? He said he owed me an explanation, and I agreed with him. If he said I owed him a gun . . .

He seemed even bigger next to me in the Alfa Romeo. He started the car and grinned down at me. "Don't look so glum. I'm harmless."

"How do I know that?"

He let the car idle in neutral and looked at me. Understanding crept into those gray eyes. Even warmth. Without any warning at all, my mind and body conjured images and feelings of what it had been like to kiss him, to have his hand touch my half-naked breast . . . *The gun, idiot!* I sat up straight: I would *have* to remember the gun.

"Trust me, Artie," was all he said before he shifted into first and edged the car down the road.

"Why can't we talk right now—here?"

"Because your entourage might come out and see us and think you need rescuing."

"Maybe I do need rescuing."

He looked over at me and flashed his most unmenacing grin. "Since when? You strike me as a woman who can cope with just about anything. We'll talk at your apartment. Court Street, right?"

I nodded. "How did you know?"

"Freckles. She talks a lot if you ask her the right questions."

"You mean you came up to her at the restaurant—"

"No, she told me everything at Rosewood."

I blinked, confused. No, it couldn't be . . .

"I asked about the lady gardener and she said you were meeting her and her friends for a drink tonight, and that you have an apartment on Court Street. No roommates. I thought she'd have told you all about me by now."

"She didn't. We—I—we didn't talk about Rosewood. You're—" I was flustered, which wasn't my usual style. "What are you doing there?"

He gave me a princely bow. "I'm a guest."

"You!"

"But of course. My name is Todd Hall. I drove in from Boston this afternoon."

For two weeks he had been a mystery. I had thought about him just short of constantly. Made things up about him. Given him last names, jobs, places to live. Decided what kind of cars he would drive and how he would look dry and neatly pressed. For two weeks, he had been mine.

Now he was taking on an identity. I had never come up with the name Hall or Boston or even an Alfa Romeo. And, most certainly, I had never imagined that he would turn up as a guest at Rosewood.

He radiated strength and power and confidence. There was nothing vulnerable about the man looming beside me. Nothing. I remembered how he had looked snuggled up against the boulder on my tiny blueberry island. This was some barely recognizable incarnation of that same man.

I wanted my hapless trespasser back.

"Look," he said, "if you're going to vomit, please do it out the window. You should at least have your Jack Daniel's over ice, Artie."

"You smug bastard." The words just tumbled out. Anger, outrage, had fast undermined my caution. *This man was a guest at Rosewood!* "Who the *hell* do you think you are? Just because you're a guest of the Harrisons does *not* mean I have to kowtow to you and—" I waved a hand. "Stop the car. At once. I don't want to talk to you. I don't *have* to talk to you."

"Artie," he said calmly, not stopping the car, "you're being an ass."

I refused to look at him. "I didn't drink the Jack Daniel's. Not even a sip. The waitress was going to pour it down your neck. I wish she had. Your note scared the living daylights out of me—"

He asked mildly, "Why should my note have scared you?"

I saw my mistake at once. He had kissed me good-bye in the lake. We had parted as friends. I wasn't supposed to know about the gun. Oh, hell. I tried to cover up as best I could. "You should have come right up to my table and said, 'Artemis Pendleton, I want to talk to you.'"

"Why? I didn't particularly want to explain myself to Freckles—"

"Her name is Nancy Lerner. And why not explain to her as well? You don't expect me to keep our little meeting secret any longer, do you?"

I regretted the question the moment I asked it. Todd said, somewhat ominously, "Yes, I do."

I changed the subject. "This is a one-way street. You're going the wrong way."

"Am I? Oh, well, Court Street is down around here somewhere, isn't it? I would have gone to your apartment in the first place, but I couldn't wriggle away from the Harrisons until eight-thirty, and that's when I understood you were to meet your little friend. I fully expected her to tell you all about the goings-on at Rosewood after you left. Frankly, I had no idea how you would react."

"What goings-on?"

He looked at me curiously. "I see I have quite a bit to tell you. Who were your other friends tonight?"

I told him, not very graciously, unable to see what difference it made or why he cared—or if he cared. At least it was a diversion.

"I take it George is the one who fell for you the instant you flashed your lovely smile. Another victim of the stern moon goddess. Well, you certainly do your name justice tonight. Pigtails and blueberry stains are not your forte."

I had changed from Adelia's prescribed "servant's whites" into fashionable gray linen slacks and a raspberry silk top but wore no jewelry and only a trace of lipstick. My hair flowed down my back.

"You're only making this more difficult," I said quietly.

"I think I was complimenting you."

He turned down Court Street without my having to point it out. I looked out my window. Even without seeing him, I reacted to his presence. Again there was that strange, indefinable stirring within me, that pull to him that I couldn't control. The Harrisons had invited Todd Hall to their estate. He would have a good excuse for being on it two weeks ago. And he would have an explanation for the gun. He was no longer hapless, but he *was* harmless.

I pointed to Mrs. Martin's pale yellow Victorian house. "My apartment's on the second floor," I said in a voice suddenly gone dry. "In the back."

It was only as we were climbing the stairs that I remembered he had told me he was trespassing. And I remembered the Dobermans. Panic rose in me, but it was too late: He was staying very close to me.

Mrs. Martin had left her back porch light on, which made the climb up the first few steps less treacherous. I could have run blindfolded up the rickety stairs, badly in need of paint and stacked with junk. Todd stumbled on a bucket of clay pieces from broken pots.

"My landlady is seventy-two and prone to calling the police when she's disturbed in the middle of the night."

That curtailed his swearing, but he muttered, "Ten o'clock is hardly the middle of the night."

My second floor porch was really more of a landing with a balustrade of wood posts, several missing, and a floor of creaky planks painted green too many years ago. There was no roof. Black boxes of marigolds sat precariously on the railing while the floor was stacked with plastic bags of peat moss, perlite, foam, sand, and vermiculite, more pots, my lounge chair, my trash barrel, and, of course, my mop. Todd stood next to a clothes rack that displayed my bathing suit, two sets of underwear, and a dishtowel.

"Is this thing safe?" he asked, gesturing broadly.

"Probably not."

I unlocked the door, kicked it open, and stood aside for Todd Hall to walk in before me.

"It's like a goddamn jungle in here."

I didn't know if he referred to the windows and shelves full of plants or the general clutter of my tiny studio apartment. I said lamely, "I get good morning sun."

"Yes, of course, that would make a difference. I should think you would feel a bit cramped."

"It suits me."

That was true. I had broken any number of decorating rules, but many of the things were mine, and, in some odd way, meant something to me. The brass bed stuffed into the alcove next to the front door was covered with a heavy lace spread, which had belonged to my parents. The big round oak table that stood in the middle of the room was highly polished and centered with a vase of wild flowers. I had decorated the kitchen alcove with calico curtains and a friend's pottery. An ugly old couch, covered with two of Grandmother's impossible afghans, and tables, stools, bookcases, wall shelves—all loaded with plants and books —overwhelmed the other side of the room. The bathroom and closet were on the far wall, the door to each covered with music festival posters. I had to shove furniture all around in order to do a proper push-up.

Ralph jumped from the refrigerator, plopped on the floor, stretched out his front legs, arched his back, and yawned.

Todd took a step back. "Good Christ, what the hell is that?"

"Ralph. He adopted me."

"Ugly devil, isn't he?"

He was. Except for a few ungodly black splotches on his face and hind end, he was white with short, coarse hair. He had the longest, gangliest legs I had ever seen on a cat, and big double paws.

"He's not particularly friendly, either," I said, "but he's good company."

Todd Hall shoved aside a bulb catalog and sank into the couch. "Could I impose on you to make some coffee?" He gave me a charming smirk. "Nothing like a nice cup of coffee to help resume a friendship."

"I don't think we've ever been friends, Mr. Hall, but if you want coffee, I'll make some."

"Anything to please me?"

"Hardly," I said levelly. I put the kettle on and dug in my cupboard for the jar of coffee I kept around. "All I have is instant."

He said that was fine. I could scrape enough out of the bottom of the jar for two cups. I decided to go ahead and make myself a cup and finish it off.

Todd fidgeted on the lumpy couch, then finally reached behind him and pulled out an open book.

"William Faulkner?" he said, eyebrows raised. "You are full of surprises. God knows what you have tucked away in here. I'm afraid I wouldn't know where to begin looking for my gun."

I dropped the spoon of coffee I had measured and watched it spill over the counter. So he knew I had it. I had to be careful. Very careful. I did not look at him.

I could sense him grinning at me. "Ah, yes. I thought you would know what I was talking about."

I cupped my hand and wiped the spilled coffee into the mug. "No, as a matter of fact, I don't," I said in the same flat tone I had been using. "You just startled me when you said *gun.* Is that what this is all about? You think I have your gun? Wonderful. Well, I don't, though I wouldn't be surprised if you carried around a submachine gun. Milk and sugar?"

"Neither," he said.

He was watching me closely. I poured the water into the two mugs with as steady a hand as I could manage after the transformation of my mystery man into a Rosewood guest, now sitting in my apartment asking me about his gun.

I set the mugs on the table. "I'd prefer to sit over here, if you don't mind."

"Near the knife drawer?" He laughed and crossed over to the table. "Or do you think you'd spill it? You're trembling, Artie."

"I'm tired," I said. "Look, now that you know I don't have your gun, you can drink your coffee and go."

"On the contrary. You do have my gun, and now that I know it, I can drink my coffee and ransack this place until I find it."

"I don't have it."

"You do." Todd narrowed his eyes at me, amused. "I suppose you'll stick to your story until I tell you I saw you find it. Oh, for heaven's sake, Artie, you needn't blush. I was two hundred yards away. Unfortunately. Now will you admit you have it?"

"I don't have it," I said. "I threw it in the lake."

"Did you now? Well, good for you. I don't believe you, of course, but it doesn't matter. I don't really want the gun. You can keep it." He sipped his coffee. "Good Christ, what is this stuff?"

"Coffee," I said.

"Damn, that's awful. Where did you get it?"

"I don't know. In Amherst, I think—"

"Amherst? How the hell old is it?"

"Two years, but it stays good."

"It does not."

I shrugged. "It all tastes the same to me."

"It must. Well, never mind. Why didn't you go to the police after you found my gun?"

"I believed your story," I said. "I checked the papers for any crimes you could have committed. Though when I heard about the Dobermans—"

"Oh, you know about them?" Todd glanced at his hand. "Vicious beasts. Damn well nearly killed me."

"Why did you lie about the motorboat? You should have guessed I would find out about the Dobermans—"

"No, at that point I had not done injury to them. I had escaped them, more or less. One had gotten my hand in his mouth. I got it out again and promptly jumped into the water, with the profound hope, I might add, that they would be less inclined to jump from a thirty-foot ledge than

I. I probably would have escaped them a second time, but you had to go skinny-dipping and find my gun."

"Why didn't you use your gun in the first place?"

"Forgot I had the damned thing. Then, of course, when I finally was compelled to fight off the beasts, my gun was in your hands and not mine."

I thought about what he had said for a moment. "Was that why you had the gun in the first place, because you knew about the Dobermans?"

"Yes, of course. Why else? For all the good it did me."

"They weren't supposed to attack. How did you know—"

"My dear, I am not one to trust anything that walks on four legs. If I had any sense at all, I would indeed have brought along a submachine gun. That, of course, brings up the central question: What was I doing at Rosewood? I suppose you want to hear my explanation now?"

"However long and embarrassing."

"I have no intention of going into all the gory details with you, but it should satisfy you to know that this whole thing has to do with Emily Harrison and why our relationship is currently on the rocks."

He stopped there and sipped his coffee. It took me a few seconds for his words to sink in. "Emily? But she—oh, dear, you're not her Boston publisher, are you?"

"I'm a publisher," he said stiffly, "but I'm certainly not Emily's."

No wonder he could quote Ovid, I thought. Damn. All thoughts of the gun, the Dobermans faded—replaced by an unfamiliar anger that I suddenly recognized as jealousy. Ridiculous! I began to arm myself emotionally. Gardeners do not allow themselves to be smitten by guests of the people for whom they work. Even smart, educated, temporary gardeners such as myself. It wasn't a question of feeling inferior to Todd Hall but of just not intending to allow things to get carried away with him . . . if I could help myself.

He had lapsed into silence, ignoring his coffee, watching me. For no reason—none at all—a shiver went down my spine and settled in the small of my back. It might have been a shiver of pure and honest lust, but it wasn't. I was alone in my apartment with a man I didn't know. Todd Hall, a Boston publisher. Said who?

Todd, I remembered, hadn't wanted Nancy Lerner to see him.

I tried not to let my sudden uneasiness show. "All right, so you're the publisher who's been seeing Emily Harrison. So what else?"

He made a face at his coffee mug and shrugged. "Nothing important."

"I'm sorry, but you'll have to do better than that!"

"Why?" he said, as if he didn't know.

"You can't be serious." I sighed. "You are. All right, does Emily know you were there?"

"That is in the category of a gory detail. I would prefer it if you did not discuss our meeting with her."

I took a big gulp of the coffee. Todd looked at me as though he expected me to keel over. I sighed again. "In essence, you want me to go on pretending we've never met."

"That's right."

"Suppose I won't unless I hear every last one of your gory details?"

"I hope it won't come to that," he said, without a hint of a threat. "Frankly, Miss Pendleton, what I was doing out there is none of your business."

That got me. My uneasiness vanished in a flash of anger. "Well, suppose I bring your gun down to the police station and let them keep it," I said hotly. "Just in case."

"Go right ahead." He smiled. "I didn't think you'd tossed it in the lake. Look, I know I've scared hell out of you several times. I didn't mean to, but my position is very awkward. All that has changed between now and the last time we met is that you know who I am."

"And you're a guest at Rosewood," I pointed out, then went on sarcastically, "I'm a big girl, Mr. Hall. You can tell me what you were doing at Rosewood two weeks ago. A tryst with Emily? Only instead of your lover, of course, you met up with three Doberman pinschers."

"And you."

I managed to ignore him. "Or were you spying on Emily? I think you should tell me."

"No."

He said it flatly, and I could tell arguing would be useless, but so were a good many other things I did regularly.

"Then I'm going to Mr. Harrison first thing Monday morning. Maybe even tomorrow. I think he should know one of his guests was prowling about his estate with a gun two weeks ago."

Todd made a sound of pure disgust and actually drank some of his coffee. Then he drew one foot up onto the chair and folded his hands around his knee. "I would appreciate it if you said nothing at all about me to anyone."

I gave him credit for his patience. "Appreciate it all you want," I countered, "but I won't do it unless—"

The foot dropped to the floor, and his right hand smacked the table. The vase of wild flowers in the middle bounced up and landed an inch off-center. So much for his patience.

"Damn it, then, go ahead and tell Richard Harrison," he yelled. "Tell everyone you damn well feel like telling. What do you think will happen? Maybe Richard will throw me out. I doubt it, but maybe. Or—"

"Not if you explain, he won't."

"I have no more intention of explaining to Richard than I do to you. That is final, Miss Pendleton."

What had happened to Artie? Of course. He was reminding me—subtly—that he was the Boston publisher and I was the gardener. I sat very rigid. "Give me one good reason why I should do as you ask."

"Because there is no reason not to do as I ask. It is a simple request. You will spare me—and, I would guess, Emily—a great deal of embarrassment."

"You would *guess* Emily?"

"I have no idea what would and would not embarrass that woman, but if this wouldn't, nothing ever will." He slid his mug across the table. It ran into the vase, and coffee spilled. He stood up. "There you have it. Either you will go along with me or you won't. I hope you will have the decency to tell me what you intend to do."

"What will you do if I say no?"

"Drive back to Boston right now."

"All right, all right. Go on back to Rosewood. I'll pretend we never met. But if you're lying to me, Mr. Hall, you can believe I'll find out and—"

"I'm sure you will, Miss Pendleton." Then he grinned, the incongruous dimple showing, and took three long steps around the table. He lifted my chin with one finger. "Thanks, Artie."

The finger traced my jawline and sent shock waves through my entire body. I wanted to resist, but I couldn't. I hadn't armed myself enough. Nowhere near enough. There was no defense against what this man could do to me with a look, a touch, a smile.

I swallowed hard. "What're you doing?"

"Have you any idea how many times I've thought about kissing you these past two weeks?"

His quiet, deep voice mesmerized me and licked my senses. So he hadn't dismissed me as easily as I had suspected—or was he telling me what he knew I longed, however inexplicably, to hear? "No," I said.

He smiled and lowered his face to mine so that I could see into his eyes. There was no mistaking the lust in them, or the warmth. I believed him then. "Neither do I," he breathed. "I lost track days ago."

My lips parted to get more air into my lungs, but he took it as an invitation. Perhaps it was. With a boldness I should have expected, he dug his fingers into the hair at the back of my neck and brought his mouth hungrily down on mine. There was nothing tentative in the way his tongue stabbed into my mouth, nothing tentative in my response. I had never wanted a man as much as I wanted this one.

I breathed deeply and opened my mouth wider, inviting deeper probing. He was still the man I had found on the island. No different. He had a name, an identity, but he was the same man. His mouth, his eyes, his big, muscular body—all the same.

And I could defend myself against them no more now than two weeks ago.

I grabbed the edge of my chair to keep myself from running my hands up and down the tempting muscles of his body. A fading voice of reason told me that responding to his kiss was daring enough for one evening. My hands tensed, my fingers dug into the seat. A less sturdy chair might not have withstood the abuse. Todd ran his fingers through my hair, then cupped my shoulders. With only the slightest effort he could have lifted me into his arms, and I would have gone to him willingly.

Before we had even become friends, we could so easily become lovers.

He pulled his mouth from mine, but I could feel his passion in his tensed fingers, see it in his dusky eyes. He looked at me enigmatically. "Maybe it all would be different if you had been a mermaid after all," he said, and let his hands drop from my shoulders.

I knew he could sense my response, see it in my desire-swollen mouth, my irregular breathing, my straining, nipple-hardened breasts. "You know, Todd," I said, wishing there was something I could do to still the sensual pulsing of my body, "if you keep kissing me, I'm going to have a difficult time pretending not to know you."

He had the gall to laugh. "Oh, Artie, I'd like to do more than just kiss you." His eyes narrowed, raking my frame, resting on my breasts. "Much more. And if I get the opportunity, I will. No self-respecting honored male guest of Richard Harrison wouldn't look at you with lust in his eyes. And I will. Believe me, sweetheart, I will."

"Just don't get me fired."

"Would it matter so much if I did?"

The phone rang, and I had to dig it out from under the couch. A drunk George invited me over to his place for a few drinks. I told him no thanks and hung up.

When I turned around, Todd had dumped out his coffee and found the fifth of Jack Daniel's I kept in the cupboard. He got out two glasses, added ice to one, filled them, and handed me the one without the ice.

"There's something else I should tell you," he said. "I wasn't going to at first, but I've changed my mind. Drink up."

I sipped the bourbon and felt it burn down into my overheated body. Here it comes, I thought: He's going to tell me he's a paranoid schizophrenic and wants his gun back so he can purge Rosewood of dogs and women. Ralph yawned on top of the refrigerator. And cats. Todd watched me with those hard slate eyes until I took another sip of bourbon. He hadn't touched his.

He had both feet flat on the floor. "Artie, I came to Rosewood with a friend."

I tried not to look too disappointed. "And what does Emily think of that?"

The Venus Shoe

"I wouldn't know."

"What's her name?"

"Artie, Artie, shame on you. Do you think I'd be here talking myself out of jumping into bed with you when I had a woman with me at Rosewood?" He smiled disarmingly but briefly. He tapped the rim of his glass with one finger, his face grim. "His name is Jack. Jack Harrison."

Shock sucked the blood out of my face. "Jack?"

"Richard Harrison's son. It seems this is the year for Rosewood reunions. First you, now Jack."

"No—no one told me."

"No one knew. Jack wanted to surprise everyone. He hasn't stepped foot on the estate in thirteen years, but I'll give him credit. He walked in as though he'd only been gone a week or two."

"But why did he come back? He vowed he wouldn't—"

"So did you."

I collapsed against the couch and tucked my knees up under my chin. So Todd knew about my parents. Of course, he would if he was a friend of Jack's. Jack. My hero. I had adored him. He would come over to the house and help my father chop wood, take me sliding in the winter and swimming in the summer, can vegetables with my mother. We were a second family to him. He was my big brother, I his little sister.

Then his mother disappeared, and I never saw Jack Harrison again. Not even when my parents died and I was left alone.

Now he was back.

"Jack came back because of you, Artemis. He hasn't told anyone as much—he wouldn't—but that's the truth."

I looked up, startled. "I haven't seen him since I was twelve!"

"I don't think that makes any difference at all to him. You're a special person in his life." Todd drank some of his bourbon and set the glass down hard on the table. "Maybe too special for my tastes, but that's neither here nor there."

"Jack Harrison means nothing to me, and I would be very happy to know that I mean nothing to him."

Todd frowned, his eyes holding me, forcing me not to

turn away. "Aren't you being a bit hard on him? You were at Rosewood when his mother disappeared, weren't you?"

"My parents were," I said stiffly. "I wasn't. We lived here in Saratoga."

Thirteen years ago Patrice Harrison—Jack's mother and R. W.'s first wife—and over a million dollars of her jewels had disappeared without a trace. The Harrisons had been invited to a dinner party that night, but Patrice pleaded a migraine and stayed home. The thieves broke into the house and, not expecting her, had had no choice but to take her with them and eventually kill her. Or so the widely accepted theory went. They disposed of the jewels very carefully, so they would never be traced.

At the time, Jack Harrison had been a freshman at Harvard and took the whole thing badly. R. W. and the police believed it had been an outside job—the work of professionals—but Jack wanted to believe someone at Rosewood had planned and executed the break-in. He pointed out that the safe had been opened without force, but the police countered that Patrice had been right there to open it for them—at gunpoint. Besides, a member of the staff would have been more likely to know about Patrice's migraine—that she would be home that evening—and called off the robbery. And finally, no one at Rosewood skipped off to Tahiti or did anything but profoundly mourn the loss of the woman whose touch—whose heart and soul—were imbued in every inch of the magnificent estate.

That was why, ultimately, Jack had left and vowed never to return. He hadn't forsaken his family, only Rosewood. The estate was his mother.

"Jack Harrison didn't come back when my parents died. I was just eighteen and left completely alone. My parents had loved him, but he wouldn't even see them buried. If he didn't come back then, when I might have needed him, why would he come back now?"

The words came in a rush of anger and bitterness that surprised me. I had hurt for my parents, and I had wanted the boy who had meant so much to them to care enough to come to their funeral. Everyone else at Rosewood had: R. W., Adelia, Emily, Marie, Bud, Nora. Everyone. But not

Jack Harrison. He didn't care enough about me, but, most of all, he didn't care enough about my parents.

Or, I had thought then and thought now, he had suspected them of being involved with the disappearance of his mother and her jewels.

"You might ask him why," Todd said diplomatically.

"I don't intend to ask him anything. I don't even want to see him."

"That's going to be difficult. He's staying at Rosewood at least through Labor Day. He's a Harrison and can do as he pleases, and you, lovely and intelligent and pigheaded as you are, are the gardener."

He gulped the last of his drink, rose, and loomed above me, tall and handsome, and completely out of place in my crowded apartment.

"Talk to him, Artie," he said quietly. "Straighten out what stands between you."

"I don't think that's possible."

"There's nothing more I can say—"

"Try good-bye."

He looked down at me for a brief, unbearable moment, then turned on his heel and left without a word.

Slowly I stretched out my legs and eyed the wrinkles in my pants. Had he noticed they were linen? The rich Boston publisher. My Ovid-quoting stranger. Why did I react to him so? Even now, after all we'd said, why did I want to hear him laugh and feel the strength of his arms around me?

I poured the rest of my bourbon in the sink and, one by one, went through my plants, pinching off dead leaves, pruning, inspecting for insects and root rot and such, watering, fertilizing. Trying not to think. Ralph watched, his tail swishing back and forth along the freezer door. He was good company, the only company I needed.

Chapter Five

I SPENT all day Sunday in Mrs. Martin's flower and vegetable gardens. She had already lectured me on the impropriety of late-night male callers, and this was my way of appeasing her. I picked some beans, summer squash, and tomatoes, and made a pot of soup. My landlady made biscuits, and we shared a peaceful meal. We were both lonely women, but neither of us said so.

I worked all Monday morning in the herb garden and had lunch on the picnic table. Nora joined me and told me everything I did and didn't want to know about Todd Hall.

He was thirty-three and unmarried. He had a doctorate in literature from Harvard and was more surprised than anyone when his father, Howard Perry Hall, retired after his wife died three years ago and made his son president of the family company.

"Doesn't get along with the father," Nora said. "But so far as I can see, he doesn't get along with anybody. One of those snotty Brahmins, that one."

Nora folded her arms across her ample bosom and waited for me to agree. Her wide, plain face told me exactly how little she liked Todd Hall. "I haven't met him yet," I said, "but I haven't heard much good about him. What do he and his father fight about?"

"Money, I would think. Doesn't run the company a bit like his father. Wants to buy out a firm up in Maine somewhere that puts out those environmental books, I think. The father says no, even though he lives up in Maine—"

"The son does?"

"No, no, he lives on Beacon Hill. The father lives in their country home, on Mount Desert Island, I think."

46

Nora started her tirade on the demise of filial respect, so I steered her, gently, to the subject of her darling Emily's relationship with this scourge of Boston.

"She's not good enough for him! That's what he thinks. The snob! Just because his family goes all the way back to the Mayflower. But she's the one who finally ended things, good for her. The only reason he's here at all is because he's friends with Jack. Wish I could do something about that, but I don't interfere. Have you seen Jack yet? He wants to see you awful bad. You were such a pair! Why, I remember . . ."

I listened to her recall a few incidents I wanted to forget before I asked her the time and said I had to get back to work.

I was beginning to regret ever returning to Rosewood.

On Tuesday, I regretted it even more.

I had spent most of Monday in my workroom and the herb garden, but I knew if the conservatory wasn't going to revert to its pre-Pendleton state, I would have to make an appearance and water the plants.

A giant coleus was soaking up a good quart of water when Jack Harrison found me.

"Artemis? Artemis Pendleton, it *is* you!" He put an arm around my shoulder and brought me to his chest. "I'll be damned."

I backed away far enough that he had to release me. "It's nice to see you again, Mr. Harrison."

"Mr.?"

Hurt washed over his face, and I felt like a fool. I had let Todd Hall rekindle the old and best forgotten imaginings of an agonized girl. Perhaps Jack had come back to Rosewood because of me, or perhaps I was only part of the reason. But my parents had nothing to do with it. Jack couldn't believe they had had anything to do with his mother's disappearance. At least not anymore. Maybe not ever.

Suddenly I remembered the thin teenaged boy who had shown me the rudiments of archery—long before I knew the mythological significance of my name—and taught me to swim. Thirteen years had added weight, a few strands of gray to his very dark hair, and a maturity to his smooth, sensitive face. I smiled at him.

The hurt vanished, and his round brown eyes danced. I could see that he had put aside the past. The vulnerability we had shared years ago was gone. And so, I knew, was my champion.

He waved a pointed finger at me. "You used to call me Uncle Jack, remember? But we'll dispense with the uncle now that you're—" He paused to smile. "Now that you're grown up. Come on, sit down and have a drink with us. I want to hear all about you. Have you met Todd Hall?"

I almost stopped dead in my tracks. Hadn't Todd told even Jack we'd met? "No, but—Jack, I can't, really. I've only just started to water the plants—"

Jack laid a hand on my shoulder. "Artemis, please," he said quietly. "It's been a long time. Too long."

This was getting awkward. I had wanted my stay at Rosewood to be temporary and painless. I had planned to work for a few months, get my life in order, and slip quietly away. But now Jack Harrison was here. With his friend Todd Hall. I put down my watering can and followed Jack meekly to the table where Todd was stirring a pitcher of Bloody Marys and looking thoroughly dashing in his muted plaid shirt and sailcloth pants. I noticed his strong arms and the breadth of his shoulders. How did publishers get such shoulders? An increasingly familiar dryness tightened my throat.

I pulled my gaze from him and told myself to behave: Todd Hall was off-limits.

"Todd, I'd like you to meet Artemis Pendleton," Jack said cheerfully. "She's our old gardener's daughter. I've told you about him. Last time I saw this one she was a gawky twelve-year-old who always wanted me to take her tree climbing."

"Then I gather she's changed," Todd said, rising and shaking my hand, which was clammy and trembling slightly. "I'm Todd Hall. Pleased to meet you, Miss Pendleton."

"Artemis," I said with a stiff smile, and sat down.

Jack poured me a Bloody Mary and dropped a stalk of celery in it. "You drink this stuff, don't you?"

I didn't. "Among friends."

"That's the spirit. Cheers and all that. Now, Artemis, I've heard all the rumors, but I want to get it straight from you. What on earth are you doing working for my father?"

The Venus Shoe

"Earning money for graduate school." I slipped into the lie so easily. I didn't want to lay my vulnerability on the table for them all to see. Money was something they could understand. "It's a job."

"But why here? It must be sheer torture for you after everything that's happened."

"Actually, it's rather therapeutic."

Jack shook his head. "I can't see how."

"I don't expect you to."

If he detected the sarcasm, he gave no sign of it. "Are you being treated well?"

"Yes, of course."

"What made you change your mind about coming back to Saratoga? I understood you said you'd never return here."

"So did you," I replied coolly. "I'm here because I need work. Why are you here?"

He leaned back in his chair and bit off the top of his celery. "Dear old Dad finally got around to threatening to cut me off. I don't blame him, really. He knew I was ready to face Rosewood again, and if I wasn't, I ought to be. Knowing you were here helped me make up my mind. If you could stand it, so could I."

I glanced at Todd and wondered why one or both of them had lied to me. Returning to Rosewood because of parental pressure was not the same as returning because of me.

"Father tells me you're studying plant science," Jack went on. "Won't any schools offer you scholarships? What about UMass—it's not expensive, and your grandparents live, what, fifteen or twenty minutes away?"

My eyes sought Todd again. He was pouring himself another Bloody Mary and pretending he wasn't listening. Why hadn't he told Jack of our meetings? Or had he, and Jack was only pretending not to know? Why?

I had to find out. "True," I said, deciding which direction my lie would take. "But UMass doesn't want me. My financial state is bad enough to deserve a scholarship, but my grades weren't all that good. I did okay on the GREs, but not so well that any graduate school will offer me financial aid. I've got two or three universities that will take me, but in the meantime I'm"—I remembered Todd's words—"saving my nickels and dimes."

Todd didn't even raise an eyebrow. Jack said, "Oh, I see. Well, good luck to you."

I said thank you and took a sip of the Bloody Mary. One round to the publisher from Boston, I thought. I hadn't learned a thing.

"You're just like your father, aren't you? I tell you, Todd, he was the quintessential gardener: surly, busy eyebrows, leather for skin, hated dressing up. But he could do anything with a plant. Spoke his mind, too. He used to call me a lazy rich boy and make me haul cow manure. And Artemis, here, is just like him."

"Except for the bushy eyebrows and leather skin, Jack," Todd said amiably.

I looked at Jack and said, deliberately, "Actually, my grandparents think I take after my mother."

Jack's smile collapsed. My father had been fifty-eight when he died, young but not as young as my mother's thirty-six. Remembering her brought a very special kind of pain for me. I knew now it did for Jack, too.

When he spoke, his voice was hushed, agonized. "You do, Artemis. She was a very beautiful woman. I loved your folks. I should have come when they died. I—I don't suppose I have any excuses for leaving you alone at a time like that, I'm sorry."

I shrugged. Todd was giving me a know-it-all look, but I ignored him. Jack *had* to have had a reason for staying away! Or so I had thought at eighteen. At twenty-five, I thought ruefully, life was so much more complex. "I managed," I said quietly.

"It must have been awfully hard for you."

"No more so than what you've been through, I'm sure," I said, and added, before he could respond, "I understand you're staying here through Labor Day?"

"Yes, I expect to. Father gets more extravagant every year, doesn't he?"

"His wife and stepdaughters have something to do with that," I said, hoping I sounded amused rather than catty. "I would love to get this whole weekend off and go hide in the Adirondacks."

"Just like your father," Jack muttered, laughing.

Todd smiled indifferently. "What, you don't want to stick around for the parade of stars?"

Jack waved him off. "Pay no attention to him. Publishers are born cynics."

"Publishers?" I sounded surprised.

"Heavens, Artemis, you are provincial. This is the Hall of Hall and Son Publishers of Boston."

Todd's eyes were half-closed. "Now, Jack, don't make the poor woman feel out of touch. Only prospective authors know me on sight, and unfortunately they make it their business to. Beautiful gardeners struggling to get into graduate school have no reason to recognize me."

I jammed my glass into my mouth and took two big gulps of the Bloody Mary. Todd had just seized his first opportunity to look at me with lust in his eyes.

"If you really want the weekend off," Jack was saying, "I can speak to Father about it."

"Oh, Jack, no. I was only teasing. I'm surprised Rosewood is still standing after seven years without a Pendleton around. Well, it's nice seeing you again, Jack. Glad to meet you, Mr. Hall."

"Todd."

I turned up the corners of my lips in a polite smile. I left my watering can and spray mister right where they were and escaped to the terrace.

But Emily was out there. This is ridiculous, I thought; I'll quit this job! I began plucking wilted petunias off the hanging baskets and prayed she would drink her coffee and leave me alone.

She didn't. She sauntered over to me and ran her fingers through her thick hair. "Did you have a nice chat with Jack and Todd? I suppose he told you his father threatened to cut him off if he didn't come back to Rosewood? Well, it's not true. Richard has never threatened to cut Jack off. Artemis, I was the one who told Jack you were here. We were at a yacht party in Newport, and I just let it slip. He said right then and there that he would come to Rosewood himself and find out what you were doing here. Those were his words exactly, Artemis. So you see," she said with a knowing smile, "you *are* the reason he came back."

The whole petunia plant came off its hanger and crashed to the terrace floor. It broke into two big chunks. I summoned all my self-control to keep from running straight to my Falcon and driving out of Rosewood forever. I looked at

Emily and said in a strained but steady voice, "Excuse me, I have to get a broom and clean up this mess."

I went into the conservatory and walked past Jack Harrison and Todd Hall, resisting the urge to take them both by the neck and demand to know what they were really doing at Rosewood.

Because I didn't believe either of their stories.

I grabbed a broom and a dustpan from my workroom and went back to the terrace. Emily, Todd, and Jack all had gone. I swept up the mess and did my best to save what I could of the petunia.

And my sanity.

That afternoon I gave Nancy Lerner a ride home and took a long walk before supper. I don't remember where I went or how long I was gone, but when I dragged myself into my apartment, I still hadn't unraveled all that bothered me about Todd Hall and Jack Harrison.

And what their presence at Rosewood had to do with me.

I made myself a cup of tea and tried to get Ralph to sit on my lap, but he preferred the top of the refrigerator. Males, I thought, scowling at him. And then I thought of Todd—not the man who owned and operated a prestigious publishing house but the man on the island, the man to whom I had been so inexorably drawn. I could almost feel his lips on mine, his soft caress on my breasts. I shifted in my chair, but the desire for a man I hardly knew and wasn't sure I could trust was there still, persistent. Long walks and pots of tea weren't enough to distract me.

But Todd Hall, I told myself resolutely, didn't care about Rosewood's newest gardener. He simply didn't!

There were two loud knocks on my door. I sat up straight on the couch. Todd? Jack?

Who cares. I yelled for whoever it was to come in.

"Artemis!"

Holly Dearborn ran over to me and was hugging me before I realized who she was.

"Damn, you look great!" she said, holding me at arm's length. "I thought you had to work for a living, but look at that tan."

"Holly, what are you doing here?"

"I'm on my way to Iowa via Saratoga. Believe it or not,

Artemis, I'm engaged to a beekeeper. Can't you see me living in Iowa, making honey and going to church on Sunday?"

I sat her down at the oak table and put on some water for tea. My college roommate for two years, Holly Dearborn was a tall redheaded artist and the very last person I expected to see in Saratoga Springs. Around Memorial Day she had written me a postcard from Jamaica declaring that she intended to remain there forever washing her hair in waterfalls. Now she was engaged to an Iowan beekeeper.

"What's his name?"

"Hans Erikson. Won't that look great on a jar of honey? I'm designing the label, of course."

"He's in Iowa?"

"Probably has the preacher picked out and the kitchen painted sunny yellow. He's the funniest guy. Strong as an ox, blond hair, but he's going bald and he's only twenty-six. Met him in Jamaica, of all places. A hundred thousand or a million or something like that of his bees had just died of cholera or smallpox—I don't know what—so he and his brother, a complete nineteen-year-old pest, took off to Jamaica to mourn. We fell in love instantly. Really, Artemis, you have to meet him."

"When's the wedding?"

"Hell, I don't know. October, November—maybe Thanksgiving Day. Wouldn't that be good and patriotic? But enough about me. You didn't get that tan pruning roses, did you? Damn, I buy tons of goop and stay white as a whore or get red as a lobster. Come on, what's your secret?"

I wasn't at all in the mood to talk about myself. I said, "It's in the blood. You look wonderful, Holly. How long have you been back?"

She lit a skinny brown cigarette. "A month. I started to get paranoid about hurricane season. I've been staying in Boston with Mum and Dad. They're off in Copenhagen now."

Holly Dearborn was the only person I knew who had grown up in Boston's Back Bay. Her family was upper class but not pretentious.

"They're convinced I won't marry Hans, of course," she

said, "and they think it's shameful that we plan to have the wedding in Iowa instead of Boston. Hans has two brothers and three sisters and God knows how many aunts, uncles, cousins, and friends that want to come to the wedding. I just have my folks and my little brother. Granny died this spring, did I tell you? And, of course, you have to come."

"I wouldn't miss it."

"You'll be my maid of honor?"

"Sure, just as long as I don't have to wear a straw hat with silk daisies."

"What?"

"Nothing."

"What about you?" she asked. "In love with anyone lately?"

Only Holly Dearborn could ask that question and make me laugh. For some unfathomable reason, I thought of Todd Hall and remembered the feel of his lips on mine, his hands on my breasts.

I said with conviction, "Definitely not."

"What happened to that ghoul who studied dead plants?"

"Dead and dying trees," I corrected amiably. "All conifers. He fired me."

She knew enough not to ask me to explain. Her only reaction was to flick a cigarette ash from her knee. "Well, this Rosewood of yours must be crawling with eligibles or whatever it is you're looking for. No luck?"

"Mr. Harrison's daughters are convinced his son returned to Rosewood after thirteen years just to see me."

"But you think they're crazy."

It was a statement, not a question, but I said, "Yes."

"Is he interested in you?"

"I don't know."

"Well, find out! You could at least have an affair and lead a gloriously decadent life for a few months." She stretched out her long legs and laid them across an adjacent chair. "Is he a toad?"

"No, as a matter of fact, he's rather handsome."

"Then what are you waiting for? You should know by now that gongs and fireworks and all that nonsense don't go off when you fall in love. Give yourself a little push. The perfect man ceased to exist in the twelfth century. Now you take what you can get and pray he doesn't have syphilis or a mother complex. Artemis Pendleton, you're blushing! Don't tell me *you* have syphilis?"

"Of course not. Remember for whom I'm named."

"In the words of Hans Erikson: Bah! Artemis, what're you so jumpy for? Have I said something? Look, if this Harrison character is a sore subject—"

"I haven't seen Jack in thirteen years."

"Then why are you snapping at me? Look, you're licking your lips like a nervous horse. What's wrong?"

"Nothing!"

She quoted Hans Erikson again.

"All right, I do have something on my mind, but I'm probably making a big deal out of nothing and—"

"And you're going to tell me all about it right here and now."

Beneath the nonchalance, the concern was there.

I told her everything, about meeting Todd Hall on the island, his bare feet, his bloody hand, his gun, the three Doberman pinschers, the meeting outside the tavern, his explanation, his kisses, and, finally, the conversation this morning.

When I had finished, I asked Holly for her advice because I knew she would give it only if I asked, and then it would be sound.

It was. "Quit Rosewood, pack your bags, and join the caravan to Iowa."

"Why?"

"Why! Because, you idiot, you are involved in a grisly little scene and you ought to get yourself uninvolved just as fast as you can."

"Oh, Holly, you're exaggerating. It's not grisly."

She glared at me sideways. "Let's see the gun."

"You don't know any more about guns than I do," I said, but I went to the closet, pulled it from under my hat, and thrust it at her. "Here."

With frightening deftness, Holly pulled out the clip and counted out six bullets. She laid them on the table. "Well, at least he didn't shoot anybody. All the bullets are accounted for."

"Holly, where did you learn how to do that?"

She waved me off. "My father's a gun fanatic. Listen,

Artemis, this is a twenty-five caliber Baretta, a lady's gun, if you will. I would think your Mr. Todd Hall could arm himself better if he anticipated doing business with a pack of Doberman pinschers. His story stinks, Artemis. And this"—she held up the gun—"makes it a grisly little scene."

My hands flew up, angrily. "I know his story stinks! So does Jack's, for that matter. But why leave? I'm not in any danger. Nobody's threatened me." I sat back down next to Holly. "I could quit my job and leave Saratoga. I know that. I wanted to when I first heard Jack was back, but—"

"But you've met him, you know he's come back because of you, and you're intrigued. Are you in love with him?"

"No!"

She eyed me skeptically. "All right," she said at length. "Is he in love with you?"

"No. At least, I don't think he is. What difference does it make?"

"It might help explain why he's lying to you. I find it difficult to believe that Todd didn't tell him about meeting you, first on the island, then outside the tavern."

"I know," I said. "So do I. But maybe they both are telling the truth. I don't know, Holly. That's the whole point. I want to know! I have to know."

"Have to?"

"Maybe that is a little strong."

"Yeah, but if this character Todd kissed me, I sure would want to know what he was up to. Why the kiss?"

"I don't know," I replied honestly. "I guess he just felt like it."

Holly grinned. "Your gorgeous face, no doubt." She exhaled a noxious cloud of smoke. "Is he scary?"

"His kiss wasn't," I said, trying to be objective. "I don't know about him."

Holly smiled and stubbed out her cigarette. "All right, Artemis. Get some hot dogs or something cooking and we'll take this thing from the beginning."

Chapter Six

For the next two hours, we picked apart every sentence spoken by or about Jack Harrison and Todd Hall. We held up each word, aired it, then put it back into context. In the end, we had consumed a broccoli and tomato casserole, and Holly had smoked half a pack of cigarettes. We had no answers.

So we went back and examined facial expressions. Could Todd have been lying about the gun, about Emily, about his explanation being none of my business, about not caring if I took the gun to the police? Could Jack have been lying about his reasons for returning to Rosewood? Did he give any hint—a flicker of an eye, a wriggle in his chair, a conspicuous clearing of the throat—that he knew I had found his friend from Boston on an island in his father's lake?

When we had examined all the facts and still could draw no legitimate conclusions, we started creating our own scenarios.

"Chances are," Holly began slowly, "we're making mountains out of molehills. The only thing—really—that doesn't add up is that Jack says he's come back to Rosewood because his father threatened to cut him off and Emily and Todd say he's come back because of you. They could be right, you know. Maybe Jack is too shy to admit it. You did give him a cold reception."

"Todd didn't tell him about seeing me on the island."

"Maybe, maybe not. It would be nice to know, though, wouldn't it?" She lit another cigarette, took a deep drag, and pointed it at me. "We have here a publisher and the son of a millionaire. What sneaky, low-down business could they be involved in? Neither of them needs money, so it can't be robbery. Murder? I don't know; maybe Jack wants to do in his father—"

"No, they get along."

"Then why the thirteen-year absence?"

"Rosewood," I said. "He was away when his mother disappeared, and he hasn't been able to face Rosewood since."

"So now he's a big boy and has come back. Interesting. What's this about his mother?"

"You remember, it was all over the papers—"

"Artemis Pendleton, thirteen years ago I was in the seventh grade learning state capitals. I didn't even know Saratoga Springs existed. Is it a long story?"

"Not really." I told her everything I knew about Patrice Harrison's disappearance, ending with, "It's a closed case as far as the police are concerned."

"Bit tragic, isn't it? Well, I don't see that it has anything to do with Todd Hall and his trip to Rosewood two weeks ago, do you?"

"No."

"You hesitated."

"I didn't mean to."

She observed me for a second or two, then went on. "All right, robbery and murder are out."

"I don't think any of them is out to commit a crime," I said. "I doubt if there even is a crime involved."

"You mean that our gentlemen are neither victims nor accomplices of a crime."

"That's right. I just think they haven't told me the truth."

"We are assuming that, you moron. What we're trying to establish is what precisely is the truth. You're saying it doesn't involve a crime. All right, what does it involve?"

"Relationships," I said. "Todd and Emily, Jack and me."

"Todd and Jack, Jack and Emily," Holly added. "That gets us everywhere, doesn't it?"

I ignored her sarcasm. "Well, Todd and Emily apparently did break up shortly after his excursion to Rosewood."

Holly sat up straight. A half-inch worth of ashes fell on her lap. "Artemis, you have not told me everything! What do you know about those two breaking up?"

"Very little. Apparently Emily initiated it because Todd

thinks she's *too* nouveau riche." I grinned at that. The Harrison fortune went back to the turn of the century, although, of course, Emily was not a biological Harrison. "He's a Boston Brahmin from the word *go*, but that's unsubstantiated rumor from the mouth of Emily's greatest fan."

"Who?"

"Rosewood's head housekeeper."

"Oh, wonderful," Holly said, dismayed. "Well, suppose —wait a minute. The gun! I told you a twenty-five caliber Baretta isn't worth a damn, really, against a pack of Doberman pinschers, and it's considered a lady's gun. How stable is Emily?"

"From what I've seen, very."

"Well, you're just the gardener, what would you know? Look, suppose Todd arranged a rendezvous with Emily at Rosewood to tell her he was breaking off their romance, and suppose Emily figured that's what he intended to do and flew off the handle. She doesn't tell him about the Dobermans, *and*—get this—she brings a gun along to their meeting." Holly took a puff of her cigarette, pleased with herself, but didn't give me a chance to respond. "Todd wrestles off her and a Doberman, jumps into the lake, swims to your island, collapses, meets you, canoes back, wrestles off all three Dobermans this time, and goes home to Boston."

I decided I'd better interrupt. "Holly—"

She didn't even hear me. "Then, for reasons unknown, Todd decides to come to Rosewood with his friend Jack. He wouldn't want to mention the incident to anyone, because Emily's a psycho and God only knows what she'd do. But he also wants to help her. Maybe that's why he's here, to see to it she gets some professional help. What do you think?"

"Well, I guess that would explain why he didn't care if I kept the gun or gave it to the police. It's possible, Holly, but—"

"So is just about anything." Holly sighed and stubbed out her cigarette in the tea mug, now almost full of butts. "May I use your phone?"

So that's the end of it, I thought. The game was fun for a while, but now it was time to call a cab and head for the airport. I pointed to the phone by the couch and watched her dial.

"Susie?"

I frowned. Another friend in Saratoga?

"Holly Dearborn. I'm doing great. Listen, you worked for Hall and Son for a while, didn't you? Know anything about Todd Hall? Yeah, right. What's he like? Is he a crank? A friend of mine is thinking of going to work for him. I see. What about lately? Would you mind calling around? Be subtle. Someone might figure out who wants to know and tip Hall off. Yeah, it's a pretty big job. Thanks, Susie."

She gave Susie my number, told her to call collect, and hung up.

"She didn't know much," Holly said, yawning and stretching out on the couch. "Saw him once in the elevator. Why didn't you tell me he's built like a bull and is handsome as all get-out?"

"I didn't think it was relevant."

"Handsome men are always relevant, you ass. Anyway, Susie—"

"Who is this Susie?"

"My cousin's daughter. That makes her my second cousin, doesn't it? You forget I'm a native of Boston. I know lots and lots of people. Susie's the only one I can think of offhand who has worked for Hall and Son. She was a secretary or a clerk typist or something. She heard Hall's civilized to work for, occasionally tactless, has male chauvinist tendencies, and is more educated and less business-oriented than his father. Your head housekeeper was right about him and Papa. They don't get along."

"Did she say anything else?"

Holly shook her head and rolled off the couch. I watched her get a pack of cigarettes out of her suitcase by the door and, still kneeling, open up the pack. She stuck a cigarette in her mouth and didn't light it until she was back in her chair next to me at the table.

I waved at the smoke. "Maybe he's as harmless as he says he is."

"He could also be a nut planning a mass murder." Holly flicked an ash into her tea mug. "The point is that you don't know what in hell Todd Blakesly Hall is."

"Blakesly?"

She grinned. "I told you, I'm a native. His father's Howard Perry Hall, and his grandfather—"

"Okay, I believe you."

"Artemis, I say quit your job, forget him, and come with me to Iowa."

"When does your plane leave?"

Her eyes opened wide. "One A.M."

"Good, that gives us plenty of time. Of course, you don't have to come, Holly, but I want to take a look at that pine grove and the area where the Dobermans were found."

Her eyes remained wide open. "You're crazy."

"Oh, Holly, you know we're being melodramatic. I'm sure we won't find a thing—I'm sure this whole business is just a lot of fuss about nothing. What do you say? I'd feel much better if I could see for myself—"

"I still say you're crazy, but what the hell." She let her cigarette hang out of her mouth and began sticking the little bullets back into the little gun. I thought she would make a good "dame" for a gangster, but, of course, her auburn hair was natural, and she would be dead before cosmetics ever touched her skin, and even then would probably leave instructions for the mortician. "Might as well bring this thing along," she said, the cigarette waggling on her lower lip, "while we're being melodramatic. Here."

"Nothing doing." I shook my head. "It's your idea. You carry it."

"Still for gun control, are you?"

"Always and forever."

She shrugged and dumped the Baretta in her canvas handbag. "We'll end up getting ourselves killed for sure. Shall we go? Or is it too early? I always imagine people doing this sort of thing in the dead of night."

"It's only eight," I said, "but the Harrisons should be sitting down to dinner now, so—"

"Our Boston publisher ought not to be taking a stroll our way. What the hell. Onward."

Chapter Seven

A NARROW dirt road intersected the highway about a mile north of Rosewood's main entrance. It led farther north, deeper into the state-owned land that abutted the Harrison estate, and then faded into an overgrown path before dying out altogether at a stone wall. But a quarter of a mile off the highway it intersected an old logging road that was little more than a break in the forest. It led southwest. To Rosewood.

And it was just wide enough for a Falcon.

I eased the car between the trees. "There's only one bad spot," I told Holly.

"This isn't it?" she said, rubbing her knee where the glove compartment had banged open.

"No, it's where we hit Harrison property. There's a rock—"

"Don't tell me, please," she said. "Isn't there an easier way to get to your pine grove? This seems a little cloak-and-dagger."

"Well, we could go back, park on the highway, and walk. It's only a couple of miles. Or we could drive in through the front gate—"

"All right, you needn't be sarcastic. You know we can't parade across the Harrisons' front lawn, and you know I don't walk more than one mile at a time." She rubbed her knee again. "Do you think Todd Hall came this way?"

I shrugged. "He had to know about it first."

"Jack Harrison."

"Or Emily. Maybe he just walked in."

"Or parachuted in, for all we know. This is crazy."

The Venus Shoe

We bounced over a rock. The glove compartment again banged open on Holly's knee. She swore.

"We're on Harrison property now," I said, and pointed to the no-trespassing sign.

The logging road ended, and we turned onto the dirt road that wound through Rosewood. It was getting dark, but I didn't dare turn on my headlights. Holly commented on that, but when the Falcon sputtered up a rise that gave a panoramic view of the lake nestled among the rolling hills, forests, and fields that were Rosewood, she shut up. A golden sunset glistened on the water, and we could see lights glittering from the main grounds across the lake.

"Quaint little place, isn't it?" she said.

I couldn't think of an appropriate response.

The road cut down the hill and through a pasture, then curved toward the lake and into the woods. Neither of us spoke. The road seemed to narrow as the evergreens thickened, and, since it was darker in the forest, I nearly missed the path—another old logging road overgrown with grass and princess pine—that led into a younger evergreen forest.

Todd Hall's pine grove.

I stopped the car a few yards from the lake, switched off the engine, and looked at Holly. She gave a halfhearted smile. Then we both got out of the car and met at the trunk. I could see Holly's pale face in the failing light of dusk.

"Eerie," she whispered. "Woods give me the creeps."

I smiled despite my own nervousness and led the way to the lake. The water lapped silently onto the rocks and pine needles.

"That's the island over there," I said, pointing. "We're on the northwest shore."

Holly stuck the end of her thumb into her mouth, bit it, pulled it out, and waved her whole hand at me. "And this is where you chauffeured our man. Well, Artemis Pendleton, it serves you right."

"What does."

"You went skinny-dipping off that island, in broad daylight, not even three hundred yards from where you had just brought a man you didn't know, a man who lied to you, a man with a wounded hand—well, it serves you right that he's come back to haunt you. Has it once occurred to you that Mr. Todd Blakesly Hall just might have joined Jack Harrison specifically to see you? How many times do I have to tell you, Artemis, that you happen to be unconscionably beautiful? Skinny-dipping! No wonder the man couldn't keep away."

"Oh, Holly, I was a mess. Sweaty, blueberry stains all over, scratches, my hair in a braid—"

"Todd was not looking at your sweat or your blueberry stains or your scratches." She shook her head with disgust and dismissed the subject. "You know, of course, we haven't the vaguest idea of what it is we're looking for. I suppose we should consider anything nonorganic suspicious. Except for dead bodies, naturally."

"That's not funny."

"I know, but at least keep on the lookout for freshly turned ground. Oh, I don't know, Artemis. Frankly, I hope we don't find anything."

So did I, but I didn't say so. "I suppose we should separate."

"Not more than five yards or I shall scream and throw a tantrum right here."

I sent her toward shore with an unnecessary warning to stay among the trees in case someone was watching. Then I set off inland, careful to keep within speaking distance of Holly, and scoured the damp, needle-covered ground.

When we had combed every inch of the pine grove, we had nothing to show for our efforts but a beer bottle—years old, I guessed—and two empty gun cartridges soggy with age. We dumped the loot in the backseat of the car, slammed the door, and then stared at each other in the darkness. There was still the area around the cabin to investigate.

"I don't have a flashlight," I said.

"It is awfully dark."

"We wouldn't find anything, anyway."

"True."

"I'm sure if there was anything out of the ordinary around the cabin, the men who found the Dobermans would have seen it," I said. "They must have looked for some sign of who the trespassers were—"

"The hell with it, then. Let's go home. Look at me, I've

been eaten alive by any number of disgusting creatures. I must have spiders crawling all over me. Did you keep running into cobwebs as thick as cheesecloth?"

"City slicker," I said, laughing. "And you're going to be a beekeeper's wife?"

"In Iowa, no less. And I talk about your lack of romantic wisdom! Do you suppose I could take a bath before I leave?"

"Of course."

She went around to the other side of the car and talked over the hood. "Can I fill the tub to the rim and use as much bubble bath as I want, or are you still so damned water-conscious that—"

"For helping me, Holly, anything. I even insist on driving you to the airport."

Holly didn't respond at once. We got into the car, and she observed me for a moment, then said, "You won't come with me to Iowa?"

"No reason to," I replied, and smiled.

"I suppose," she said, unconvinced.

"Did you see what I did with my keys? I thought I left them in the ignition." I felt on the dashboard but came up with nothing but dust. "Look on the floor, will you?"

Holly got down on the floor and started feeling around with her hands. "You'd love Hans's younger brother," she said, not looking up at me. "He's rather a farm boy, but he's built like a tree trunk and has impeccable manners."

"He's also nineteen."

"I did tell you that, didn't I? Well, I'm sure Hans has friends who are just as upright and funny and male chauvinistic as he is and pretends to be. No, huh?" She looked up from the floor. "Have it your way. You usually do. Artemis, there's not a thing down here but old maps and . . . oh, my God."

"What?"

Then I followed her gaze and turned around to look out my open window.

Todd Hall stood there with my keys in one hand and a gun—no little twenty-five caliber Baretta—in the other. The gun was leveled at my head.

"Well, Miss Pendleton," Todd said evenly, "you have a

charming propensity for turning up in the wrong places. Who's your friend?"

His deep, sober voice and the "Miss Pendleton" made me only slightly less nervous than the gun. What a fool I'd been not to think this man could be scary! He was scary all right. Scary as hell. "Holly—" My voice cracked; I swallowed and tried again. "Holly Dearborn."

"All right, Holly Dearborn, you will very slowly remove your hand from that bag of yours and then pass it to me. Do not get up from the floor until you have done that."

Very, very slowly, Holly did precisely as Todd ordered. I didn't take my eyes from the black hole that glared at me through the window until she handed me her bag. For once, I didn't notice the breadth of Todd's shoulders or shiver with desire just because he was near. I shivered with fear, cold, hard fear. I passed the bag to him.

The gun disappeared.

"I'm sorry I had to do that, but I'd rather not be killed by some hysterical woman. Now, what are you two doing here?"

Raw anger mingled with my relief. "Holly is not the hysterical type, and neither am I!"

"One can never tell," he said unapologetically. "Now—"

"Never mind what I'm doing out here. What are you doing out here—with a *gun*, no less? Damn it, Todd Hall, you nearly scared me to death!"

He just couldn't help himself. He smiled. "Darling, if anyone could take the scare you could. Now, are you going to explain or shall I get out my gun again?"

He was having the time of his life. I said sourly, "Holly's on her way to Iowa. I was just showing her where I work. She—"

"I suppose you always have your friends gather garbage in the forest," he said, glancing at the beer bottle and gun cartridges in the backseat. "How much did you tell her?"

"Nothing."

"Then explain why she was carrying my gun in her pocketbook."

"What difference does it make what I told her? She's going to Iowa. She's not going to tell anybody about—"

"Damn it, Artemis—"

"Don't damn it me, Todd Hall. You just threatened me

with a gun. Why? What are *you* doing here? And give me back my keys."

"First you will tell me what you were doing."

"I told you."

He bent down and placed his forearms in the window, his face, angry but controlled, just inches from mine. "Miss Pendleton," he said, more than a trace of strain in his voice, "this is not some silly Nancy Drew mystery. I asked you to please stay out of my affairs."

"Don't wax Brahmin on me, Todd Hall. I can do as I damn well please. You're the one who stole my keys and came creeping out of the woods. If you hadn't, Holly and I would be on our way back to Saratoga now."

"You were looking for something," he persisted. "What?"

"Buried treasure. For God's sake, isn't it obvious? I thought we might find some clue as to what you were doing out here, that's all. As you can see, we didn't find—"

"All right, listen to me, both of you. Go back to Saratoga. Go to Iowa. Go wherever the hell you please, but stay out of this affair. Do you hear me?"

"Loud and clear." Holly finally spoke, sitting on the seat next to me, not sounding anywhere near as afraid as she looked. "My plane leaves for Iowa at one this morning. I plan to be on it and take Artemis with me if I possibly can."

"Excellent idea," Todd agreed. "I'll be glad to pay her way."

"I am not going anywhere until I know what you're up to. Why the gun? There aren't any Dobermans out here. Why—"

"Artemis, will you please not press the man?" Holly pleaded. "Let's just go, okay? Mr. Hall, if you would please give me back my bag—you, of course, can remove that filthy gun—then we will be off."

The Baretta came out of the bag, then disappeared, I assumed, with the other gun. Todd handed me Holly's bag, which I handed to her. She was looking every bit as terrified as I felt.

Todd ran his fingers through his hair and breathed a sigh of exasperation. "I'm sorry," he said, as if he meant it, which I doubted. "I should have let you go on your merry little way, but I wasn't sure what you were doing out here. This whole affair is bordering on the ridiculous. I know you want an explanation, Artie, and no doubt you deserve one—"

"But you won't give me one."

He didn't smile, but there was something in his eyes that I was still too angry to want to notice. "That's right."

"You must know I'm going to go straight to the police and tell them all about you and your stinking guns."

Holly squelched a protest and instead opted for a glare that told me exactly what she thought of my tactics. Todd, however, chose to be remorseful.

"I don't blame you, Artie," he said, "but I would appreciate it if you didn't."

"Then you'd better do some explaining."

"No. For your sake and mine, no."

"Tell me now or tell the police later," I persisted.

"Artemis," Holly said, grabbing me by the arm. "He still has your keys. Will you just do as he says?"

But Todd leaned forward and dropped the keys in my lap. His teeth were clenched; his nostrils flared as he controlled his temper. Kissing me was obviously not on his agenda, but for some stupid, suicidal reason I wanted him to stick his head through my window and press those delicious lips of his to mine. I willed myself back to the real world.

"Do as you damn well please, but don't come crying to me if you're the one who ends up doing the explaining." His voice matched his hard, uncompromising look. "Good night, Miss Pendleton. Miss Dearborn, my sincerest apologies. Have a good trip to Iowa. And if you can possibly do it, get this woman to go with you."

I opened my mouth to ask him what he meant, but he was already gone. "Miss Pendleton!" I snorted, and banged my fist on the steering wheel.

Holly exhaled in a long, cathartic moan. "Damn, I've never been so scared in my life. Why in God's name did you keep after him, Artemis? Do you realize what he could have done to us? Have you any idea—" She stopped and fell back against the seat, limp. "I don't want to think about it. Let's just get out of here."

I started the Falcon and edged it slowly out of the pine grove and onto the dirt road.

"Well," Holly said at length, more calmly, "so much for fun and games. What are you going to do now?"

"I don't know."

"He can't be dangerous. He scared the living daylights out of me, but I'm sure he meant to. He had us right there, for God's sake. Two guns and—he *is* built like a bull, isn't he? And you flapping off your mouth. I bet it took every ounce of control for him not to smack your mouth shut."

I chewed on my lower lip. "Then you don't think we should go to the police?"

"I didn't say that. I said I don't think he is dangerous, but what I think and what is are very often two different things. He *did* threaten us."

"He thought you would shoot him."

"As you so nervelessly pointed out, I am not the hysterical type."

"He doesn't know that. What do you think he meant when he said I would end up doing the explaining?"

Holly shrugged. "I think he was referring to your relative social positions. He's a publisher and you're a gardener. He could tell the police some tale and brush you off as a pest."

"Why not tell me the tale? Why take the risk that I would go to the police?"

"He obviously doesn't want to tell you anything unless he absolutely has to. He's letting you decide whether or not to go to the police, but he's betting you won't."

I frowned. "Should I?"

"I don't like the idea that he was sneaking around with a damned thirty-eight."

"Was that what it was?"

"Damned right. I don't know what the hell he thought he was going up against, but—well, it looks as though my theory about Emily is out the window."

"Not necessarily."

"But probably. That doesn't answer your question, of course. Should you go to the police? Well, I don't trust our man Todd. He's up to something, and he hasn't even begun to tell you what it is. I still don't think he's dangerous, but no matter how much this all is none of your business, you are involved. You can't change that. No matter what you say, Artemis, you can't go on being the deaf and dumb gardener. You have to tell either the police or Mr. Harrison—preferably both. I don't see any way around it."

The moon chased away a cloud and peered down at the Falcon. I was driving fast now, with the headlights on, my concern for stealthiness shattered by the confrontation with Todd Hall.

What Holly said made sense, but I knew what I had to do. "I think I'll go along with him one last time."

"You mean you're not going to tell anyone about him?" she asked in disbelief.

"For now."

"Do you mind telling me why?"

"I don't know why."

"You didn't believe that tripe about his being sorry, did you? Loving God, Artemis, don't tell me you're falling for him! I know he's convincing and as handsome as the devil, but—"

"I am not falling for him. I don't even think I like him, and I didn't believe him. That's not the point."

"Then what, pray tell, is?"

"All right, suppose I do go to Mr. Harrison or the police. Maybe they'll believe me just enough to call in Todd. What does he tell them? Some story that has nothing at all to do with the truth. They believe him, send me off, and either he goes back to what he was doing in the first place or just quits and goes home. Then we never find out what he's up to. But suppose I don't say anything. You said yourself that Todd can't be dangerous. Well, I agree. That means we don't have to worry that he'll go off and murder someone—"

"Don't say *we*, Artemis."

"All right, all right. *I* don't have to worry that he'll go off and murder someone. If I lie low, either I'll find out what he's up to on my own or he'll go and hang himself—"

"And you'll save yourself from challenging the iron will of Todd Blakesly Hall," Holly pointed out nastily.

"I don't care about that, and you know it."

"I do not."

"Then you go to the police—or R. W. I don't care. But I'm not. I want to know what Hall's up to and if Jack knows about it." And if, I added silently, it has anything to do with me.

Holly sighed, but I knew I had won. "And how do you propose to find out?"

"I'll think of something."

That was good enough for her. She was still disgusted with me, but I could tell she thought I'd never come up with a plan to uncover Todd or the activities at Rosewood, and therefore would stick to my affairs and leave him to his. But, of course, I did win the argument, so she sulked all the way back to Saratoga.

When we reached my apartment, she informed me that she wanted to go straight to the airport—she would endure the cobwebs and spiders—and I could go up and get her suitcase and handle any heavies lurking in the bushes. I muttered that the only heavies within miles of here were in her head and left her in the car.

I ran upstairs, grabbed her suitcase, and ran back down. I dumped it in the backseat and hopped back in the front. I pretended that I had hurried out of disgust with her, rather than with a case of the jitters.

"See," I said, "no heavies."

Holly was not encouraged.

I got onto the interstate. We were about thirty minutes from the Albany airport, and I didn't intend to spend the entire time with Holly Dearborn scowling silently next to me. I threw a monkey wrench into her annoyance by apologizing for dragging her into my affairs. I pronounced *affairs* with as good a Brahmin accent as I could. Holly responded with a terse, but effective, obscenity, then laughed.

"Are you going to tell Hans?" I asked.

"Good God, no," she said. "He'd either ship me to the nuthouse or grab a shotgun and go after Todd Hall himself. Probably both. He's so law-and-order, bless his incorruptible heart. But you listen to me, Artemis Pendleton, I am calling you every single night until Todd Blakesly Hall is back in Boston tending to his publishing house. If I suspect you're in trouble, I'm phoning in the police. Understood?"

I smiled. "Actually, that's rather comforting."

"Good."

We both decided enough had been said about Todd, so I asked her about Hans. She told me all about their romance in Jamaica, and, by the time we arrived at the airport, I was convinced she was genuinely in love with her beekeeper and might even marry him. I was glad for her, but tonight her happiness seemed to accentuate my own aloneness. If anything happened to Holly, I was sure Hans would avenge her death and remain celibate for life. If anything happened to me, people would just shake their heads and say I was better off and should have been in the car with my parents that day in May.

"Why are you so gloomy?" Holly asked. "Are my stories that boring?"

"Just feeling sorry for myself. Sometimes I feel so damned alone. I'm not unhappy, but occasionally—"

"Occasionally you wish you weren't dealt such a bitching unlucky lot in life. I don't blame you. The least you could have are bunches of cousins and uncles and aunts to run to instead of just your grandparents." Her tone softened as she went on. "You're a hard-ass, the worst I know, and I guess I would be if I had to contend with your looks and your past, but don't be afraid to let your guard down once in a while. People will understand."

"Thanks," I said.

"Hell, if I were you, I'd find out if Jack Harrison's a good guy and tell him your fears and troubles and—"

"And I'm staying out of this mess, remember?" I laughed and turned into the airport. "Want me to drop you off first and hunt up a parking place, or—"

"Just dump me at the proper door, or is there only one? Whatever. Go on home and scrub off your spiders and cobwebs. I'll just be standing in lines." She gave me a hug. "I feel so guilty leaving you here. Todd Hall's an animal, you know that? I know he's handsome and rich and probably leaves you panting for more when he kisses you, but he's trouble."

"Holly, I'll be fine."

"Do you like it better when he calls you Artie or Miss Pendleton?"

"Holly!"

"Well, if you change your mind and want to come to Iowa—"

"I'll let you know."

She got her suitcase out of the backseat. "But you won't change your mind. It's just as well you're the last of the Pendletons, I'm sure. Let me know the finale to this affair, will you? And, damn it, plan to be at the wedding!" She smiled and, leaning over her suitcase, gave me another hug. "Be careful, okay?"

Holly pushed open the door and dragged her suitcase behind her. Another good-bye, another admonishment about Todd Hall, and she turned up the sidewalk. I watched her stumble past an old man, wave at me, then disappear inside the terminal. Her plane would leave in thirty minutes.

In forty-five, I was home in bed.

Chapter Eight

Fifteen minutes later I was sitting on the couch in my dark apartment without a stitch on, yawning a hello into the telephone. A deep masculine voice on the other end woke me up.

"Hello, is this Artemis Pendleton?" it said.

"Yes."

"This is Hans Erikson. May I speak to Holly, please?"

"She's already at the airport." I glanced at the digital clock glowing 1:31 across the room. "Her plane left thirty minutes ago."

His sigh betrayed annoyance. "But she left a message saying she would be staying with you a while longer. You mean she isn't?"

"I don't understand. When did she call?"

"About twenty minutes ago. She spoke to my mother."

My thumbnail went into my mouth. Holly had to be on that plane. If not . . .

"She's not backing out on me, is she?" Hans asked stoically, but I detected an undertone of fear.

"No, no," I assured him. "She probably just missed her flight. We—we were running late. I just got home myself, so she hasn't had a chance to get hold of me yet."

"Would you have her call me when she does reach you? I'll wait up."

"Yes, of course."

"Sorry to have bothered you. Good night."

I grunted and hung up.

Where in hell was Holly?

My stomach told me where, but I had to be sure she hadn't simply missed her plane before I went to the police.

I switched on a light and tore at the phone book for the number of the airport. I stiffened my fingers to keep them from shaking and dialed. Eighteen rings later a woman answered, and I asked her to page Holly. Yes, I would hold. I watched three minutes flick away on the digital clock. The woman told me Miss Dearborn had not answered the page.

I hung up.

She wasn't at the airport. She wasn't on her plane. She wasn't here with me.

Todd Hall.

He had decided she knew too much, met her at the airport, forced her to call Iowa—

I closed my eyes to arrest the approaching panic. The son of a bitch had lied to me and tricked me into complacency, and now he had Holly.

Suddenly my panic turned to anger.

I got into a pair of jeans and found a sweat shirt in a basket of clean laundry. I had it in hand when I heard the quiet creaking on the stairs to my apartment. I felt the familiar lump of terror in my throat, the knees of jelly, the feet cemented to the floor.

I listened to two more creaks. Then I collected my wits and scrambled to the kitchen alcove where I jumped onto the sink and yanked the screen from the window above it. I threw the screen to the floor and crawled belly-up and feet-first out the window. I flipped myself around as my toes latched onto the rickety, ivy-covered fire ladder that clung precariously to the side of the house. I dropped my sweat shirt ahead of me. I slid most of the way and jumped the last six feet, landing with a soft thud in Mrs. Martin's flowerbed. It smelled of dahlias.

From upstairs came the cracking of wood and the mutter of men's voices. I kept in the shadow of the house and ran toward Court Street.

Sheer instinct dropped me to my hands and knees.

I crawled under a lilac and poked my head around a drainpipe. At first I didn't notice it. I was looking for a dark gray Alfa Romeo, not a BMW. It was parked in front of my Falcon. I couldn't see the license plate, and I wasn't sure whether it was dark blue or dark green. But it was there, a BMW, with a man in the driver's seat, his back to me, his head turned toward Mrs. Martin's house.

I shuddered and turned back.

How many men did Todd Hall have working for him? And where was Holly? Dead in the trunk? Already deposited in a ditch and—

I didn't finish the thought. I was already racing across the narrow side yard to a row of hedges, which I negotiated as quickly as I could. I landed squarely on my back in a tomato patch, still muddy from its nightly watering. I ducked and, staying within the shelter of the hedges, scurried down the length of the yard, trampling prickly cucumber vines in my bare feet before making a ninety-degree turn between two rows of shoulder-high corn. The damp stalks scratched my naked breasts and made me itch all over, but I ignored the discomfort.

I emerged from the corn patch, mangled a garden of petunias and portulaca, and finally thrust myself over the row of hedges that separated the yard from Phila Street. I landed hard on my feet.

I resisted the urge to pause and catch my breath. Instead I broke into a dead run. My bare feet absorbed the painful shock of every step, but there was nothing I could do but grit my teeth and keep running. I pulled on my sweat shirt, wet and muddy from the romp through the neighbor's yard, and tripped on a crack in the pavement. I managed not to fall and only gave a casual glance at the gush of blood from my left big toe.

A car screeched on Court Street. I knew the man in the BMW was after me.

I got to the corner of Circular and Phila and dropped flat behind the nearest tree in the nearest yard. The BMW paused at the intersection, then went straight, up Phila, toward downtown Saratoga. I leaped up and continued running left on Circular, also toward downtown.

Then the BMW was on Circular, headed for me.

I dove into another lawn, behind another tree. The BMW sped past me.

This time I waited. The BMW turned around again and came back down Circular. I ran through the lawns on Circular until I reached the corner at Spring Street. I glanced over my shoulder. The BMW again was speeding down Circular.

I cut across the yard at the corner of Spring and Circular

The Venus Shoe

and scrambled down Spring. The BMW passed me. I heard the screech of brakes.

I knew I was caught.

Then there was a branch of a maple in front of me. I didn't break stride or look back or think. I simply grabbed the branch with both arms, swung myself onto it, and started to climb. I paid no attention to the scratches of the rough bark on my feet and hands, the near misses of my groping feet, the height I was gaining. I kept my eyes glued to the street below, watching for the headlights of the BMW. They appeared, and, high in the maple, I stopped.

Two doors slammed shut. I inhaled deeply through my nose, held in the air, then exhaled, slowly and silently, through my mouth.

I was standing, my arms wrapped around the trunk, both feet on the same thin branch. I didn't dare move. I heard street shoes strike the sidewalk. I glanced down. The massive old maple occupied half the width of the sidewalk and overhung the street. Had it not been for the thick foliage and branches, I would have had the perfect vantage point. As it was, however, I could only see a small patch of sidewalk below me.

And the gleam of headlights from the street.

I unwrapped one arm from the trunk and, pivoting slightly, stretched sideways over the street.

The BMW was stopped on the opposite side of the street. Two men were bent over the open window on the driver's side. One was big, too heavy to be Todd Hall. The other was tall, but too thin to be Todd Hall. They spoke in an unintelligible rumble. When they stood up, I lost them in the foliage, but I thought the big one had a beard and the thin one sparse, curly hair.

The BMW drove off, and I heard the two men cross the street.

I returned to my previous position and posted watch on the patch of sidewalk below me. They never appeared in it. For thirty minutes, they paced up and down the sidewalk. I envisioned them peering into yards and porches, behind fences, trees, bushes.

And I wondered what I had done wrong. I hadn't gone to the police or Richard Harrison. I hadn't found anything in the pine grove that would damn Todd Hall. I hadn't told anyone—except Holly Dearborn—what I knew about him. I hadn't even pressed him too hard for an explanation.

What had I done?

And Holly. What had been her transgression?

She had been right, and I had been a fool. We should have gone immediately, directly, and without hesitation or debate, to the police and R. W.

Why had I trusted Todd Hall?

The men gave up their search. The BMW crept alongside the sidewalk directly below me. I could see the top of the car, but I still didn't know if it was blue or green.

"Not a damned thing. Christ, she has to be somewhere. I know she came down here."

"Maybe she's in the park."

Congress Park, I thought. Not a bad idea, only it was on the other side of Circular Street, and I doubted I could have crossed in front of the BMW.

Apparently the low, even words that followed—I was sure they came from the driver—agreed with me, because they were answered with, "But Jesus, we've looked everywhere. She's probably seen us and got the plates memorized and is on her way to the police—"

That was all the driver needed. The car door opened, then slammed shut, and the BMW sped off.

I didn't move. For fifteen minutes, I stood motionless in the tree and waited for the BMW to return. Finally, I unglued my arms from the trunk and crawled down the ladder of branches.

Was the BMW lurking around the corner, the men waiting for me to come out of hiding?

I dropped to the sidewalk. The numbness of desperation was gone, and I felt the pain that shot up from my raw feet. But I summoned whatever stoicism I had remaining, stood right up without so much as a groan, and started back up Spring Street.

The safest place to go, I decided, was not downtown to the police station but back to my apartment. The men from the BMW would not risk returning there. They could not know, as I did, that Mrs. Martin was spending a few days with her sister. They would expect her—or even a neighbor—to have heard the commotion upstairs and called the police.

They would not be there waiting for me.

Chapter Nine

I PLACED a hand on the railing at the bottom of the stairs to my apartment and listened. Nothing. I picked up the garden spade leaning against the house and slowly, without turning on the porch light, mounted the steps.

My door stood open. I could see the shadow of the safety lock where it clung dutifully to the doorjamb and the splintered hole it left on my door.

I swallowed in a dry throat and raised my spade.

Terror burned in my eyes and pounded in my ears, but I stepped inside and, spade held high and steady, tried to spot the enemy among the shadows of my apartment.

"Is anyone in here?"

My voice rasped, but my hand crept confidently along the wall for the light switch.

"Artemis? Oh, God, Artemis, is that you?"

The light was on, and Holly Dearborn was rushing from the bathroom. She dropped her butcher knife, and I dropped my spade. We met in the center of the room, hugged each other, and sobbed with relief.

After a while, we sat down at the oak table, wiped our tears, and asked each other what had happened. Not until then did I notice the raw pink lump above Holly's right eye.

"My God," I said, appalled. I ran to the refrigerator, got out some ice, wrapped it in a dish towel, and handed it to Holly. "You first."

She took the dish towel and placed it on the lump. There were cuts on her knuckles. Her fingers were shaking. She was sucking on her upper lip. Her auburn hair was disheveled. Everything about her suggested that she had been through far worse than I.

"Are you hurt?" she asked, her voice disconcertingly calm. "Maybe we should call the police now and—"

"We will," I said decisively. "But first, what happened to you?"

She nodded meekly.

"Holly, are you going to be all right?"

"Yes, I'm sorry. I just—it doesn't make any sense."

"Why don't you begin at the beginning," I said. "Do you want a glass of Jack Daniel's?"

"No, I'm all right." She laid the dish towel of ice on the table, got out a cigarette, lit it, and took three quick puffs. "After you dropped me off at the airport, I went inside and checked in, found out where I was supposed to catch my plane, and bought a cup of coffee from one of those filthy machines. I wasn't there fifteen minutes when I heard your name paged over the loudspeaker. Naturally, I went to see what was going on. Well, wasn't there a nice little note for you? 'Artemis,' it said, 'please meet me at the east end of the parking lot. It's urgent.' Urgent was underlined, and it was signed Jack. Lovely, eh?"

"Jack?"

"Harrison, I assumed."

"Do you still have the note?"

"No. I'm getting to that part." She sucked on her cigarette and leaned back in her chair. "I didn't know what to think, of course. At this point I had talked myself into believing our man Todd was as innocent as the driven snow and you were perfectly justified in not going to the police. I just didn't know what to make of this note. So I asked the clerk to describe the man who left it. He said he didn't see him. The note apparently was left while his back was turned. That made me very suspicious, needless to say. The clerk didn't seem to think anything of it. But, can you believe this? Stupid me went out to the parking lot, anyway. Don't ask me what I was thinking."

"But, Holly, Jack Harrison would have waited for me inside the airport. He wouldn't write a note."

"Precisely," Holly said dryly. "Provided Jack Harrison wrote the note."

"Oh, God."

"I was about two-thirds of the way to the east end of the parking lot when three men jumped out from some cars and tackled me."

"Holly!"

"Yes, I know. Twenty-five years I've lived in Boston and never have been mugged. But, of course, this was no mugging. There were two big beefs and one little guy. They knocked me down and dragged me out of sight between the cars and proceeded to wrench my elbows to my ears. Well, while they were wrenching, you'll be pleased to know they kept asking me what I had done with the jewels and where the hell did I think I was going."

"Jewels? Holly, what jewels?"

She held up a hand. "Let me finish. I managed to pull my face off the asphalt and scream—well, it seemed like a scream at the time, but it certainly didn't attract any attention. They merely wrenched my arms harder and told me to shut up and tell them what I had done with the jewels and—get this—kept calling me Artemis Pendleton."

"But Holly—"

"You don't have any jewels. I know that. These goons, however, thought I was you and you knew about their goddamn jewels. I finally got out something to the effect that I was not Artemis Pendleton. I think I even denied knowing you existed. It didn't get me very far."

"Why—"

She held up a hand. "Then this voice came out of nowhere—very literate and quite commanding it was. I gather he was the boss goon. I remember exactly what he said: 'Let up a little. She's not Pendleton, you fools.' They let up—precious little. One kept a hand on my neck so I couldn't look up and see their faces. So the voice goes on to tell me that no harm will come to me or you if we would just cooperate. All you had to do was tell them about their jewels, and all I had to do was tell them where you were. Then I could go about my business, and you could go about yours. Coward that I am, I told them you had dropped me off and I didn't know where you were going. I should have said you were on your way to Alabama or something—"

"That wouldn't have done any good."

"I suppose. Anyway. The little guy searched my bag and found my name and address and my plane ticket. Thank

God I still didn't have the Baretta! Then the voice came on again. He was pretty damned persuasive, let me tell you. He said that if I wanted you and my family to remain unharmed—those were the words he used—that I should just go on to Des Moines and forget this whole 'unfortunate incident.' He emphasized that I shouldn't worry about you. He also made it very clear that going to the police would only get you and my family hurt and wouldn't get him caught. So, then one of his goons knocked me on the head and left me lying there. When I came to—it must have been just a second or two later—they were gone."

"Holly, for God's sake, why aren't you in Iowa? Your parents—"

"Are in Copenhagen, and I would love to see them track down my little brother. An idle threat. If the police can't catch this guy—and I'm more than willing to believe they can't—then why should he go murdering people? For revenge against someone who happened to be in the wrong place at the wrong time? He's smarter than that. I wasn't worried about me or my family, only you. My hiding in Iowa wasn't going to do you one damn bit of good. I had already checked in and everything. I just didn't board the plane. Artemis, how could I have? With this lump on my head and you being chased by a carload of creeps?"

"So you called Hans and told him you weren't coming for a few days."

She stared at me. "Yes, how did you know?"

"He called. I'll get to that. Finish your story."

Holly stubbed out her cigarette on her old plate of broccoli-and-tomato casserole. "Actually, I tried to call you first," she said, "but you weren't home yet. I should have called the police, but I wasn't thinking too clearly. I called a cab instead, then Hans's mother. I tried you a few more times while I was waiting, but no answer. For all I knew, a whole other set of goons had already grabbed you. Finally, my cab came, and I came directly here. I started up the steps, but I heard someone ransacking your apartment, so—"

"What?"

"He didn't really make much of a mess, did he?"

I glanced around the room. For the first time I noticed the two open bureau drawers, the books thrown on the floor, the mattress askew on my bed, the clothes basket dumped on the cedar chest, and the crooked couch cushions.

"No," I said dully, "I guess he didn't."

"Well, of course, I tiptoed back downstairs. I hid in the shrubs and prayed to God you weren't dead. Maybe five minutes later he came down and went around front. I was in the side yard; you know, this one here"—she pointed to the wall with the kitchen and bedroom alcoves—"so I sneaked up behind a lilac and watched him. He was there maybe a minute before a BMW picked him up."

"Did you recognize him?"

"Yeah, more or less. He was the little guy who searched me: dark hair, big nose, I think. I never got a good look at him. There are four men after us, Artemis: my little guy, two big beefs, and the one with the literate voice."

My throat was tight. "Todd?"

"I don't know. Maybe. I was hurting at the time, so I didn't pay too close attention to what he sounded like."

I nodded, but my heart was sinking fast. "Anything else?"

"The BMW was blue, but I couldn't see the license plate."

"Are you sure it was blue?"

"Of course."

My smile was feeble, but the thought was there. "You're the artist."

"Well, anyway, once they left, I came crawling up here. I was scared to death, Artemis. I thought they'd killed you or kidnapped you—I didn't know what the hell I'd find. When I saw the open window, I thought you might have escaped, but I just didn't know. Then I heard you coming upstairs, only I didn't know it was you, so I grabbed a knife and hid in the bathroom. Damned if I knew what to do." She grinned, and a little color appeared in her cheeks. "We're lucky we didn't kill each other."

"I'm sorry, Holly," I said. "I never should have said a word to you about any of this."

"What good would that have done? I still would have answered your page and gone out to the parking lot and been mistaken for you and gotten beaten up. The only difference is I wouldn't have been an ass for doing it. Christ, I should have known better! So forget it. What's done is done. I'll let you know when I want your guilt. Now, what's your story?"

I told her as succinctly and as fully as I could. When I had finished, we sat in silence for a full minute. I could feel Todd's lips warm on mine, see the incongruous dimple in his cheek, hear his deep laugh. But the truth was staring me in the face, and my father had always said only fools ignore what's in front of them. "Todd's the only one who knew we were going to the airport."

"But it doesn't make sense!" Holly said. "He had us. If he thought you had the jewels, why would he let us go?"

"Something changed his mind," I said. "After we left, something happened that made him think I had found these jewels."

"*What* jewels?" Holly asked irritably, but didn't wait for me to reply. "Hall can't be a jewel thief, for God's sake! He's a publisher! Well, I say we call the police and let them sort out this mess."

"What would we tell them?"

"Everything, you idiot."

"What about Todd?"

"We don't know he's our fourth man, but I'll bet the police can find out for us."

"Why should we speculate?"

"Damn it, Artemis, look what happened here tonight!"

I ignored the growing irritation in her tone. "It doesn't seem Todd Hall's style to hire three men to do a job he could have done himself. All he had to do was knock on my door and say, 'Artemis Pendleton, where are my jewels?' And I'd have said, 'What jewels?'"

"Wait a minute!" Holly sat up straight. "Suppose he had these guys watching you and told them that if you did anything suspicious to haul you in for a little talk. Now, what did you do? You went up to your apartment—alone—and came down with a suitcase. They didn't know about me and my trip to Iowa. Hall did, but he was at Rosewood and had no chance to communicate with them. So they follow us to the airport, and I get out—"

"But I didn't. They would have seen me drive off."

"Not necessarily. Maybe they weren't following too closely. All they know is that a female with a suitcase goes into the airport. So they try this note from Jack to woo you into the parking lot. Only the female with suitcase is Holly Dearborn and not Artemis Pendleton."

"They're pretty dumb, then."

Holly shrugged. "I never have given thugs much credit for brains."

"All right, it's possible. So how does Todd fit in?"

"There are three possibilities." She counted them off on her long fingers. "One, he doesn't. Two, he hired all *four* men and the boss goon is someone else and actually answerable to him. Three, he hired three goons to watch the house, they alerted him, and then followed us to the airport. He met them there and let them know they had the wrong woman."

"It's got to be one or two," I said. "Why would Todd bother racing back to Saratoga to rout me out of bed if he knew we'd just done exactly as we told him we would do?"

"Those men knocked me in the head, Artemis. And, if nothing else, Todd proved he wasn't a nice guy back there in the woods. Maybe he could count on me going on to Iowa, but he knew I'd get in touch with you sooner or later and tell you what happened."

I was silent.

"Call the police, Artemis," Holly said quietly.

I said nothing.

"Artemis!"

I sighed. "What if they don't believe us?"

"What do you mean? I have a lump on my head, and you've got bloody feet and a torn-up apartment to prove our story. Why wouldn't they believe us?"

"Oh, they'll believe we were chased and beaten up all right, but suppose they don't draw the same conclusions we have? Suppose they call it harassment, nod their heads, and say they'll keep their eyes open?"

"That's better than nothing."

"And meanwhile Todd gets away and we never find out a damn thing about what he's up to and whether or not Jack Harrison knows about it or is involved."

"So?"

"So I want to know."

Holly kicked out her legs and ran both hands through her hair. Then she growled in exasperation.

"I'm not saying I won't call the police," I went on. "I'm just debating how much to tell them. I don't want to tell them about Todd, Holly. I'm sorry."

She closed her eyes. I knew her head was pounding with pain, but I also knew I had to have my way. She said quietly, "Why?"

"I'm not sure."

"You are. You just won't tell me."

"You're already too involved."

"Artemis, either I am involved or I am not involved. There isn't any 'too' about it."

I closed my eyes, trying to blot out the pain and fatigue and, most of all, the memories. Finally I looked at Holly. "All right," I said grudgingly. "I think Todd Hall might be trying to find out what happened to Patrice Harrison."

"Jack's mother—the one who disappeared with over a million in jewels? Oh, wonderful, Artemis. Wonderful."

"Todd must believe my father had something to do with the robbery and Patrice's disappearance."

"And Jack Harrison's the one who put him on the trail."

"Exactly. When I met Jack this afternoon I thought—I thought I was wrong. He seemed so glad to see me. But that could have been an act. Don't you see? He can't creep about the woods without good reason, especially if I might run into him and get suspicious. But Todd could."

"And he reports back to Jack," Holly added. "Then they must think—Artemis, they must think you know your father was involved. . . ."

"But he wasn't!"

"Jesus."

It was as close as I'd ever heard Holly Dearborn come to praying. I closed my eyes again and breathed deeply, steadily, slowly steeling myself against any rush of emotion. Todd Hall and Jack Harrison believed that my father had killed Patrice Harrison. They believed that I had come to Rosewood for the jewels that Martin, fearing discovery, had never been able to bring out of hiding.

Martin's daughter would know where to find them.

How Jack must have hated me! How he must have been retching inside during his performance that afternoon! And Todd was his ally. Now all the comments he'd made and the questions he'd asked on the island began to make some sense. He didn't want me to know what they were after. Of course not. And neither did Jack.

It all made such perfect sense . . . except why Todd had kissed me. . . .

I opened my eyes and smiled at Holly, but I knew my face was pale. "You okay?" she asked.

"I'm fine."

I poured myself a glass of Tennessee bourbon and dialed the police station.

The police dusted my apartment for fingerprints and believed everything I said. My story included all the essential facts: my visit with an old friend, our trip to the airport, the footsteps outside my apartment, my escape via the kitchen window and subsequent flight through the streets of Saratoga. I said the car was a blue BMW. I said there were three men for sure, one big and heavy, another tall and thin, a third small.

If the goons found out about my talk with the police, they would think their scare tactics had worked and never give a thought to my not mentioning the fourth man. After all, Holly hadn't *seen* him. For all she knew for sure, the voice *could* have come from one of her attackers. And I couldn't mention him, not until I knew for certain he wasn't Todd . . . or wasn't hired by Todd.

I said Holly Dearborn had called me between flights in New York to tell me about her ordeal and was en route to Iowa.

I related what happened to her in such a way that the police wouldn't go through all the trouble of contacting her in Iowa. I didn't have her number, I said, and she didn't want her fiancé to find out what had happened.

I sounded confused, innocent, as though I had no idea in the world why these men had broken into my apartment and tracked down my friend Holly.

Utterly convincing.

Holly, meanwhile, was walking around the block cursing my soul and smoking the last of her cigarettes. She hated letting me have my own way. "Bull cookies they'll believe you," she had said in her inimitable style.

They believed me.

August, Sergeant Dick Warner said, is crazy month in

Saratoga Springs. Too many people in town, not enough police officers to keep an eye on them all. Lots of men on the lookout for attractive women. Two attractive women alone? Sitting ducks, he was sorry to say. His conclusion: sexual harassment. Maybe we'd encountered them earlier in the evening and—unknowingly, of course—offended them, and they were getting their revenge. Or maybe they were just drunks cruising the streets and happened to spot us. Maybe this, maybe that. They wouldn't be back—not likely, anyway. And anything they'd said to us about jewels and whatnot was doubtlessly a ploy, a scare tactic.

Sergeant Warner promised to increase patrols of Court Street for the next few days and keep a lookout for a blue BMW and the men I'd vaguely described. But, of course, it *was* racing season.

In the meantime, he said, I should get a new door.

Chapter Ten

Holly returned from her walk, and together we made our plans. They were sketchy at best, but we didn't have too many options. Holly called Hans and told him the most convincing lie I'd ever heard, while at the same time reassuring him of her undying love. Then, confident that we would succeed, we slept, Holly on the bed, me on the couch. Sun streaming through the window above the couch woke us just after seven. I made tea while Holly showered. Then she made toast and more tea while I showered.

Finally, at eight o'clock, when we were cleaned, dressed, fed, and bandaged, I called Rosewood.

"Nora? Artemis. Listen, can you tell Jeff I won't be in today? I—"

"Are you sick?" Nora asked, concerned.

"No, no. Some idiots broke into my apartment last night and chased me into the streets. It's a long story. I'm all right, but they ruined my door and tore up the place a bit. It—"

"You called the police, didn't you, honey?"

"Yes, of course, but there's not much they can do—"

"Never is. You would think—"

It was my turn to cut her off. "You will tell Jeff, won't you? He doesn't get in until nine, and I have to order a new door—"

"Are you all right? Maybe I should call Bud and have him go down there."

"No! Nora, I'm fine," I reassured her. "Tell Jeff I'll try to get there by this afternoon."

"You take all the time you need, honey. I'll handle

Jeffrey Chapman. I hate the idea of you being alone down there—"

"Thanks, Nora. 'Bye."

I hung up and turned to Holly. "Well, the word is out."

Holly was lying on the couch with an ice pack on her bruised forehead and a bottle of aspirin on her lap. Her enthusiasm for our plan waxed and waned with every throb of her poor head. Right now it was waning. "You really think she'll tell Todd?"

"Not directly, but he'll find out. Ten to one he'll be pulling up behind my Falcon within the hour."

Holly moaned and took off her ice pack. "I hope to hell you know what you're doing."

"It's what I have to do, Holly. My father wasn't a murderer and a thief."

"Let's just hope our man doesn't bring his thirty-eight. I guess we'd better get to our stations."

It was only forty minutes, and it wasn't Todd Hall who arrived.

Jack Harrison, frowning and obviously absorbed, turned up the walkway to my apartment. I was assuming a relaxed, unworried position on my lounge chair in front of Mrs. Martin's vegetable garden. I had a leaflet on toxic fruit-tree pesticides on my lap and a glass of Jack Daniel's in my hand.

"Hello, there," I said with a coolness I did not feel. The bastard. The spurious, two-faced bastard. My father was not a murdering thief! I smiled my goddess-of-the-hunt smile. "You're not going to tell your father you caught me sitting in the sun when I was supposed to be watering his plants."

Jack rushed over to me. "Artemis! Nora told me what happened. Are you all right?"

"Just a stubbed toe." I pointed to my bandaged foot. "Nora exaggerates."

"A stubbed—oh, I see."

Perspiration glistened on Jack's pale brow. He was dressed sloppily, in a work shirt and jeans, and looked upset. Genuinely upset. Had I misjudged him after all? I threw my legs off the end of the lounge and asked him to sit down. He refused. I shrugged and watched him pace nervously beside me while he wiped his brow with the palm of his hand. Suddenly it occurred to me that he was far more upset than my story to Nora had warranted. He knew something. At the very least, his friend Todd had told him about the goings-on in the woods last night.

"Look, Artemis, Nora was awfully sketchy," he said, raking one hand through his hair. "What happened?"

I took what I hoped was a nonchalant sip and not an eager gulp of bourbon. Did he know already? I admonished myself to be objective—or at least calm and collected. "There's not much to tell," I said. "The police think I was just being harassed. It's not the first time. I remember once in college—"

"Artemis, please!"

Jack rubbed the back of his neck as though it were stiff. Then he said, gravely, "I think you'd better tell me what happened."

I told him exactly what I had told the police. There was no mention of Holly, now hiding in the backseat of my Falcon, or of Todd Hall.

"You see," I said in conclusion, "it's all so silly. I'd just as soon forget the whole thing."

Jack stuffed his hands in his pants pockets, then removed them. "Artemis, this may not be as silly as you think."

"Oh?" I smiled. "Why, do you know someone who drives a blue BMW and is missing some jewels?"

He stiffened but said smoothly, "No, but I wish I did." Then he sat at the end of the lounge and stared at his hands. At length, he turned to me. "Have you told me everything?"

"I told you, there wasn't much to it."

His eyes softened. "Artemis, I'd like to help. I care about you—"

"Thank you," I said, hoping that the shrug of my shoulders conveyed a familiarity with men who cared about me. "But there's really nothing you can do."

"Are you still angry with me?"

"For what?"

"For not contacting you in thirteen years, even when your parents died—"

"Oh, stop it, please!" He was good, too damn good. I was doubting myself already. But all the evidence pointed to the simple fact that Jack Harrison suspected my father of murder and me of such greed and callousness that I had come to Rosewood for over a million dollars in jewels. "I'm not the twelve-year-old girl who used to idolize you, Jack. You hurt me, but that was a long time ago. You hurt my parents even more, did you know that? Why? Why didn't you ever contact them?"

Jack lowered his head. "I'm sorry, Artemis. It's all I know to say."

Did I dare believe him? "Why did you come back to Rosewood?"

"What? Oh, because I wanted to see you. You knew that, didn't you?"

"It's what I've been told, but why didn't you tell me so in the first place?"

He smiled, sadness in his sensitive, handsome face. "Because I felt like a fool. The gangly twelve-year-old I had left had turned, thirteen years later, into an intelligent, cool beauty. I was shocked, Artemis. That's all."

His tone hadn't changed, but I knew he was hedging. He wasn't telling me everything. After all, he had yet to explain his friend Todd and the goings-on out at the lake. I didn't for a single moment believe that he didn't know about them.

"Why did *you* come back to Rosewood, Artemis? I've been trying to understand it, and I just can't."

So now, I thought, we were getting down to the nitty-gritty. "I told you. I needed a job. Do you think there's some other reason?"

"I do. You don't need this job, Artemis. The University of Massachusetts has offered you all but the sun and the moon to attend its graduate school. So has the University of Michigan, Duke—"

"How do you know?"

"Father was thinking about giving you a scholarship. He asked me to look into it. So I called your grandparents and found out everything. Six universities, Artemis. Six. Every one of them has offered you a full financial-aid package."

"All right, all right—"

"Why did you lie to me? You said your grades were poor, yet you graduated summa cum laude—"

"What difference does it make? I'm here. I came back here because I needed to see Rosewood again. That's all, Jack. Is it so hard to believe?"

He shook his head painfully.

"Then why keep after me? Jack—never mind."

He placed a hand on my knee and looked at me intently. "You won't let me help?"

"Help me with *what?*"

"Artemis, those men last night—"

"—won't be back, according to the police."

"That isn't the point," he said. "Artemis, have you told me everything?"

I looked at him sharply. I was sure at last. Jack still suspected my father—and perhaps even my mother—and he still suspected me.

"Yes, I have."

"Look, maybe it would be a good idea if you stayed at Rosewood until the police come up with something."

So he could keep an eye on me? Make sure I didn't steal any jewels? "I don't need your help, Jack."

"Don't get your back up," he said, smiling thinly now. "I'm not going to force you to do anything. Look, I've got to get back. If you change your mind or need me for any reason, call. Okay?"

I didn't expect him to abandon ship quite so quickly, but I'd found out all I expected to—and more than I'd wanted to. I nodded at him and thanked him for his concern.

He patted my knee. "Get some rest and don't worry about anything."

What was that supposed to mean? "Right," I said hollowly.

"Jack Harrison, I presume?" Holly said, curling up on the lawn after Jack had left. "Or another of your rich admirers?"

"You know perfectly well I have no rich admirers."

"No, I know of your *aversion* to rich admirers. He's not bad, you know. Not our he-man Todd, but he'd certainly do for a brief affair, winter in the Caribbean, say—"

"Holly!"

"Oh, all right. He drives a white Porsche—not a blue BMW, thank God. As far as I could tell, he came alone and wasn't followed. And the next time you want me to hide in your car and play spy, make sure it's not parked in the sun. I feel like a tomato left to rot on the vine." She lit her last cigarette. "Well?"

As accurately as I could, I repeated my conversation with Jack.

"Knows all your weak spots, doesn't he?"

"He thinks I'm holding out on him."

"Well, you are."

"I just don't understand what their game is!"

Holly inhaled on her cigarette and blew the smoke at the sky. "Or they yours. They do seem convinced you know where Patrice Harrison's jewels are."

I groaned, disgusted. "How could they be so stupid!"

"Look, Artemis, you can sit here all day and think up all sorts of explanations, but the only way you're going to find out which is right is to ask this Jack, or Todd. Take your pick. Me, I'd talk to Jack."

"I don't want to talk to either of them."

"Of course you don't. Apparently they suspect—or suspected—your father of murder and you of being a little thief, in which case this must all be some sort of grim misunderstanding you'd better settle right now. You don't have any choice, Artemis." She slid her fingers through the grass. "Damn, I wish I had another cigarette. You'll make a chain smoker of me yet. Oh, well, Hans will put a stop to it. Speaking of whom, I suppose I should give him a call."

After she'd gone, I lowered the lounge until it was almost flat, and thought about what to do next. Should I do as Holly suggested and lay it all out on the table for Jack? No, better to confront both Jack and Todd, together, on my terms. How could they believe my father had killed Patrice Harrison?

I gulped the Jack Daniel's.

"Bourbon before lunch? I'm surprised at you, Artie."

I looked up at Todd Hall and suddenly nothing else mattered. My first impulse was to leap up and throw myself into his arms and tell him everything. I wanted to trust him. He was so damned big and strong and confident, and I had been alone so long. His linen pants outlined the muscles of his legs, his white pullover shirt the muscles of his shoulders. Slowly, methodically, I reminded myself of his two guns, my questions, and the men who had invaded my apartment and beaten my friend.

Todd gave me a mock smile and a bow, and dropped a blue morning glory on my lap. I crushed it and threw it to the ground.

He laughed. "Always the little fire-eater."

"You lied to me."

"I did, didn't I?" He shrugged, put his foot on the edge of my lounge, and leaned over. "But, of course, you lied to me."

"You deserved to be lied to!" I narrowed my eyes at him and knew I was not afraid of him . . . and wondered if I was being very foolish. "Why did you send those men after me?"

"I did not send them."

No! I wanted him to say he'd sent a few of his friends out just to scare me—us—a little so I would go to Iowa with Holly. But that was ridiculous. The men in the BMW had meant business. It had never made sense that Todd had sent them, no matter what he suspected about me and my father. I could see that now.

Still . . . "But you had to! You were the only person who knew I was going to the airport."

"Was I?"

He pushed my feet aside and sat down at the end of the lounge. I wondered if it could hold both of us and, for a fleeting moment, even imagined us crashing to the ground and landing in each other's arms. My body trembled not with fear or anger, but with a sudden, insatiable yearning to meld myself against Todd and lie against him for a long, long while, forgetting this whole mess.

He fastened his eyes on me with the no-nonsense air of a proper Bostonian. I thought he would notice my telltale tremble or my shallow breathing or at least read my mind, but I was wrong. I might have been facing him across a conference table in the headquarters of Hall and Son Publishers instead of across several inches of a flimsy lounge chair. He was all business—and more than a trifle irritated. That, too, I could see in his eyes.

"I suppose no one could have followed you," he went on. "Your maroon Falcon with its Massachusetts license plates and bald tires is so unremarkable, you know. Use your head, for heaven's sake. Do you actually believe I would need to *hire* someone to get information from you or scare the hell out of you or do whatever those men meant to do to you? Have you forgotten I had you and that friend of yours at *gunpoint?*"

I gave him a white-hot look. "No, I haven't forgotten!"

I swore under my breath, furious with myself. I had told Holly I could remain cool under the worst of his arrogance. No, damn it, it wasn't his arrogance. It was my stupidity, my incomprehensible susceptibility to the man sitting beside me. I didn't want to trust him, tell him anything, or, worst of all, care about him. There was too much risk involved, too great a chance of being hurt. But it couldn't be helped. The more I saw Todd, the more I was drawn to him.

He sighed impatiently. I had the feeling I was wasting his time. "The point is, Artie, that you have these men after you—"

"Did Jack tell you?"

"Of course Jack told me, you little idiot!" Then he paused and drew in a breath that told me more than any words that he regretted his outburst. He pulled in his lips. His eyes softened. He went on quietly, "We're all caught up in this damned mess, Artie, and it's my own damn fault you're involved. I should have gotten you out of here while I had the chance."

"You never had the chance," I told him stoically. "I lost my father when I was eighteen, but even before that he never told me what to do. Don't think you can."

"The hell I can't! I've half a mind to haul your little ass—"

"Don't even think about it."

"Don't be so goddamn bullheaded, Artie. I know some of what's going on and you don't know a damn thing."

"Because you haven't told me!"

"And I don't intend to!"

"Who's being bullheaded?"

"It's for your own damn good."

"Was sticking a gun in my face for my own good?"

"Yes! Besides, it wasn't loaded."

"How the hell was I supposed to know that?"

"Artemis, for God's sake, listen to me. Jack and I didn't

hire those men. *We don't know who they are.* I don't know what you've figured we're up to, but will you please believe me? We're not going to hurt you. We're on your side."

"As the saying goes, with friends like you, who needs enemies?" I got off the lounge and gave Todd what I hoped was a contemptuous smirk. I had believed every word he said, but my heart was pumping furiously with fear and confusion. "I'm out of this, as of now. See you."

I flipped my braid over my shoulder, threw back my head, and marched across the yard. Then I started up the stairs. With control. With dignity . . .

I was three steps from my porch when I realized Todd was behind me, and Holly was inside and not in Iowa, as I had told Jack, and Jack had presumably told Todd.

Which would say loud and clear that I hadn't told them everything.

I stopped dead and turned around. "Look," I began reasonably, "except for a few inconsequential details, I told Jack everything that happened last night. Honestly. I didn't see any faces or hear any voices that I recognized. The BMW was blue and new, but I never saw the license plate. I don't care what you and Jack and these goons are up to. I really don't. As far as I'm concerned, our deal still holds. I don't know you except as a guest at Rosewood."

Todd didn't move.

"Please. Go."

"I wish it were that simple," he said heavily. "But it's not—and you know it, Artemis. I would like to talk to you."

For the moment his irritation was gone. A beguiling softness had come into his eyes: They reminded me of the ocean on a cloudy afternoon in November. Better to outwit a cold-hearted, arrogant son of a bitch than a man with sensitive eyes and a need to make amends. Still, Holly wasn't in Iowa. I shrugged as nonchalantly as I could and made a move to go back downstairs.

He said quietly, "In your apartment, if you don't mind."

"No!"

I bit my lip, but the word was already out, too suddenly, too emphatically, and far too loudly. Todd eyed me suspiciously. When I just stared at him guiltily, he grabbed my elbow, turned me around, and pushed me in the direction he commanded. "Upstairs."

So much for sensitivity and making amends. Wait until the dear man finds Holly, I thought, dreading the moment.

There was no sign of her beyond the little mound of cigarette butts on her tomato-and-broccoli casserole plate.

I wrestled my elbow from Todd's grip. "What the hell's the matter with you?"

"Why didn't you want me up here?"

"You don't trust me—and I don't trust you."

He glanced around the room, still disheveled from last night's marauder. Unexpectedly, he laughed. "You're damn right I don't trust you—it's hard to trust a smart-ass woman who thinks you're some kind of hood. I never know what in blazes you'll do next. I'm a mild-mannered publisher, Artie."

I gave him a dubious look.

He grinned, and the dimple was there, but only for an instant. He was serious again. "I wish this were all just a silly adventure, but it isn't. Look, I'd love to let you stay here with all your clutter and greenery—and that beast of yours." He pointed at Ralph atop the refrigerator. "But my sense of duty forbids it. Enough's enough, sweetheart. Start packing. I'm paying your way to Iowa."

"No."

"You don't have any choice in the matter," he said wearily.

"I can take care of myself."

"Damn it, that's not the point! Look around you, for God's sake. Those men meant business. They broke into your apartment and chased you into the streets. They beat up your friend. Isn't that enough? I don't know who in hell they are, but it's my fault they're after you—and yours for sticking your nose where it doesn't belong. *You're going to Iowa.*"

I lifted my chin and regarded him with supercilious calm, belied by the turmoil raging inside me. A part of me wanted to let this strong, capable man put me on a plane to Iowa and go about his skullduggery without my censure, approval, or involvement. But I couldn't let that happen. In my own way, I, too, was strong and capable, but, more than that, I needed to retain control over my own fate. No one—not even a man who'd made my blood boil with desire from the moment I'd seen him—was going to force me to do anything.

"I'm not going to Iowa. This affair has as much to do with me as you and Jack. More. You two think Martin Pendleton had something to do with the disappearance of Patrice Harrison and her jewels and that I came to Rosewood to recover the jewels." There. I'd said it. I hadn't intended to, but I was relieved to have it out in the open at last.

"Thought, Artie. Thought."

"I'm staying."

Todd stood very still and stared at me, every muscle in that considerable body tensed. I wasn't sure he was breathing. I met his penetrating, slanted eyes with an outward calm, but my skin was prickly, my heart thumping in my throat.

His eyes traveled up and down my body and rested on my eyes, which, I suspected, hinted at what was raging behind them. I didn't turn away but saw immediately that he was just as adamant, just as uncompromising as I.

"We're wasting time," he said in an even, deadly voice. "If you're not packed in ten minutes, you'll go as is. You *are* going, Artie—now more than ever. You might as well accept it."

All I could think of was escape, but he was between me and the door.

A glimmer of amusement danced briefly in those slate eyes. "Don't try it, Artie. I'm bigger than you."

"I told you, Todd: I'm out of it."

"After what you just said? Jack is waiting for you outside."

I gave him my best bullheaded look.

"We can stand here and argue for ten minutes, but then you're going downstairs, and Jack is driving you to the airport, putting you on a plane, and waving you good-bye."

"I'm not going. Todd, please try to understand—"

"I know I must seem like a perfect bastard to you, Artie, but I'm doing what I have to do." His eyes were on me, his mouth determined, his words very deep, almost in a monotone. "I happen to think your life is more important than your pride. If you want to hate me, go right ahead. Maybe that can be straightened out later. I have no control over those men. If they want to break in here again and kill you, then they're going to do it without asking me if it's all right. If you don't want to go to Iowa, then pick another place. Chances are you'll be back here in a week."

I looked at Todd, standing erect in front of the door, hands in his pockets, too accustomed to getting his own way, too handsome, too sensual. How was I supposed to think clearly? I turned on my heels and flounced into the bathroom.

Holly was stretched out in the tub with the shower curtain drawn and the butcher knife across her lap.

"Give me the knife," I said impulsively.

"You're an ass, you know that?"

"Give it to me."

"He'll only take it away. Besides, I agree with him."

"You—Holly!"

That I whispered my outrage did not lessen it, but Holly waved a hand dismissively. "Look at this thing rationally, if you can. I know your ego is involved, but facts are facts, and Todd's right. You can't stay here."

"He doesn't really care what happens to me. Neither does Jack."

"Maybe not in the sense you mean, but I get the feeling your fate is tied to theirs. At least go to the airport with Jack. Maybe he'll talk. For God's sake, Artemis, he can't very well force you onto a plane! Todd knows that. He's just being an animal."

"Why?"

"Because he thinks you're stubborn and feisty and would have a lot more fun dragging you out of here by your heels."

I sat on the toilet and frowned. "I don't trust him."

"Oh, hogwash."

"He won't listen to me."

"That's because all you do is hiss and grumble. Have you tried tears? No, of course not. But I'll bet he'll melt at the first sign—"

"It'll be a rainy day in hell, Holly Dearborn, before I try to get my way with tears! *Especially* with him."

"Ah, then you do like him." She stretched out, relaxing in the tub. "I wasn't sure. Usually sick plants get more of a rise out of you than a healthy male. Todd, I see, has penetrated your scientist's objectivity."

She was talking just above a whisper, probably hoping Todd would hear her. The traitor. "Give me the knife," I said.

Holly gave me a disgusted look. "So you've dug in your heels, is that it? I know better than to argue with your I-can-take-care-of-myself routine. Go. Do as you please." She handed me the knife, blade first. "Just don't maul him."

I smiled weakly and took the knife, but already I knew it would do me no good.

It clattered to the floor when Todd burst in. He hauled Holly out of the tub with one hand and jerked me by the shoulder with the other. In far too short a time and with far too much ease, he had us both on chairs at the oak table, me glowering at him and Holly cursing us both.

Jack Harrison sat opposite us, his eyes lowered.

"Jack, I'm sure there's a plane Miss Dearborn is about to miss," Todd said, not even breathing hard.

All three of us looked up at him.

"If Miss Pendleton would like to go, she may. As Miss Dearborn astutely pointed out, you can't force her on a plane."

I opened my mouth to speak, but Holly was quicker. "Suppose *I* don't want to leave?"

"I can't look after you both."

"You have such a charming way about you, Mr. Hall," Holly said dryly. "But I assure you, I am not going anywhere until I know Artemis will be all right."

Jack cut in smoothly. "We can't make any guarantees, except that we will do our best to protect Artemis."

I nearly retched.

Holly crossed her arms. It was her turn to dig in her heels. "You think she's in danger, don't you?"

"If she stays here, yes," Jack said mildly.

"Then make her come with me, for God's sake! Tell her what's going on—"

"We will, but—"

"Good. Tell us both. Now."

Jack looked to Todd for help, but instead it came from me. All I could see was the raw lump on Holly's forehead.

"Holly," I said quietly, "I'll be all right. I'll leave Saratoga, I promise. I've been wanting to go camping in the Adirondacks. I—I don't want anyone getting hurt just because I stay here."

Todd's mouth twisted doubtfully to one side. He knew I was lying.

"Why the sudden change of spirit, Artemis?" Holly asked skeptically, her arms still crossed. "If you're protecting me—"

"Oh, Holly. Look, I'll get the explanation from these two, leave Saratoga, and call you tonight. I don't want you to worry about me."

"And you don't want to worry about me. Why not get the explanation now?" She uncrossed her arms and threw them up in the air. "Oh, all right. I can't buck all three of you. I warn you, though, if you don't call me tonight, I'm phoning in the police." She looked from me to Todd to Jack. "I mean what I say."

Holly and I embraced. Behind the encouraging smile she gave me, I could see the exhaustion and the fear that were still there. I needed an ally. I wanted her to stay. I knew that all I had to do was say so and she would. But I couldn't justify that. She belonged in Iowa with Hans. I smiled back.

I told Jack to buy her a pack of cigarettes—no, two—and watched through my broken door as they left.

Chapter Eleven

I LEANED back in my chair, crossed my ankles, and looked up at Todd. "Well," I said, resigned, "where are you taking me?"

"Boston."

"I see."

"If I were in your situation, I would get the hell out of Saratoga."

"Just what is my situation?"

"You're Martin Pendleton's daughter. Let's just leave it at that, all right? Throw a few things together. I'll clean up your dishes for you."

Martin Pendleton's daughter. Oh, God!

I got my grandmother's old suitcase out from under the bed and started gathering up clothes from the floor, the cedar chest, and the open drawers. I wasn't choosy. I just grabbed what was handy and dumped it in the suitcase. Todd ran water in the sink. The silence was worse—far worse—than our arguing.

"What are you going to tell my landlady?"

He rinsed off a plate. "Nothing."

"I'll leave her a note—"

The plate clanked into the strainer and, with some distaste, he started tackling the casserole pan. "She doesn't need to know your comings and goings."

"She'll worry, especially when she sees that door! Damn it, if I want to leave her a note I'll leave her a note! She'll have to feed Ralph. You *do* want me to make my exit look natural, don't you? If I leave Ralph to starve—"

"Throw the damn beast out and let him fend for himself!"

I plopped down on the bed, dug a scrap of paper and a pencil out of my nightstand drawer, and printed a perfectly normal note to my landlady. Todd dried his hands as he walked over to the bed. He tossed the towel over his shoulder, sat down beside me, and plucked the note from my fingertips. He read it and tore it up.

"I'll see to it your beast gets fed and Mrs. Martin doesn't worry. I'll also get your door fixed. But no note."

Far too aware of his nearness, I crossed my arms over my breasts. "Just because I agreed to leave town doesn't mean you can arrange all the details for me," I said, my teeth clenched. "What do you think gives you that right?"

"This!"

He curved an iron arm around my waist and shoved me—gently but insistently—onto my back, easing his weight on top of me in that same, smooth motion. There was an instant, a single second, when I could have stopped him . . . if I had wanted to. But I didn't.

The body pressing into me was all hard and thoroughly male. I could hear him breathing. I could see his pulse beating in his throat.

"I wanted you the first moment I saw you," he rasped, "and I want you now, more than ever."

"Todd, it can't . . ."

My voice trailed off, and his mouth found mine. His hot, wet, tensed tongue parted my lips and pierced into my mouth, stealing my breath and drawing a moan from deep in my throat. Both his hands were on my waist now, lifting the edge of my shirt. The feel of his strong palms and fingers on my skin made me gasp with surprise and sudden, erotic delight. He seized the opportunity when my mouth widened with my gasp, and plunged his tongue deeper, hungrily.

"Do you see now why I can't let you stay?" His voice was very low and ragged. His hands edged up under my shirt, his fingers slipping under my bra. "I haven't been able to sleep because all I can do is think about you—think about touching you here, everywhere."

I groaned as my body began to pulse with the same urgency as his. Blood poured into my most secret places. All of me—all of him—was tensed, determined, radiating the rawness of our need.

The Venus Shoe 105

With purposeful, hot kisses, he blazed a trail along my jawline and throat while his fingers located the clasp of my bra.

"I've wanted you to do this for so long," I whispered against him. "After you'd gone . . . during those two weeks I kept thinking about you."

"Darling, I could hardly think of anything else but you—no matter how I tried not to."

I held back, not touching him, but exulting in the feel of him. My mind knew nothing but the aching need within me. My body wanted nothing but more of him. His kisses descended, hot, purposeful, maddening.

"You do want me—" I choked.

He moaned his answer as his lips reached my breast, working their way to the already straining pink nipple. He took it in his mouth and began nipping, tugging, and sucking until at last I cried out wordlessly and clasped him to me. It was happening, it was true! Neither of us could deny now what had erupted between us on the island.

"I want you, Artie," he whispered. "Can you feel how I want you?"

My hips and pelvis rocked against him. He pressed down hard, so that I could feel his swollen maleness, ready to drive into me, so perfect.

"Yes, I do! Oh, yes—please, Todd, please . . ."

But suddenly, with a groan, he pulled away, sprang up, and leaped off the bed.

I sat up quickly and rearranged my clothes, not embarrassed but bewildered . . . and aching. I watched him, breathless with arousal.

He raked his hair, pacing in front of me. "I'm sorry," he said curtly.

"Sorry! A minute ago—"

"Never mind a minute ago! I had no right to touch you."

I stared at him, shocked, my breasts still straining inside my bra, heaving as I tried to steady my breathing. And all over my body tingled with the memory of his touch. "I *wanted* you to touch me, Todd," I said quietly.

"Damn it, I won't make love to a woman who has another man in love with her—and might be in love with him herself!" He flew around me with fury and controlled passion burning in his eyes, in every tensed muscle. "Damn it, I won't."

"What?"

"Finish packing," he growled, and turned away.

There was no use trying to talk to him now. He was still on fire . . . and so was I. I snapped my suitcase shut. "I'm finished. How am I going? By bus or—"

"Alfa Romeo," Todd said curtly. "I'm driving you."

"There's no need."

"I'll carry your suitcase. You're hobbling around enough as it is."

"Todd, I can drive myself to Boston."

He paid no attention to me whatsoever. I gave up and followed him downstairs. The Alfa Romeo was parked behind my Falcon, where the BMW had been parked last night. I shuddered. I wasn't quite so hell-bent on taking care of myself at that moment. Maybe getting out of Saratoga *was* a good idea.

"You know, I can just go in my car," I offered lamely. "There's no point in your driving all that way to Boston and back. You are coming back, aren't you?"

"Yes." Todd dumped the suitcase in his trunk. "The door's unlocked. Go on, get in."

I started to argue, but Todd wasn't even looking at me. I did as he said. I thought he was angry at himself this time, not me. He was only taking it out on me. And I didn't understand: no one was in love with me, at least as far as I knew. And even if someone was, since when was Todd Hall so damn virtuous?

He got in beside me and started the engine. "Don't sulk, Artie. You can't always have your own way."

I looked out my window and wondered how such an insufferable, unpredictable man could have driven me to the threshold of passion only minutes ago. He was impossible. I reminded myself of the disparity in our incomes, if not our brains and stubbornness, and told myself I should be glad the scene upstairs had ended so abruptly and, according to my body, prematurely.

"Why did you lie to the police?"

Back to business. "I didn't," I said, still not looking at him.

"Oh? Then you told them Holly wasn't in Iowa?"

"No, but—I just didn't want to involve her any more than she already was."

As soon as the words were out, I regretted them. I shot Todd a look, and he glanced sideways at me. "No," I said. "It's not the same."

"And why not?"

"You didn't involve me intentionally. It wasn't your fault we ever met on that island. And last night wasn't your fault, either. You've as much as said so. Anyway, it was inevitable I'd be involved."

"I said I didn't know who the men were. I don't know if their coming after you was my fault or not." His words were clipped, businesslike. "What makes you so sure your involvement was inevitable?"

"Jack—and you, too—thought I was going to lead you to his mother's jewels."

"But why should a carload of thugs come after you?"

"How would I know?" I turned back to my window. We were on the interstate now, and Todd was driving fast. "I'm the one who doesn't know anything, remember?"

"And that's the way it's going to stay, I'm afraid. Jack asked me not to tell you anything for the time being, and I agreed."

"Do you always do everything Jack says?"

He glanced at me while the car veered into the left lane and sailed past a tractor trailer. I thought we were going for the median, but the Alfa Romeo settled into the middle of the lane and stayed there. There was no expression on Todd's face. "In this case, yes," he said at last.

"We're at an impasse, Miss Pendleton." He glanced over at me again, and this time there was a tiny gleam in his eyes, a half-smile twitching at the corners of his mouth. What a devilishly handsome publisher he made, I thought. "Get some sleep if you can," he added.

Questions pounded in my head, my toe hurt, and I was being driven to Boston by a man who had held a gun on me less than twenty-four hours ago. Less than an hour ago that very same man and I had practically been in the throes of ecstasy. It was madness! But, as Todd said, we were at an impasse. I curled up as best I could and went to sleep, warmed and comforted by the memory of my Ovid-quoting stranger's arms secured around me. . . .

When I awoke, Todd was driving out of the Newton tollbooths and onto the Massachusetts Turnpike extension. I sat up and rubbed my neck.

"Well, hello," Todd said cheerily.

"You're in a good mood," I pointed out sourly.

"It's been a very pleasant drive. Did you sleep well? You snore, you know."

"I don't."

He laughed. "And I thought you believed everything I said. We can stop for lunch if you're hungry. I don't think I have any food at the house—"

"What?"

"Well, I might have a can of tuna or something—"

"Todd, what are you talking about? Are you saying I'm going to be staying at your house? Nothing doing. You can put me up in a hotel."

"Hotels are expensive, Artie. Besides, a little exposure to Beacon Hill society would do you a world of good. Now, are you hungry or not?"

I could see he was teasing, but I said, "I don't need any exposure to Beacon Hill society, and no, I'm not hungry."

He started to say something but concentrated on his driving instead, his face hard. I regretted being a sourpuss. Still, what choice had he left me? I looked out my window. It was a bright, sunny day with a clear blue sky, warm but not humid. An autumn day. A day for bicycle riding through the mountains. And here I was . . .

I wanted to apologize to Todd. I wanted him to apologize to me. Oh, damn, I thought, I'll never survive a week alone in his house. I wanted to be where the action was.

It was my *father* people had suspected of being a murderer!

It was *I* they had suspected of being a sneak thief!

And Todd Blakesly Hall was a bully who had even less business being in Saratoga than I did. He wasn't going to let me decide my own fate. And yet I, fool that I was, couldn't help but feel a tiny twinge of satisfaction—something indescribably warm within me—in knowing that I did not daunt this man.

"I prefer to be accepted and treated as an equal, you know," I said, breaking the heavy silence.

Todd didn't look at me. "You're still not going back to Saratoga with me."

"Not being able to get me off your mind is not a fair reason to hijack me to Boston."

"Who said anything about being fair?"

Insufferable, I thought, fuming. The Alfa Romeo negotiated the insane streets and rude traffic of Boston with impressive speed and agility.

"Men worship you, don't they, Artie?" he asked in his half-teasing, half-unsympathetic voice.

I said nothing.

"You're so damned beautiful and look so charmingly helpless," he went on, his tone unchanged. "Being an orphan doesn't hurt. But, of course, you're actually feisty, intelligent, and independent. In short, a handful." He smiled, downshifting to turn behind the Massachusetts State House. "I've known all that from the very beginning, Artie. What helpless woman would think she could knock out a big lug like me with a little rock?"

He paused, and I wriggled uncomfortably in my seat.

His voice deepened as he grew more serious but not much more sympathetic. "None of which has a single thing to do with your staying in Boston. In your position I'd willingly agree to be dragged out of town."

"You're not in my position," I pointed out.

He grinned cockily and left that as his answer.

Beacon Hill was a maze of narrow streets, brick sidewalks and elegant urban town houses in the heart of the city. The streets were lined with parked cars, but there was almost no traffic. Oddly, it was quiet.

I refused to be impressed. "A few trees might help," I said.

Todd pointed to a thin maple held up by string. "There."

"That's a sapling. I'm talking about mature trees."

"They're around." He drove down Mount Vernon Street. "See, here—elms. We've been trying to save them from Dutch elm disease."

"Caused by the fungus *Ceratocystis ulmi.*"

He gave me a dry look. "Of course."

The Alfa Romeo slowed and turned onto the cobblestone circle that was Louisburg Square. Holly had once said the rest of Boston could collapse all around it, and Louisburg

Square would never change. From the looks of it, I thought she was right. Todd parked in front of a small statue of Christopher Columbus that stood at one end of a trim, private park in the middle of the square. The park was enclosed by a high wrought-iron fence. "To keep out dogs or people?" I asked.

Todd grinned down at me. "Both."

He got my suitcase out of the trunk and led me to a three-story brownstone with long windows, black shutters, and a big oak door with brass trim. It looked remarkably like all the other houses in the square.

"You don't like it?" Todd asked at my frown.

"I expected something more ostentatious."

"Simple elegance is the telltale mark of breeding," he said with an exaggerated Brahmin accent and grinned, unlocking the door. "I've always wondered what my neighbors would do if I hung bright orange drapes in all my windows."

He went in first, setting the suitcase on the bottom step of a mahogany staircase carpeted in dark red. The small foyer had cream-colored walls and gleaming hardwood floors. I followed Todd down the hall to the kitchen, also small but surprisingly functional, with white fixtures, open shelves, and brightly flowered curtains in a window of dead and dying plants. Todd gestured to them.

"You can rescue the critically wounded and toss out the rest while you're here," he said. "Vile things. Don't live too long without water, do they?"

Beginning to relax, I smiled and said, "No."

"Coffee?"

"No, thank you."

He was already digging in the refrigerator for a bag of beans. "It won't be anything like the swill you served me." He nodded to a door in the far corner. "You can wash up in there, and there's a bath upstairs if you need it."

The washroom was tiny but somehow held a washer, a dryer, a sink, and a toilet. There were plain white towels folded on a shelf and a dead begonia hanging in the shuttered window, not bigger than a square foot. I splashed cold water on my face, but the reflection in the mirror still stared back, gaunt and tired. Todd was right: I did look helpless. At least he had claimed he knew better. What I needed to do was exchange the braid for short, wispy curls, the yellow oxford shirt for a low-cut silk blouse, the blue slacks for something in linen, and the flat-heeled shoes for some sexy sandals—

No! No way. I am what I am. And I like it—or so I told myself.

Todd was hanging up the kitchen wall phone when I came out of the bathroom carrying the dead begonia. I dumped it in the wastebasket and asked Todd whom he had called.

"Leslie. I left a message for her to look in on you—"

"Who's Leslie?"

"My sister. She's a first-rate bitch and doesn't know a thing about what Jack and I are doing at Rosewood. I'd prefer it if you kept it that way."

"That won't be difficult," I said.

"If you suddenly disappear, I've asked her to call me."

"Won't she think that strange?"

"From me, no." Todd got two mugs out of a cupboard and set them on the counter. "You can do as you like, Artie, just don't turn up in Saratoga."

I sat at the simple pine table. "What if I do?"

Todd had his back to me, but he turned around with the coffee pot in hand, and said confidently, grinning, "I'll kick your pretty little ass in. Cream and sugar?"

I shook my head. He looked so damnably capable and efficient, so sensual and impossibly male. My senses reeled with the tangible memory of what he had done to them . . . and what he was doing to them now, just by being near. When he was gone, I would be able to think.

And hadn't I just told him that was unfair reasoning? I almost laughed. But it was true. Without Todd Blakesly Hall distracting me, I would be able to regain a proper perspective on who he was, who I was, and why there could never be more between us than a frustrating physical tension. And then, that accomplished, I could curse his soul and do as I pleased. I didn't need to account to anyone. I didn't want Todd to worry about me.

I simply wanted to find out what was going on at Rosewood.

"Will Leslie be staying here?" I asked.

"I haven't asked her to. She has her own place on the waterfront."

"Oh, you get the family company and the family house. I thought primogeniture went out of style after the Revolution."

"She's a vice-president," Todd said, and set the two mugs on the table.

"Yes, but you're the president."

"To my eternal damnation, yes. My father and Leslie are two halves of the same nut. We're constantly at odds—"

"Doesn't she have a useless doctorate in literature from Harvard as well?"

Todd didn't take offense at my sarcasm. "No, she has a master's in business administration from across the river. Boston University."

"Then she should be president."

"Over my dead body." He gave me a sudden, sharp look. "How the hell do you know I have a doctorate?"

"Nora."

"Gossipy old woman. She's hated me ever since I broke off with Emily."

"She says Emily is the one who broke off your little romance."

Todd grinned, unembarrassed. "Does she?"

"Yes, she thinks you treated Emily badly, and you're a snob."

"I am, you know."

"A Brahmin through and through, even a family tree that goes back to the Mayflower—"

"You disgrace us. The Pilgrims were riffraff. The Halls sailed to Boston with the Mathers." Todd took a sip of coffee and dropped the subject. "Look, there really isn't much food around. I have an account at the grocery at the corner of Cedar and Pinckney. They'll deliver. I'll leave you some cash as well."

"I don't want your money."

"Then I suppose you brought your own?"

Always so capable and efficient. I sighed. "I'll pay you back."

"As you wish."

"Where do I sleep?"

"In my room, if you like." He smiled, amused. "Or if that idea offends, use the guest room. Both are on the second floor. I'd prefer it if you didn't use the rooms on the third floor."

"Why?"

"They're my father's, if you must know."

"Oh." I tasted the coffee. It was hot and smooth, better than my old instant, but I would always prefer tea. "Will you call me?"

"No. You'll be safer that way."

"Why am I in danger?"

"You're not, as long as you stay out of Saratoga and those men who paid you a visit last night don't find out you're here."

"Do you know who they are?"

"I told you no."

"But—"

"Artie, I promised Jack. If you insist that I talk, I'll only tell you another lie. Trust us, please."

I put my elbows on the table and sank my head into my hands. Todd reached out and ran his index finger lightly down my nose.

"You don't have to be afraid, Artie," he said quietly. "Everything will be all right. It's just very important that those men don't make a connection between you and us."

"I don't want to stay here."

"I know you don't, but will you?"

I sighed, then nodded slowly.

"Good." The bantering grin was back and with it the incongruous dimple. "You'll be back to your weeds in a matter of days. Here's three hundred dollars. That should get you through the week. Buy yourself a sexy dress and go see the sights."

"I have clothes."

"All chosen to make you blend into the crowd, I'm sure, but with your looks, Artie, that's a hopeless cause. The right dress and you'll have men trailing after you by the score. Nevertheless, I'm still betting you'll end up a very sour old maid. Well, I've got to get back. Don't forget to call your friend tonight."

I made one last, desperate stab. "Would it be any different if I were a man?"

"Darling dear Artie, it would be different if you were

anyone but you." He smiled and, standing up, gave me a paternal pat on the cheek. "Behave."

"Damn you."

Todd laughed, but he didn't turn and leave as I expected. "Maybe I'll stay and show you to your room after all, Artie."

I crossed my arms on my breasts. "I thought you didn't have time."

"I'll make the time, damn it," he said, the laughter gone. He pulled my arms apart, cupped my elbows, and hauled me, not ungently, to my feet. I lost my balance and toppled against his hard length, feeling his arms circle around my waist. His hands rested lightly on my sides just above my hips. I don't think either of us breathed. His voice was lower, quieter when he spoke. "I don't want to leave you like this, Artie."

Awkwardly, tentatively, I placed one hand on each of his muscular shoulders. I stared at my fingers, outstretched against the fabric of his shirt. I couldn't look at him. My nails, I observed, were those of a gardener. I sighed and said plainly, "I'm sorry to be so obstinate, but—"

"You want to know what's going on," Todd finished for me.

Now I looked at him. Fear and confusion suddenly filled my eyes with tears, but his eyes were that warm November gray, not laughing, not angry. "And I want to help," I added, my throat tight, unyielding, fighting a sob. I thought I sounded like a three-year-old wanting to help her mother bake biscuits.

But if I did, Todd didn't tell me so. "Darling, I know," he said, shifting his arms upward, one tightening around me, the other moving up my back, drawing me closer so that I no longer could stand there with my elbows crooked and my hands primly on his shoulders. My fingers slid down his back as my arms went around his entire breadth, and I buried my head in his chest. I felt his mouth on my hair. The tears had vanished, and the longing of a few hours ago returned, flooding my senses. I felt secure. Maddeningly secure. Todd Blakesly Hall was a rich Boston publisher who was trying to take control of my life, and I was letting him.

I lifted my head off his chest and hardened my expression, trying to ignore the fluttering in the pit of my stomach, the tingling throughout my body that said I wanted this man. "I can find my way around."

"Artie, Artie," he said, amused, exactly as though he knew what I was thinking. "I feel good in your arms, too, you know."

"Do you?" I asked, not expecting an answer. Unique events had brought Todd and me together, and I suspected—perhaps we both suspected—that a return to the ordinary would drive us apart. I didn't know what was making me feel so secure in his arms. Nothing conscious, for sure. Everything I *knew* about Todd should have made me want to run. "I'm much better with plants than people," I added obtusely.

A small smile was on Todd's lips, and he slowly lowered his face to mine, giving me every opportunity to back away and escape. I didn't. I held my breath and exhaled in a satisfied sigh only when his mouth finally touched mine. I could feel my body lose its rigidity as I sank against him and parted my lips so that our kiss could do more than merely relax me.

His mouth opened into mine, our tongues exploring and tasting, arousing. Would he pull away this time? Would I? I slipped my hands under his arms and eased them around him, so that my fingers could stroke the hard muscles of his back. I was aware only of our kiss, the taste of his mouth, until suddenly I felt his hands warm on the bare skin of my midriff. A pang of desire stabbed through me, and I groaned, our mouths still joined, until I could feel his fingers creeping up my stomach under my bra, and covering my naked breasts. He caught a nipple between two fingers and teased it to a hard peak.

"I don't want to keep you from anything," I whispered, my head falling back from his mouth, against his upper arm.

I could feel him shudder as his tongue flicked longingly against mine, our lips not even touching. But he pulled my shirt down and stood back, and I fought for control. This was to be the end of it. He would go, and I would stay in Boston, alone, confused, resentful.

His breathing was quick and ragged, obvious desire in

his every feature. "I need you, Artie," he said quietly. "I need you now. I can't fight it anymore."

I took his hand. "Neither can I."

Together we walked upstairs and, in his elegant, masculine room, slowly undressed each other. Time seemed unimportant. Rosewood was far, far away. In that room, at that moment, only Todd and I existed. Every touch, every move, every look made me want him more. When we were naked and he wrapped his arms around me, I knew that this was right. We wanted and needed each other.

"You're beautiful," he whispered.

He smiled simply, meaningfully, and it was as though I had never heard those two words before. For the first time in my life, I really wanted to be beautiful.

I placed my hands on his shoulders and ran my fingertips down his chest, reveling in the mat of hair and the hard, firm muscles. "I thought all publishers were skinny and wore little wire glasses," I teased, letting my hands wander lower, to his taut, smooth midriff.

"And I thought all gardeners were crochety old men with bushy eyebrows." He pressed me into him, rubbing his swollen maleness against the very part of me that ached for him. "Two myths shattered."

I moved against him, and we both groaned with pleasure and anticipation. There would be no more teasing. We tumbled onto the bed, breathing each other's names, kissing madly.

Quickly his hands coursed down my abdomen and around to cup my naked buttocks, kneading them, while his mouth worked its gentle, erotic wonders on my breast. Then one hand slipped between my thighs, and I groaned aloud as two strong fingers probed the sensitive heat of my womanhood. Nothing could stop us. I *wanted* nothing to stop us. I told Todd so, not in words, but with my body, accepting his touch, pleading for more, wrapping my arms around him so that I could feel the passion stiffening his body.

"I've wanted this for so long," he rasped.

His tongue and lips were in my mouth, on my cheeks, my ear, my breasts. "Me, too," I cried, "oh, Todd, me, too!"

His hot, provocative mouth moved slowly across my stomach, downward, lower and deeper, nipping and lap-

The Venus Shoe

ping until I was tensed and damp and pulsing for more of him. I ached to be filled. My fingers dug into his thick hair and tugged, gently but firmly, until at last he kissed a wonderfully torturous trail back to my mouth.

I grabbed at his hard buttocks, urging him, telling him what I wanted and how badly. He knew. For an instant his eyes sought mine. Then he entered me with a hard, jabbing thrust. I cried out, gulping for air, and rubbed my hands up and down his strong, naked back, exulting as his magnificent maleness filled me.

In the next moments of wild thrashing and mindless, endless ecstasy, all the years of control ended. The crystal cocoon in which I had tried to encase my life crashed into tiny slivers. I cared again. I was alive. With his body pounding passionately into mine, with my body answering with frightening abandon, I took from Todd and gave to him.

I had been alone for a long time, dependent upon and answerable to only myself for a long time. Giving up some of myself to another human being made me feel stronger and less alone. Whatever Todd believed about me, whatever role he played in the events at Rosewood, he had ignited some spark within me that had been cold and dead for far too long. I needed a warm body to love.

But I thought of this only after he had gone, only after we had reached impossible limits and exploded again and again. Together we fueled a refiner's fire that tempered our fierce, unyielding independence and forged us together. Our lovemaking joined us harmoniously, naturally, without struggle. And yet the problems at Rosewood remained.

In the glowing aftermath of our lovemaking, I knew that Todd was as stubborn and independent and unused to compromise as I was. I didn't want him to protect me from my life. I wanted him to share it. I looked at him and smiled, seeing a man I could argue with and love for all time.

He smiled back and left quietly, a kiss his only promise.

Chapter Twelve

I WAS having a good cathartic cry at the kitchen table when, perhaps thirty minutes after Todd left, I sensed someone standing in the doorway. I looked up. The arrogant stance, the gray eyes, and the square jaw were Todd's, but Howard Perry Hall was neither as tall nor as broad as his son. He stood staring at me in his conservative light gray suit with his white hair neatly combed and his arms folded across his chest.

"My, my," he said in a tone that was neither concerned nor sarcastic, but a cross between the two. "Who are you, young lady?"

"I—oh—" I pulled a white napkin from the holder on the table and wiped my face. "A friend of Todd's."

"I see." He cocked his head slightly and took a step toward me. "Do you have a name?"

I hesitated at the patronizing tone he used, then said, "Artemis Pendleton."

"Miss Pendleton, I am Howard Hall. Is my son here?"

I held the napkin tightly in my hand. "No."

"Oh?" An eyebrow arched, just one. I don't know how he did it. "When will he return?"

"I don't know," I said, "exactly."

"Perhaps you could give me a general idea—today, tomorrow, a week?"

His words were sarcastic, bitingly so because they were so politely spoken. I sniffled and tried to regain my composure, but the man had caught me off guard, crying, and totally unprepared for explanations.

"A week," I said. "I think. He didn't say. I—I'm on vacation. Todd said I could stay here."

The Venus Shoe

"Miss Pendleton, the last I heard from my son, he was in Saratoga Springs, New York, visiting a—er, friend of his."

"He's still there. I mean, he's on his way back there. He—"

"He drove you all the way here and then turned around and went back to New York?"

"Well, yes—or no." My hand fell to the table. "I really don't know, Mr. Hall. We met at Rosewood. I mentioned that I—that I was spending my vacation in Boston, so he offered me a ride and said I could use his house. I accepted."

Todd's father looked me up and down with the effrontery of his son. "I see."

I was about to protest that I didn't think he saw at all when the front door slammed and a woman yelled, "Father?"

Leslie Hall was flushed and breathing hard when she reached the kitchen. Again I recognized the square jaw, but her eyes were blue and almond-shaped. She was a couple of inches shorter than I, round but not heavy, and had the short wispy curls—dark with red highlights—that I had thought would make me look more capable. Leslie Hall looked very capable. I guessed she was near thirty, a woman as comfortable with the vice-presidency of a publishing house as she was with slamming her leather pocketbook on the table and glaring at me.

"Damn," she said. Then she turned to her father, and her expression and voice both softened. "Father, I'm sorry. I tried to get here first. Todd called me at work, but I wasn't in. I came as soon as I could. Have you two met?"

"After a fashion," Howard Hall said wryly.

"Then you're not upset?"

"Why on earth should I be upset? This is Todd's house. He may lend it to whom he chooses." But it was clear Howard was upset. "I shall check into a hotel at once."

"But Father—" Leslie turned and stared at me. "Didn't you tell him?"

"Tell me what?"

Leslie turned back to her father. "This is the girl Todd's going to marry."

Howard Hall didn't even bat an eye, but it took every remaining ounce of nerve I had to keep me from running straight out of that house.

"Indeed," he said mildly. "Well, Miss Pendleton, it seems my son has offered you more than a ride and the use of his house for your vacation. I am going upstairs to wash. I will meet you in the front living room in thirty minutes. You will explain then. Excuse me."

When he had gone, Leslie Hall leaned against the stove and crossed her arms. "My brother is an idiot," she said. "Well, who are you?"

"What did Todd tell you?"

"A lot of rot."

"Please—"

She sighed disgustedly and pulled a message slip from the pocket of her dress. " 'A woman will be staying at the house for a few days,' " she read. " 'Please keep an eye on her. She's one of those Cinderella types. Let me know if she gets scared off and beats a path home. Am in love with her and intend to marry her. Todd.' There you have it."

"Oh," I said dumbly.

"Damn, why do I always have to come between those two?" She hit the oven door with the back of her hand. "Didn't Todd say anything to you about Father?"

"No."

"I can't believe he forgot. Father always spends the last two weeks of August in Boston. Here, in his own bedroom on the third floor—" She banged the oven door again. "Damn that Todd! He should have known not to send one of his playthings around when Father's here."

"I'm not Todd's plaything," I said firmly. "I—"

"It doesn't matter what you are. We have to mollify Father before he has apoplexy. I should let Todd fry in his own fat this time."

The Hall family, I decided, was a pugnacious lot.

"Look, I'll be happy to leave—"

"Oh, no, you don't. There's one thing I've learned about being in this family: Keep the peace between father and son. What did you tell Father?"

I told her.

"That's salvageable—barely. We could claim shyness. Were you crying? Damn. All right, look, go on upstairs and change. You aren't dressed for a proper introduction to your future father-in-law. I know that's a lie, but it's our best bet. And take your hair out of that braid, for God's sake. I'll make tea. You'll have to follow my lead."

She was didactic, uncompromising, and arrogant. Just like her brother, with whom I had just had the most rousing bout of lovemaking I had ever hoped to experience. I was glad I had had the foresight to make his damned bed. Oh, God, but I missed him! My Pendleton common sense told me to walk out the front door and say the hell with Todd Blakesly Hall and his family, but I went upstairs. My suitcase was lying on the four-poster cherry bed in the guest room on the second floor. I cursed my everlasting soul because at that moment I knew I was falling hopelessly and recklessly in love with the president of Hall and Son Publishers. I smiled and allowed myself a little hope. Maybe Howard Perry Hall wasn't as ferocious as he pretended to be.

I washed my face, combed out my hair, and sprinkled my wrists with the Chanel perfume that was in the bathroom. Then I found a white satin top I had bought in an antique clothing store, and a white cotton skirt. My sandals were inappropriate, but they were all I had. I shrugged and got dressed.

Howard Hall was already sitting on a love seat covered in maroon velvet in the front living room when I came downstairs. He held a cup of tea. My stomach wound itself into several knots, but I smiled and followed his gesture to a chair that matched the love seat and was kitty-corner to him. It was uncomfortable. I imagined that was why he had chosen it for me.

"Well," he said, uncrossing his legs, "what sort of rubbish have you and Leslie decided to tell me?"

Leslie strode in with a silver tea service, which she placed on the coffee table in front of him. "Don't be ridiculous, Father," she said. "She's shy. She had no idea you were here. Can you imagine if your fiancé's father walked in and you hadn't been introduced—"

"This whole affair has hardly been a paradigm of propriety," Hall said distastefully. "Todd should have stayed and introduced Miss Pendleton himself."

"I agree, but he was in a hurry to get back." Leslie poured a cup of tea for me and refilled her father's. "He had business at Rosewood, remember?"

"Business, my foot! I am not a senile old fool, young lady. Todd went to Rosewood to take up with that Harrison girl again. He changed his mind and ended up with—this."

"Father!"

He turned to me. "Miss Pendleton, obviously you are not a closet poet or one of Todd's glamour women, and certainly you are not his fiancée. I tend to believe that what you told me initially is true. Todd discovered you were vacationing in Boston and, forgetting that I was visiting from Maine, offered you the use of his house."

"Father, that is not what happened," Leslie said.

Her father ignored her. "Why were you crying?"

I nearly dropped my cup on the thick Oriental rug. "Do you always ask such personal questions?"

"When it suits me. Has Todd treated you badly? Has he led you on?"

"Oh, you—" I stopped and instead let a sigh register my disgust with Howard Perry Hall. Like father, like son. I meant to tell him he could go to hell, but a glance at his miserable daughter pacing in front of the marble fireplace changed my mind. "As unlikely as it might seem to you, Mr. Hall, your son Todd asked me"—the untrue words came hard—"to marry him. I was crying because he had just left and I would be staying here alone for a—a while."

"I see."

He certainly did. He knew I was lying. Leslie, however, seized the opportunity—fragile as it was—to make peace in her family. "Her father is a classics professor at Skidmore," she said eagerly.

"Is he really? Did you attend Skidmore as well, Miss Pendleton?"

I nodded.

"And what was your major?"

Leslie answered for me. "Literature."

Howard Hall's eyes, amused but indulgent, were on me. I shrugged. He was a snob, she was a crab, and Todd was a bastard for putting me in this position, but since I had to choose between them, I chose Leslie and foolishly decided to embellish her lie. "Slavic literature," I said.

"Indeed. Which author is your favorite? Solzhenitsyn, Tolstoy, Chekhov?"

Leslie gave me a deadly look. Well, so much for her, I

thought. "Actually, I concentrated on Bulgarian and Latvian poets."

"Can one specialize at the undergraduate level?"

"Not really, but one can at the graduate level," I said, mimicking his Brahmin formality.

I could see he didn't believe I was old enough to have been to graduate school. With my disheveled braid, I hadn't looked twenty-five. "Then you have your master's?"

"Yes, of course." I took a sip of my tea and settled in for a contest of wills between Howard Hall and myself. Sooner or later he was going to have to admit he knew I was lying or I was going to have to admit I was lying or—well, for now I was enjoying myself. "From the State University of New York. I'm planning a trip to Sofia to begin research on my doctorate."

Horrified, Leslie set her cup and saucer on the mantel and bit her thumbnail, obviously waiting for the outraged protestations from her father. But Howard smiled and said, silkily, "Then you and Todd do not intend to marry immediately?"

"Oh, I'll be back by Thanksgiving. Bulgarian winters can be rough, I hear."

"Yes, of course."

"I think I'd like a spring wedding."

"That would be—pleasant. What do your parents think?"

"They don't know yet," I said. "I'm not sure how they'll react. They're both such snobs, you know, Father being a classics professor and Mother a dance instructor—"

"A dance instructor."

It wasn't a question. He was tasting the words, hoping they might come out as something else. I smiled. "Oh, yes. Slavic dance. That's where my interest in Slavic literature comes from. Anyway, they were hoping I would marry an academic. I know Todd has his doctorate, but he is still a businessman."

That struck a nerve. Howard Hall set his cup and saucer on the coffee table. He had had enough, but he wasn't ready to admit anything. "Leslie, would you please call the Ritz and reserve a room for me? Miss Pendleton, I would be charmed if you would join my daughter and me for dinner tonight."

"Mr. Hall, I don't need this whole house to myself. I

shouldn't impose on you this way. Look, I have a friend who lives in Boston—on Marlborough Street. I can stay with her."

"You will do no such thing."

Leslie intervened, desperately. "Father, why don't you just stay here? There's plenty of room—"

"I do not think it proper for a man nearly seventy to share a house with a girl barely out of her teens. Now there will be no more discussion. Please see about a room, Leslie. I am going upstairs to pack."

He stood up and started toward the door, but I stopped him. "You're behaving like a spoiled little boy, Mr. Hall," I said. "I am going to call my friend and—"

"What is her name?"

"Holly Dearborn. Her father is Arthur. Look him up in the phone book. I am not lying to you. I know Todd hurt your feelings, but that's no reason to be silly. If anyone stays in a hotel, it will be me."

He scoffed at me, then ignored me altogether. "Leslie, call the Ritz."

Then he turned on his heel and went upstairs.

"Jesus," Leslie said.

"I'm sorry."

"Spare me, please. You didn't even try." She sighed at the ceiling. "Oh, well, why should you? What's it to you if those two go to war? But the least you could have done . . . Bulgarian and Latvian poets, a spoiled little boy—"

"He knew I was lying."

"Yes, but at least he was going along with you. Now, did you see that look? Jesus. I suppose he'll drag it out of me who you are." She stared at me. "I don't even know. Who *are* you?"

"I'm a gardener at Rosewood—"

"What!" Suddenly her face paled, and the capable, fearless vice-president of Hall and Son looked even more miserable. "You—you're Jack's gardener, aren't you? Artemis. Damn."

I went over to her, but she drew away from me and, clasping her fingers together, slid down onto a chair. I could recognize cold, hard fear when I saw it. "What's wrong?" I asked. "What did Todd tell you?"

"Nothing, nothing at all," she said quickly and uncon-

The Venus Shoe

vincingly. "He and Jack are out on a lark, and I know better than to stick my nose in." She licked her lips and changed the subject. "Is this Dearborn woman for real?"

"Yes," I said absently. Then, ignoring Todd's request to keep his sister out of our mess, I added, "What do you mean, a lark? See that bandage on my foot? Look here, scratches, bruises—I got them escaping from a carload of goons who broke into my apartment last night. I'm sure Todd and Jack know why they're after me, but they won't tell me. Will you?"

Leslie's face was ashen now. "Are they all right? You didn't—" She swallowed. "Jack and Todd—"

"Of course, they're all right! I'm the one who got routed out of bed."

Leslie's face told me everything I wanted to know. Jack—or Todd—had told her they suspected that my father had killed Patrice Harrison and that I was after her jewels. If they'd changed their minds, they hadn't told Leslie Hall. She was afraid of me. "Look," she said, "if—if they haven't told you anything, they must have a good reason."

"What is it?" I asked, not trying to scare her more.

But I did. She drew back farther in her chair. "I don't know. Really, I don't. Jack just told me—he told me he was going back to Rosewood because of you."

"Why because of me? I haven't seen him for thirteen years. Why, all of a sudden, the interest in Artemis Pendleton? Don't panic, Leslie, I'm not going to torture information out of you."

"I don't know anything!"

"You know more than Todd thinks you do."

"Please, believe me. I don't know anything."

"Okay, okay, I believe you." I had been afraid too many times the past few days to capitalize on someone else's fear. "Here, I'll leave quietly. Tell—"

"Where are you going?"

I thought quickly. "The Dearborns', I guess. Tell Todd and your father whatever you want. I'm sorry if I upset you. Tell Todd I left, and you couldn't stop me. This whole mess is his fault, anyway. Are you sure you're all right?"

She looked at me, confused.

"Jack was wrong about me," I said emphatically. "Very wrong, but I think he knows that now. It's too bad he and

Todd haven't told you. Sorry I caused you so much trouble. 'Bye."

"Wait! What are you talking about? Look, I'd like to know what's going on."

"I know how you feel. So would I."

"Why did Todd bring you here? Of course, they must have been wrong about you—I'm sorry. I . . . you can't leave. Todd will be furious."

Now the poor woman didn't know whether to be afraid of me, Todd, or her father—or all three of us. I knew how she felt. But I also knew there was little I could do to help her, except get out of her life.

"Good," I said. "See you, Leslie."

Unlike Todd, she knew better than to try to stop me.

Chapter Thirteen

I USED some of Todd's money to take an interminable bus ride into Albany, and arrived a little after ten. I felt my confidence surge. I was in control again.

I called Holly from a pay phone. Hans answered and, very formally, accepted the charge before passing the phone to Holly.

"Artemis! Where are you? God, I've been worried sick. Todd called and—"

"What!"

"He said you'd disappeared from his house in Boston. He thought I might know where you'd gone, the fool. He was livid. Said he'd kick your ass in yet."

It used to be little and pretty, I thought with a pang.

"I'm sorry, Holly." I explained quickly my meeting with Howard and Leslie Hall—and Leslie's obvious fear. "I had to leave."

"I guess so," Holly agreed heartily. "Where are you now?"

"Albany."

"Artemis, for God's sake! What are you going to do?"

"I don't know exactly, but I sure as hell don't want anyone to know I'm here—especially Todd. What else did he say?"

"Very little that I'd bother to repeat. He was in an ugly mood, absolutely breathing fire. He's worried about you, though. I think you ought to let him know you're all right."

I frowned. "Is he calling you back?"

"I don't know. He just asked me if you had called, and when I said no, he swore awhile, told me more or less what had happened, swore some more, and hung up. If he does call, do you want me to tell him—"

"Not to worry," I said. "But don't tell him I'm headed for Saratoga. Say I mentioned going camping. All he's really worried about is that I don't show up at Rosewood. Tell him I won't."

"Will I be lying?"

I hesitated. "No, no, you won't."

"Now you're talking sense. I've a good mind to hop a plane back—"

"No!"

I could almost see her grin. "I didn't say I would. Hans wouldn't stand for it now that I'm here in his clutches. Take care, will you? Keep me posted. And remember, Hans and I are here if you need us."

"Thanks."

I hung up and called a cab to take me to Saratoga.

I asked the driver to circle my block twice and watch for a blue BMW or a dark gray Alfa Romeo, but neither of us saw one, so I paid him with Todd's money and got out in front of Mrs. Martin's house, the only dark one on the street. My lips were dry, but licking them didn't seem to help. I told myself I wasn't afraid, but that was just splitting hairs: Dreading a confrontation with Todd Hall and fearing one amounted to the same wobbly knees.

And then, of course, there were the men in the blue BMW. . . .

The cab drove off. I stood on the curb, suitcase in hand, waiting for one of the six men I didn't want to see to come bounding out of the shrubs. None did. I brought my suitcase to my Falcon and set it beside the trunk.

No keys. I swore. That meant I had to walk down the dark path to Mrs. Martin's dark backyard, up the dark stairs, and into my dark apartment. I had no choice. I left the suitcase where it was and, with a resigned shrug, proceeded.

A brick held my door closed. At first I kicked it aside, but then I picked it up and carried it inside with me. Not breathing, I stood in the doorway.

The apartment was empty. I cradled the brick in one arm and crept in the dark to the nightstand beside my bed.

I groped for my keys. A cup crashed to the floor, splattering tea on my feet. I flung a sock to the floor.

Then I remembered the keys were under a philodendron. I clenched them victoriously and hurried out, replacing the brick on the way. I was glad I hadn't needed it.

The darkness and my sore feet prevented me from running, but soon enough I was unlocking my trunk and tossing my suitcase next to my sleeping bag and austere but functional camping equipment. There was a tent, cooking utensils, a tiny propane stove; with Todd's money for food, I would survive. I shut the trunk and went around to the front door, which, as usual, was unlocked. I hopped in and coaxed the Falcon to a start.

When I came to the stoplight at the intersection of Broadway and Circular, I allowed myself a sigh of relief and pride.

"Jesus Christ." Todd's face appeared in my rearview mirror. "What the devil have I been lying on for the past half-hour?"

"Books," I said dully.

"I know they're books, for Christ's sake, but do you have to keep the entire set of the Encyclopedia Britannica back here?"

"They're horticultural reference books."

"Of course. Well, hang on, Artie, I'm coming up front."

He threw one jean-clad leg over the seat, bumped his head on the map light, which he cursed soundly, and, dragging his other leg behind him, slid down onto the seat.

"Haven't done that since I was nine."

Expressionless, I stared out the windshield. Seeing Todd wasn't part of my plan. During my flight from Louisburg Square, I had convinced myself that that afternoon was nothing more than a physical release for us both and that Todd Blakesly Hall was far too domineering, possessive, and rich for an independent woman such as myself. We would never really get along. How could we?

But now, with his big body looming beside me, I knew all of that was nonsense. In spite of everything, I was deliriously glad to see him.

He was not, however, deliriously happy to see me. "You've a green light. Let's not sit here and cause a traffic jam. Here, turn into that lot." Then he added ominously, "We have a few things to discuss."

It was the parking lot of a small restaurant. I left the car running. Todd told me to shut it off. I shut it off. Then he looked at me coldly and said I was an irresponsible, untrustworthy, miserable, goddamn pest, and he would like nothing better than to cart me back to Boston and make love to me until I couldn't think straight, but first things first.

"You're all bluster, Mr. Hall," I said, holding back a laugh. "So Leslie called you?"

Even in the dark I could see the sudden gleam of amusement in his eyes. "No, Father did. He was glad to be rid of you, but he thought I should know he had run my fiancée out of the house."

"He's a horrible old man," I said. "He knew perfectly well I was not your fiancée. That was a dumb idea, you know."

"I thought it would work on Leslie. I forgot about Father."

"It wouldn't have worked on Leslie, either. She knew—"

"I did send you into a den of lions, didn't I?" Todd interrupted. He did not sound apologetic. "You could have at least told them where you were going."

"I did—even if it was a lie. . . ."

"Yes, and Leslie called the Dearborns and found out they are in Copenhagen, their daughter is in Iowa, and the boy who answered the phone—presumably the son—had never heard of you."

"The little liar. He's probably turned the place into a hotel for all his friends while his parents are away—"

"Artie, I told you to go anywhere in the world except back here."

"And I didn't listen to you."

"Obviously."

I shot him one of my fiercely independent looks. He had a foot slung over his knee and gave no indication at all that he didn't enjoy trying to run my life—or that he intended to stop anytime soon. "I didn't plan to stay," I said evenly. "I came for my car. Then I thought I'd go off and hide in the woods somewhere—"

"The Harrisons' woods?"

"No," I snapped, angry that he could see through me so easily. "It doesn't matter now, does it? What are you going to do with me? I won't go back to Boston. Your father's a beast. He knew I was lying, but he led me on."

"That's his Brahmin breeding."

"It's his nasty sense of humor. I won't go back."

"I won't ask you to. First—"

"What did you tell your father?"

"Nothing much. I stuck to my story, which wasn't easy. I sidestepped the issue of your Bulgarian and Latvian poets." I could see Todd's grin in the dark. "You didn't make things any simpler for me, did you? Father, of course, declared we both were lying. He said you were quite a pretty little thing—not the usual sort of tramp I bring home—but a bit of a snip. His words. He added, with his usual arrogance, that you wouldn't marry me or I wouldn't marry you, whatever the case may be, that he really didn't care, and, finally, that we could both go to hell."

I dismissed the last with a wave of the hand. "Your father doesn't swear."

"Only to his son," Todd said with a touch of bitterness. "Artie, there is one more thing. Father wanted to know why and how you put the fear of God into Leslie. He said she was trying to hide it but wasn't doing very well. I thought I told you to keep her out of this. What did you do?"

"Growled and bit her neck. What do you think I did? Nothing! She started to crumple up once I told her my name—"

"Oh, I see. Jack must have—" Todd stopped and gave me a quick upturn of the lips that I supposed was a smile. "It doesn't matter. Well, what am I going to do with you? Will you go on and get out of Saratoga or am I—"

"No," I said, "I want to stay here."

"Let's not play that record again, Artie."

"You don't have the right to make me leave, Todd."

"You can't stay."

"What do you suppose our men in the BMW are going to think if I suddenly disappear?"

"That's not your worry, Artie," he said curtly. "All I want is for you to be safe."

"Thank you very much, but that's not *your* worry, Todd. Look, if I just go on acting as though I haven't the slightest idea why those men broke into my apartment I *will* be safe. I've called the police. Now I should simply order a new door and go back to work."

Todd shook his head so self-confidently I could have kicked him. "No."

"I won't be your prisoner," I informed him quietly. "I won't be protected. My father and mother died tragically at Rosewood seven years ago. I came back to get in touch with their lives and put the past behind me. People can think what they will. I won't run."

"It's not a question of running," he hissed. "It's a question of being sensible!"

I pursed my lips stubbornly. "If you want me back in Boston you're going to have to take me at gunpoint, and when I get away I'll go straight to the police and charge you with kidnapping."

"Artie the fire-eater."

I looked at him and saw he was smiling; grudgingly, but the dimple was there. "The insidious Hall charm. You and your father would make a great pair of bookends." I paused. "I mean what I say, Todd."

He settled his hand on my shoulder and extended his fingers along my neck. His thumb gently traced my jaw and touched my lips. I heard him take a deep breath. "Did this afternoon mean nothing to you, Artemis?"

"It meant everything," I replied honestly.

"Then why are you doing this?"

"It has nothing to do with what happened between us." My voice was steady, but already my throat was getting constricted. I felt warm all over, receptive. His thumb traced my chin. "Todd, you know I'm not some fair and innocent damsel waiting for her knight on a white horse."

"I know darling, but I can't think when you're around—"

"It's not easy for me to think when you're around, either. Hasn't it occurred to you that I might worry about *you?* You may be built like a bull and have an arsenal of weapons at your disposal, but you're still a Boston publisher—not a guerrilla."

His hand slipped away. I felt cold and empty without it but said nothing. Todd looked out his window. I could hear

The Venus Shoe

him breathing steadily. Then he held his breath for endless seconds, blew it out in an angry stream, and turned back to me. In the darkness his face was especially uncompromising, his jaw set and determined.

"I shouldn't have expected you of all people to run to safety at the first sign of trouble. I'm not sorry, Artie. Don't mistake me. I think you're crazy as hell. But you're right: I can't make decisions for you. I can only care very deeply about what happens to you." Those slate gray eyes narrowed and held mine. "You'll be completely on your own."

Now that he had seen my point I wanted to kick him out of the car and race back to Boston and Howard Perry Hall, but I resisted the impulse. "It's better that way," I said, ignoring his look of surprise. "If the men in the BMW have connections at Rosewood, I'll probably be watched. That's why I plan to stick to gardening and leave the sleuthing to you and Jack. I do trust you, you know."

"I still don't like it."

"You don't have to like it."

He looked at me sharply and seemed to reconsider our bargain; I almost wished he would. "All right," he said. "There's a gun in the backseat under one of your tomes—"

"Why would I need a gun?" I frowned. "Do you always carry one around?"

"Artie, please. Do whatever you'd like with the damned thing. I also think you should accept Jack's offer to stay at Rosewood. It'll be more difficult for anyone to bother you there with guests and whatnot roaming about, even if— well, never mind. I think you'd be safer at Rosewood."

"Especially since the only spare room just happens to be above yours," I said.

"I wouldn't know," Todd replied. "I told you, Artie, you're on your own."

"Sure, and if I were being beaten to death above you, you'd roll over and go back to sleep. Your ogre act is wearing a bit thin, don't you think?"

A little grin escaped. "I thought you weren't interested in knights on white horses."

"I'm not. All I expect is human decency."

His arm shot out, and I felt his fingers dig into the curve of my shoulder. "So do I," he said harshly, and yanked me half onto his lap, so that his breath was hot on my face when he spoke. "Do you know how worried I was? Do you have any idea at all?"

I shook my head insolently.

He crushed me to him and covered my mouth in a kiss that was fierce and passionate even before it began. I reached up and clung to his neck, responding with a hunger that would last a lifetime. My mouth opened. My tongue darted into his mouth. My body shuddered and trembled with the need to be loved and touched. That afternoon had been but a beginning.

"I haven't necked in a car with a pretty woman in years," he murmured, and, as he straightened up, I could see the flash of his grin in the darkness. "You know, darling, even after this afternoon you still look like a virgin moon goddess."

"Which I'm not," I said, glad the darkness hid my rare blush. "Otherwise I'd have turned you into a stag by now."

His grin broadened. "For seeing the beautiful goddess disrobed? You'd better get used to it, Artie."

"No one calls me Artie, you know."

"I do." He released me altogether and rested his palms casually on his knees, as if he were unaware of the electric current that traveled between us. "Jack's going to have ten fits, you know. I'll have him pick you up in the morning—"

"Why? I should report to work as usual," I said, slightly breathless. "He can repeat his offer while I'm at Rosewood. I don't want to fuel any rumors."

"You won't be able to avoid that."

I sighed. "I'll manage. Where's your car?"

"I can walk from here. You're not going back to your apartment, are you?"

I hadn't thought of that. "No, of course not. I'll find a place to sleep. Don't worry about me."

"Is it so awful having someone worry about you? You know, Artie, you'd like Maine. You'd have the whole place to yourself—"

"That's what you said about Boston," I reminded him. "Thank you, Todd, but I'm staying."

He narrowed his eyes at me. His gaze was sober, searching for a weakness—an uncertainty—that I forced my face not to reveal. We both knew he could make me go to Maine or anywhere else. I had to convince him I could handle what I proposed to do.

And, in so doing, convince myself.

"As you say," he began, touching the door latch, "it's your life."

I didn't watch him leave or say good-bye. I heard the door shut and stared at the center of the steering wheel for a full minute. Then I started the car and went to find a place to sleep.

Chapter Fourteen

I SLEPT in my car, parked under my massive maple on Spring Street, and woke up early enough that I could have a big breakfast at a restaurant on Broadway. I got a few strange looks when I went into the ladies' room wearing a wrinkled white satin top and white skirt and came out wearing a white cotton shirt and white pants. If anyone had asked, I would have said my name was Emily Dickinson. I grinned at that, went out to my Falcon, and drove to Rosewood.

Nora was in the kitchen scrubbing a big copper pot. Her wide, plain face beamed when I said a cheerful good morning. She hugged me and made me sit down to coffee and a sweet roll and tell her all about "it." I gave her a clipped version of the truth, picked at the roll, and ignored the coffee.

"You poor dear," Nora said, placing a plump, worn hand on my shoulder. "Bud just about died when I told him what happened to you. He doesn't like the idea of you living alone like that. Neither do I. It's not safe anymore. And the police! They won't get those men, you wait and see. They don't start working until somebody gets killed, and even then, likely as not, they won't find out who did it. Bud wants you to go on and stay with him for a while."

"That's nice of him," I said noncommittally.

"He looks out for you."

"I know."

I quickly finished off the roll before Nora could start on one of her lectures. She always gave me three choices. One, get married. Two, go back to Hadley and my grandparents. Three, get a roommate. I never argued with her. It was fu-

The Venus Shoe

tile. I would just cut her off gently, without hurting her feelings, and go about my business.

Which is exactly what I did now.

I went to work. It was the last Thursday of the month: fertilizer day.

I was on my little stepladder fertilizing a hanging pellionia when R. W. Harrison came up behind me. I climbed down, set my watering can on the floor, wiped the palms of my hands on my pants, and took his outstretched hand. It was soft and manicured—like the rest of him. R. W. had always reminded me of a poet: thin gray hair, a pinkish face always freshly shaved and lotioned; his son's friendly, sensitive smile. He wasn't an inch taller than I, and his body, sagging slightly now in the usual places but still trim, had never been either frail or brawny. It was his eyes, dark and alert, that shattered the stereotypical image of a poet. Those eyes made Richard Winthrop Harrison look every bit the owner of a worldwide chain of hotels—and God knew what else—that he was.

His smile showed his concern. "Artemis, it's good to see you," he said in his refined monotone. "Jack told me about your ordeal. Well, you don't look any worse for the wear, as usual. Ah, you're blushing. There is some of your mother in you after all! She never could get used to the idea of her beauty either, poor woman." I thought he was going to begin a reminiscence that would be painful for both of us, but he caught himself in time. He snapped himself up straight. "Well, Jack tells me he offered you a room here at Rosewood and you turned him down flat. I insist you change your mind."

How clever of Jack and Todd, appealing to R. W.'s guilt, I thought.

"I *expect* you to come to me for help," he went on. "You know that."

"Thank you, Mr. Harrison. I—"

"At least stay until the police have a chance to round up some suspects or dismiss the matter entirely."

I laughed, surprised that I felt so comfortable with this man. "I'd be happy to stay," I said. "I'll speak to Jeff about deducting room and board—"

"You'll do no such thing. See Nora about a room." He took my hand into both of his. "And, Artemis, if there is anything I can do for you—anything—you just let me know. I mean that."

I tried to read his eyes. Did he know the real reason Jack had returned to Rosewood? Had R. W. also suspected that my father had murdered his first wife and stolen her jewels?

"Is something wrong?" he asked.

"No." I smiled. "No, not at all. Thank you, Mr. Harrison."

He returned my smile, patted my hand, and let it go. On his way out, he plucked a wilted fuchsia blossom.

At lunch I drank a cup of tea on the picnic table in the herb garden with Nancy Lerner. She ate a carton of yogurt and couldn't wait to tell me the latest gossip. "This morning I was cleaning the dishes off the table in the conservatory," she began, tucking her feet under her on the bench. "Emily and Marie were standing at the door to the terrace, talking." She presented me with one of her dramatic pauses. "About you and Jack."

"Me and Jack?"

She nodded vigorously. "Emily thinks you're after Jack —and she thinks you're milking Mr. Harrison because he feels guilty about your parents and all. Honestly! She said you were a gold digger. I wouldn't be telling you this, Artemis, except that if you're staying here and everything, I thought you might want to know the general twist of the gossip. It's disgusting. I mean, maybe you are after Jack, and maybe you aren't, but I know one thing for sure: It wouldn't matter to you if he had ten million dollars or just ten dollars."

"Oh, it matters," I said with a hollow laugh. "I almost always prefer the man with just the ten dollars. Thanks for the warning."

We went back to work. I spent the afternoon avoiding people and analyzing every twist and turn of events of the past few weeks. I wasn't very successful at either. When five o'clock finally came, I drove back to Saratoga. My apartment was as I had left it. I cleaned up, finally measured for a new door, called the building supplier and ordered one of solid oak, and fed Ralph. Then I called Holly.

"Well, I suppose it's more sensible than staying alone in

that apartment," Holly said when I had told her of my plan to stay at Rosewood. "But you don't know who those goons in the BMW are—or what they'll do next!"

"I'll be all right," I said, confident. "Are you having a good time?"

"Of course. We just got back from a tour of half the state. Not really, but it seems like it. Flat, Artemis. F-l-a-t. Flat."

I smiled into the phone. "Do you like it?"

"I love it. I think I'll become the Grandma Moses of Iowa. I'm eating like a pig, too. You would not believe Hans's mother. I swear she hasn't ever stepped out of the kitchen. I heard from my folks, by the way. I think I've finally convinced them I intend to marry Hans. Did my little brother really deny you? I'll shoot him. I'm gabbing like an idiot! Artemis, are you sure you're doing the best thing? You could be wrong, you know. Maybe this all has nothing to do with Patrice Harrison and your father and—"

"It does."

"Always so sure of yourself. Do you have a plan?"

"No," I said truthfully. "I have to play it by ear."

"Wonderful," Holly said.

"I don't really plan to do anything. I told Todd I'd leave the sleuthing up to him and Jack."

"But you won't." She didn't wait for an answer. "I told Hans everything, you know. He thinks you're a bad influence on me, but, of course, he offered to come help you. So did his brother. Artemis, he is awfully cute—"

"I'm sure he is, Holly. I'll call you every day until this is settled. If I don't call—"

"We'll come to the rescue—the Erikson boys, their sidekick Dearborn, and their forty million bees."

"Is that how many there are?"

"More, probably. I don't make it a point of counting the little horrors. We'll have honey at the wedding."

"I'll be there."

There was a short pause. Then Holly said heavily, "You'd better be."

I hung up and wrote a note to Mrs. Martin. Todd or no Todd, I didn't want her to worry if she returned to find her upstairs apartment broken into and no sign of her tenant. I left the note in her mail slot and, eating two of her tomatoes and one of her cucumbers for supper, went back to Rosewood.

My room was in a small suite originally used by maids in the attic. Nora said she lived there when she had first come to Rosewood. It was accessible only by the rear stairs, which meant I could sneak into the kitchen without any fanfare instead of parading up the main stairs.

I let the chef know I was here and disappeared for the night.

Yellow-flowered wallpaper; low, slanted ceilings; and simple pine furniture gave the room a country flavor. It shared a bathroom with two other tiny bedrooms, both unoccupied. The rest of the rooms in the sprawling house were spoken for for the "big" weekend, which was just as well. I liked the privacy of the fourth-floor attic.

I unpacked and set up my things in the bathroom. Todd's Baretta went under the mattress. I hated touching the thing, but I didn't think I should leave it lying around in my car. If anyone searched my room, however. . . .

I leaned my head on the window casing and stared outside. The sun was still bright in the sky, but it was dipping into the hills beyond the lake. I couldn't quite see the lake itself, but I had a splendid view of the barns, the stables, and the greenhouses across the lawn, northward, and, below me, the rose garden and the terrace. I could hear the chatter three stories below as the guests began to assemble for cocktails.

Finally I got out my nightgown and a book and went in to take a long, hot bath.

Then I wrote a letter to my grandparents that was cheerful enough but an utter lie. I read some more Faulkner, watched the sun set, thought of six different plans of action, and decided none of them was any good. Finally I gave a bored sigh and went to bed. I missed Todd, and I wanted him—I wanted him very badly, so much so that I scrunched up my pillow and curled up against it, as if he were there, big and solid beside me.

Chapter Fifteen

At first I thought the siren was part of a dream. Then I prayed it was. It wailed, waned, wailed again, and then stopped altogether. I leaped to the window. Red and blue lights flashed in the distance, through the trees, across the yard, way down. . .

By the lake!

I don't remember running down the three flights of stairs or if the kitchen was light or dark, but there were several people coming in from the hall. I remember that, because one of them called to me. "Artemis, don't go down there!"

But by the time the words reached my consciousness, I was already lifting my nightgown to my knees and running through the herb garden.

Don't go down there. Why? Someone was dead! Todd, Jack—

I slipped in the dewy grass, fell to one knee, and got back up again. I was by the rose garden. I avoided the brick walkway and instead cut diagonally through the yard, following the lights to the boat house.

I shoved my way past the dozen or so people gathered in front of the canoe rack. I think it was Marie who first yelled for me to stop, but soon others joined in.

Finally Jack grabbed me, but he was too late.

I had already seen Bud McCarty's body. It was stretched out on the sand, grossly bloated, purple in the flashing light. Two ambulance attendants lifted it onto a stretcher. No one was calling for resuscitation or asking questions or saying much of anything. It was all too obvious. Bud McCarty had drowned.

I screamed.

Jack's arms went around me, and I cried.

Behind me, a woman was speaking to Jack. "Perhaps you ought to take her up to the house."

I pulled my head off Jack's chest and glared at the woman, an ambulance attendant with long dark hair and a blunt face. "How did he drown?"

"We don't know—"

"He was a good swimmer. He wasn't careless. How could he have drowned?"

"We don't know," she said again, patiently. "There will be an autopsy in the morning. Are you a relative?"

I shook my head. She turned to leave, but I said to her back, "Was it an accident?"

Jack pulled me to him. "Artemis—"

The ambulance attendant pivoted and gave me a sharp look.

"She's in shock," Jack said quickly. "I'd better take her up to the house now."

"But if she thinks—"

"She doesn't."

I opened my mouth to say something, and so did she, but we both saw Jack's determined face and thought better of it. She went back to Bud. I stared up at Jack. He was pale, and the hands clenching my elbows were shaking, the knuckles white in the light of the moon and the ambulance. I said quietly, "Bud was murdered, wasn't he?"

"Artemis, please!"

"Tell me."

"Not here."

I yanked my elbows free. "I'm going to the police."

"Artemis, for God's sake, please—"

Todd appeared at Jack's shoulder. He looked tired but not afraid or bitter or even particularly sad. "As always, Artie, you have a charming sense of timing," he said wearily. "Uncross your arms, pull in that jaw, and come along. Jack, your father took Adelia up to the house. She's hysterical. You'd better stay here until things are settled."

"Young Harrison stepping into his father's shoes." Jack's voice was a bitter whisper. "All right, I'll see if I can get these ghouls moving."

Todd reached for me, but I shrank away.

"Artie, if you don't come here—now—I am going to knock you over the head and pretend you've fainted. We will talk but not here." His eyes narrowed. "Unless you want Bud's murderer to go free."

"Then—"

"Let's go, Artie."

I couldn't think clearly. Part of me said go, part of me said stay, but most of me said to forget it all and weep for the friend I had just lost. Todd's arm went around my shoulder, and I let him guide me back to the house.

I stared at the ground. When we came to the crest of the slope above the lake, I looked back over my shoulder. Two men were shoving the shrouded stretcher into the ambulance. They closed the door.

Bud McCarty was gone. Two hot, wretched tears dribbled down my cheeks and dropped onto the cool grass. They would be the last tears I would shed for him. Yet the mourning would go on.

And I would find out who had killed him.

I wiped my face on the sleeve of my nightgown, refused Todd's arm, and walked straight and steady to the house. In the kitchen, Todd pulled out a chair at the table and poured me a glass of Jack Daniel's.

"Drink it. All of it."

I did.

Then he poured himself one, downed it, and poured another. "I'm sorry about Bud," he said flatly. "But don't ask me what happened because I don't know. Maybe he was involved in our little problem, and maybe he wasn't. We'll see if the autopsy turns up anything."

"You said he was murdered."

"Lied to you again, Artie. If I hadn't, you'd have gone blabbering to the police and put yourself right back into danger. If the autopsy shows Bud was murdered, you won't have to go to the police. I will. But right now they think he had a heart attack and fell out of his boat and drowned. He was an old man, Artie. I know it seems awfully coincidental, but it could have happened that way."

I bit my lip and looked down at my feet. They were wet, and little pieces of grass stuck to my heels. My toe was bleeding again, but it didn't hurt. "You don't believe that," I said.

"It doesn't matter what either of us believes. If the autopsy doesn't prove he was murdered, how will we?" Todd thrust the bottle of bourbon into my lap. "Here, go on up to bed and get drunk. You've had one hell of a goddamn day."

He got up and started toward the hall door.

I said in a voice just loud enough for him to hear, "You owe me an explanation, Todd. Maybe you didn't before, but you damn well do now. Bud McCarty was like a second father to me. He was with me all through my ordeal when my parents died. Jack wasn't, and I didn't know you. I owe him. Todd, if anything happened anywhere near the lake, Bud would know about it."

Todd stopped dead but didn't turn around.

"You—and presumably Jack—searched for Patrice's missing jewels around my father's cabin on the lake, didn't you?" I went on.

"I think we'd better have a talk."

"I thought you would."

"Your room is safest. If anyone sees us, look faint and I'll say I'm staying with you until Jack can get here. That should jibe with current gossip."

We met no one. When we reached my room, Todd closed the door, turned on a light, and poured himself another glass of bourbon. I sat on the bed with my back against the headboard, my knees drawn up under my chin, and my glass of bourbon sunk into the pillow next to me. Todd sat on the other end of the bed and leaned back on his elbows. The incongruous thought occurred to me that he looked very handsome in his navy blue turtleneck. I took a sip of Jack Daniel's and wondered if I was in shock.

Todd sighed at the ceiling. "Artemis, Jack and I came to Rosewood to find out once and for all what happened to Jack's mother. Can you imagine what it's been like all these years not knowing? He's had theories over the years—lots of them—but one that's troubled him more than any other."

"That my father stole the jewels and murdered Patrice."

"Exactly—and your showing up at Rosewood stirred up that theory again. All we hoped to do was to prove conclusively that Martin Pendleton had killed Patrice Harrison and maybe get our hands on the missing jewels. We figured you were our only potential 'enemy,' but we were hardly worried about your doing us any harm."

"Didn't it ever occur to you that I'd come back to Rosewood simply to come to terms with my own past?"

"Yes, it did," Todd admitted. "We thought perhaps you suspected what your father had done and needed to come to terms with it. Jack didn't know for sure if Martin was involved with his mother's disappearance, but he had to find out. It had been weighing on him far too long. You can understand that much, can't you, Artie?"

"No, I can't," I said stiffly. "My father was not a murderer."

"Jack had fair enough reason to think he was—or at the very least that he knew far more than he was letting on." Todd looked at me measuringly. "Are you sure you wouldn't rather wait until morning? You've had enough shocks for one day."

"I can handle a few more." He looked unconvinced, so I added, "I'm numb, Todd. Bud was my father's best friend. He adored my mother and treated me like a daughter. It doesn't really matter that I've hardly seen him for seven years. I loved him, and I'll miss him. But I've learned to deal with these things as much as anyone can."

"You should cry and get it out of your system."

"I did." I smiled. "You can't measure the quality of grief by the quantity of tears. I can control my emotions when I have to."

Todd smiled back at me. It was, I thought, a remarkably gentle smile. "All right, if that's the way you want it. Jack suspected your father because of the white lady slipper."

I stared at him. "The what?"

"Christ, I hate this. Shortly after Patrice disappeared, your father began a quiet search for a white lady slipper."

"So what? He was a gardener, and white lady slippers are very rare. He always had a thing about wild flowers."

"Yes, but the white lady slipper was Patrice Harrison's favorite flower, a fact known only to him, Jack, and presumably Richard."

"Again, so what? Maybe he was planning to cultivate one in Patrice's memory."

"I don't think so, Artie."

"Why?"

"Shortly after Patrice disappeared, Martin called Jack and asked him if his mother had ever taken him to see a white lady slipper on the property. Jack said no and asked why. Martin said he couldn't explain, asked Jack to keep their conversation confidential, and hung up."

"That's hardly enough reason to suspect somebody of *murder!*"

"Probably not, but Jack was young—and, as you can imagine, pretty distraught. He called Martin back, but Martin wouldn't explain anything else and suggested Jack just leave the thing be, that—as you just suggested—he only wanted to plant white lady slippers as a memorial to Patrice. There was nothing Jack could do to disprove him, but he didn't like the furtiveness of the entire conversation or its taking place so soon after Patrice's disappearance. And it seemed to him Martin was looking for a particular white lady slipper—one at Rosewood—and not just *any* white lady slipper, which is all he would need for a memorial. He mentioned to his father that he'd spoken to Martin about the flower, but Richard seemed completely unconcerned and in fact assumed Martin *was* simply planning a memorial. No one else at Rosewood knew anything about it, so Jack kept his suspicions to himself."

I couldn't look at Todd as I said quietly, "So Jack swore off Rosewood because he thought my father was a murderer."

"No one supported his theory that it could have been an inside job, Artemis," Todd said patiently. "The police had done a thorough investigation and come up with nothing, and his own father saw nothing suspicious in Rosewood's gardener's quiet search for a rare flower. Jack was just a boy, for God's sake. What else could he do? He couldn't very well announce to the world he suspected a man who had been like a second father to him of murder because of a damned flower, could he? So he kept his mouth shut and left."

"Well, it's a good thing! He'd have sounded like a fool. For heaven's sake, Todd, how could a flower be the key to a murder?"

He looked at me steadily. "You don't remember anything about your father and his white lady slipper, do you?"

"No."
"When do they bloom?"
"May and June, sometimes July."
"What month did Patrice disappear?"
"In the spring sometime. I don't know the exact date."
"June eleventh. When did your parents die?"
I didn't answer.
"Well?"
"May twenty-fourth."

Todd paused while I propped up my bourbon glass on my knees and stared at it. "Think back, Artie," he said.

Tears sprang up in my eyes, and my lower lip began to tremble. I shut my eyes and bit my lip. Then I relaxed.

"You know, don't you, Artie?"

I nodded. "My parents never liked for me to go to Rosewood," I began, "but every now and then they would let me visit Bud. One afternoon, Bud and I went on a walk around the lake. We stopped for a picnic at my father's old cabin. Most of the walls have caved in, and it's pretty much a wreck, but it sits in a clearing near the lake. But you've been there."

"Yes," Todd said at my pause.

"After the picnic, Bud said he'd better get some rest or he wouldn't make it the rest of the way. He made a joke of it. So I went exploring. I—I found a white lady slipper. I showed it to Bud because I knew they were so rare. I didn't know my father had been looking for one. Bud suggested I tell him about it. I never thought twice about it. My father was a gardener, so naturally he would be interested."

"Did you tell him where it was?"

"Yes." I gulped the bourbon. "I told him about it that evening, and he said he would go see it in the morning. I—don't know if he ever did. He—he—"

"He and your mother were killed that next day," Todd finished for me.

"Yes."

"Apparently he went to see the white lady slipper and came back very excited. He grabbed your mother, told Richard he'd be back in an hour, and left. We don't know where he was going or what he planned to do, but Jack figured his mother must have outfoxed Martin six years earlier—at least partially—and at last he had found the jewels."

My knees dropped into a tailor squat and I leaned forward. "But Jack wasn't even there!"

"His father told him everything. Before he went to look at the flower, Martin said to Richard, 'Artemis has found the white lady slipper. After all these years, my little girl has done it.'"

"Would he say that to Richard Harrison if he thought he was about to find a million dollars in jewels and run off to Tahiti or something?"

"He was excited, Artie. It'd been six years."

I snorted with disbelief.

"At any rate, he took off into the woods and before Richard had any idea what was what, Martin and Nellie Pendleton were dead. Jack was sorry—sorry for his mother, sorry for your parents and you, sorry for himself because he would never know what actually had happened."

"None of this makes any sense!"

"Maybe it doesn't now, Artemis, but it did then—at least to Jack. Obviously he wondered if he was right or wrong, but what could he do about it? Nothing. All concerned were dead."

I scowled. "What was his theory?"

"He figured your father had been blackmailing Patrice for one reason or another, but she finally rebelled the night of her disappearance. Martin wanted a million dollars in jewels as a payoff. She hid the jewels and got herself killed because she double-crossed him. She died before he could find out what she'd done with them. It was a reasonable theory, Artemis."

"No, it wasn't. Ever," I said, adamant. "You're assuming Patrice chose a white lady slipper to bury her jewels under or near, aren't you? Why? She must have known my father knew it was her favorite flower. And obviously he knew to look for a white lady slipper. How? Would she tell him if he was blackmailing her? And why hide the jewels way the hell out there by the cabin?"

Todd nodded with understanding. "Perhaps Patrice didn't know *who* was blackmailing her. The demands could have been made by letter—or even phone. The cabin could have been a drop-off point. Maybe this had been

The Venus Shoe

going on for years and the jewels were to be the final big payoff, who knows? Patrice would drop off the jewels and Martin would pick them up at the cabin. Obviously things didn't work out the way either of them planned. As to his knowing about the white lady slipper, suppose Patrice mentioned to someone at Rosewood—Richard, even—shortly before she disappeared about the white lady slipper, made a small issue out of it so whoever she spoke to would remember. You know, something like, if I die I'd like dozens of white lady slippers planted over my grave. And since she didn't know who was blackmailing her, she tipped off her trusted gardener. That's what Jack always believed."

"My father wasn't blackmailing her!"

"I think we can assume that now, Artie," Todd said quietly.

"Why didn't Jack just ask me to show him where I'd found the white lady slipper so he could see for himself that his slimy ideas were all rot?"

"At the time, you were an eighteen-year-old girl who had lost her parents," Todd explained. "He didn't want to ruin your life. You were alive, they were dead. It's that simple. If he was wrong about your father, fine. But what if he were right? There was nothing he could do, except maybe find the jewels, but what would it do to you to find out your father was a murderer?"

"How noble of dear Jack."

"Yes, I think so," Todd said, oblivious to my sarcasm—and my bitterness. Then he grinned. "I'd have taken you by both your pigtails and made you bring me to the white lady slipper—and made you do the damned digging. Tainted blood, you know. Don't be angry with Jack, Artie. Even he can't live up to your expectations."

I gave Todd a sour look, but his grin was infectious, and nothing he said had altered my reaction to him. It wasn't just physical now: It was emotional as well. I knew my timing was awful, but I was falling in love for the first time—the only time—in my life. Strangely enough, I thought Bud McCarty would have approved. "You haven't finished," I said.

"Yes, I know." He sighed, and I could see that he was tired. A man had died tonight. We both had seen him, and neither of us would forget. "All right. Jack told me the whole tale over gin and tonics off the coast of Newport. He had heard you were just back at Rosewood, and all the old wounds were opened up again. He was hesitant about interfering, and thought perhaps you were just there to put your past behind you, but when he looked into your situation he got suspicious."

"My six scholarships," I said.

"Right. You'd sworn off Rosewood the same way he had, but suddenly you changed your mind and took a job there, despite lucrative scholarship offers. He wondered if you'd guessed the 'truth' about your father in much the same way he had. I was the one who suggested you might have come back to Rosewood to do a little treasure hunting."

"Collecting my reward for having been orphaned?"

"Why not? I insisted that if you were indeed treasure hunting you already knew all about your father and had accepted it. Now you were reaping the unjust rewards of his avarice—or whatever. Jack just wanted to try to put a period at the end of the whole tragedy if he possibly could, but he was afraid of upsetting you if he was wrong. I informed him in no uncertain terms to get on with the search so he could beat your little ass to the treasure."

"How nice of you," I said wryly. "How did you know to go to my father's old cabin?"

"That was my idea. Jack drew me a map of Rosewood and we pored over it and the facts of the case. Your father had gone out to the lake that morning, and the day before you and Bud had taken a walk out there. We ruled out the sections closest to the boat house and the main grounds. I asked Jack if there were any buildings around the lake, and he thought about it and came up with the cabin. So I said that's where we'd go. We walked in from the road and got on the path just below the pastures."

"So Jack *was* with you!"

"Yes, of course. The Dobermans attacked us soon after we came to the clearing where the cabin stands," Todd said. "Jack knocked one over the head with a rock while the other two came after me. Fortunately, I was on the ledge above the lake, so I simply dived in and prayed the water would be deep enough. Once in the water, of course, I was presented with the problem of getting back out again.

The Venus Shoe

Jack hid himself in the cabin, so I knew he would be all right. It would have been challenge enough to climb back up that ledge without a bleeding hand, but with it, it was impossible. You know that area, don't you? It's all rock and sand and hill in the inlet where the cabin is. I could have come onto shore on the point, but it doesn't have much cover."

"So you tried to swim around the point to the pine grove."

"Right, and when I realized it couldn't be done, I took refuge on the nearest land—your island. I managed to tie up my hand before I collapsed. I'd been up all night, and the damn beasts did quite a job on me. I never even heard you, until, of course, you roused me out of a sound sleep."

I stretched out my legs till my toes nearly touched Todd's thighs. "Didn't Jack worry?"

"Some, but there was nothing he could do. He was still dealing with the Dobermans. They didn't exactly run along on their merry way, you know. I did finally rescue him."

"Killing one—"

"Darling, it was him or me."

"When did you tell Jack about meeting me?"

"As soon as I could." Todd added more bourbon to his glass. "His Artemis Pendleton, said I, was a beautiful, fiery little thing who wore her hair in a pigtail and was perfectly satisfied picking blueberries in the hot sun and eating vegetables straight out of the garden, dirt and all. I added, most adamantly, that I doubted you would skinny-dip in the middle of the same lake where you knew a million dollars in jewels were buried. Either the jewels were there and you didn't know about them, or the jewels were not there. In any case, I told him we should abandon this foolishness and go back to Boston."

I frowned. "Why didn't he?"

"He did."

"Well, why didn't he stay there?"

Todd hesitated, then shrugged. "What the hell, I've told you everything else," he said. "Jack decided that any normal person would have gone to the police after finding a strange man and a gun on an island in a private lake. I, of course, told him you were not necessarily a normal person."

"Didn't you tell him about our deal?"

"Yes, but he couldn't believe you'd stick to it, not after finding the gun." Todd smiled, amused with himself. "He doesn't know how I can be with beautiful young women."

"Revolting, intimidating, arrogant—"

"That's not what you said last night." His chuckle was low and incredibly seductive, but he quickly cleared his throat. "Anyway, Jack was still suspicious, but there was really nothing we could do about it. But a week or so later, Emily came to town for dinner. She couldn't seem to shut up about you. Why had you come back? Nobody could figure it out. Why would anyone as gorgeous as you be content to work as a gardener? I could see it was getting to Jack and I tried to change the subject, but then she told the tale about the Dobermans. Obviously, you still hadn't said a word about me. I think that's what triggered Jack's decision to come back and see you for himself."

"So you both came back to Rosewood to terrorize me," I said, suddenly exhausted.

"No." Todd was patient. "But I was curious why you hadn't turned in my gun. Artie, for God's sake, what innocent trespasser would carry a gun?"

I shrugged. "I wondered."

"Well, when I realized you were indeed just keeping your end of our bargain, I did my best to shut off my suspicions and went back and told Jack and shut off his. We settled down to enjoy our vacation."

I made a very skeptical face. "Tuesday night you were prowling around the woods with a gun," I pointed out. "That doesn't sound like a vacation."

"Just looking around. At this point, we had nothing specific to go on. I was in the woods down the road when your Falcon puttered by. I had brought along the gun, in case I happened to be wrong about you, and you turned up with my Baretta. You had me going then, Artie. I didn't know what the hell you were up to. I could have kicked myself when I realized you and your friend were just playing detective."

"For the—" I sighed angrily. "Do you know how many times you had me scared half to death?"

"You never acted it."

"What was I supposed to do, shiver and faint?"

"No, but you weren't supposed to smart-mouth me, either."

I scowled.

"To continue, when you and Holly went on your way, I again went back to Jack and told him we were as wrong as we could possibly be. We agreed to forget the entire thing once and for all."

"But what about the men in the BMW?"

"It's my guess, Artie, that whoever they are, they have similar ideas about you that we had. They've blamed you for killing the dogs—God knows how you could have done it—and thought you were looking for the jewels. I would also guess they saw you leaving the pine grove and decided you must have found them."

"But I didn't find them!"

"Of course not."

I sighed, my eyes heavy, burning, but sleep was a long way off.

"Bud—could he have guessed what was going on and wanted to protect me or something . . . ?" My voice lowered, and I couldn't seem to get enough air. "Oh, God, what if they murdered him because of me!"

"Artie, we don't know even that he *was* murdered," Todd said in his take-charge voice. But he went on more gently, "We'll just have to wait and see what turns up in the autopsy. I know it isn't easy, darling, but—" He stopped abruptly and stared off into space, frowning. Then he said decisively, "No. We won't wait. All this has gone far enough. I'm going down to see the police and tell them everything."

"Do you think they'll believe you?"

He smiled. "Of course, they'll believe me. I'm a mature, respectable Boston publisher."

Then, without any warning, Todd leaned over and kissed me, for a very long time. He would have left it at that if I had wanted him to. But I didn't. I grabbed his hand and kissed it. "I don't want to be alone yet," I whispered.

He twisted my fingers around his and pressed them to his lips. "Are you sure?"

I nodded, never taking my eyes from him.

Todd stretched out on the bed beside me and, with two fingers, slowly traced the outline of my face until he touched my lips. I kissed his fingertips, then drew myself against him, one arm circling his hard middle, and kissed his lips, savoring the escape of my own rising desire. Bud McCarty was dead, but Todd Hall was alive and I needed him. I wasn't afraid to admit it, even to myself.

"Oh, Todd," I whispered, "I need you so much."

I felt his hands on my buttocks, then his fingers catching the hem of my tangled nightgown as he slowly lifted it upward. I rolled on my back and helped him get it over my neck and shoulders. He dropped it on the floor and turned back to me. The night air cooled my overheated body, but a different kind of warmth took over as Todd gazed at my nakedness.

"I wish you knew how beautiful you are," he said, his gray eyes smoldering cinders now. "I want to make love to you, Artie—"

"Then do," I said, choked, "because right now I only want to be loved—and to love you. Please—"

He cut me off with a plunging kiss as he placed a hand on each side of my head and hovered over me. Wildly he kissed my chin, my throat, then lower, to my breasts. My fingers raked his thick mass of hair as I groaned and arched against his probing, tantalizing tongue. He sat up on his knees and pulled off his shirt so that I could touch every muscle, every hair on his broad chest. He whispered my name over and over again as I kissed every inch of his torso, until, finally, I came back to his mouth and we smiled and tasted each other again.

Then I lay flat on my back and raised my arms overhead, signaling that my body was his as much as my own, that I wanted only him. He gazed at me and placed the outstretched palm of one hand on the curve of my stomach. My breasts were swelled, taut with desire, but he bent over and kissed them again, catching the nipple between his teeth so that my entire body tingled somewhere beyond excitement. I wanted nothing more than to feel the strength of his body against mine, in mine. He lifted his head from my breasts and traced them with his fingertips, then brushed his hand down my stomach, to my legs, and then, gently, into the moistness between my thighs. His lips followed the same trail, and when he rose to pull off his pants, I could hardly breathe and, gladly, could not think.

But suddenly from somewhere within me came the sob, deep, bitter, frightened, wrenching. Tearless. I looked up at Todd, frozen beside the bed. "Please," I begged, "I want to forget—"

He sat on the edge of the bed and brushed the hair back off my face. "No, Artie," he said quietly. "When we make love, it should be because we both want to remember."

I closed my eyes against the rush of consciousness. "I'm sorry."

"There's no need to be sorry," he said gently, and I could feel his weight lift off the bed. "Sleep, Artie. I'll leave you the bottle."

I didn't open my eyes until I heard the door shut.

Chapter Sixteen

TODD or Jack or someone might have come up to tell me how the police had reacted. I sat up until just before dawn and waited patiently in a full lotus position. After all, I thought, Todd would need time to find Jack, fill him in, drive to Saratoga, and get hold of the right police officers. Probably he would have to get someone out of bed.

When the first light of morning crept into my window, however, I flung my pillow across the room and crawled under the covers. I didn't retrieve the pillow. I just lay on my forearms and cried. I cried for Bud McCarty and Martin and Nellie Pendleton and Patrice Harrison, and I cried for myself. I was so tired of being alone! Here I was lying up in the attic, forgotten, useless, alone. But don't disturb poor Artemis! She's had a rough night. Let her sleep.

Sleep!

I didn't want anyone feeling sorry for me.

I didn't want to feel sorry for myself.

I rolled onto my back and felt the tears stinging my cheeks and wondered what kind of damn fool would fall in love with a man like Todd. What else did I expect? I asked myself bitterly. He had taken over again, assumed I wouldn't mind waiting up in my room while he straightened things out.

Well, I did mind!

Bud was dead. Drowned. Murdered.

My body shuddered with sobs, but still Todd didn't come. I got up and retrieved the pillow, then hugged it close to me. I wanted to be loved and needed, but, perhaps, even more than that I wanted to need, I wanted to love.

But I was so afraid because I needed and loved Todd and I could so easily lose him . . . like Bud, like Dad, like Mom.

And, damn it, I was angry because he didn't come, because he knew I could point out the white lady slipper in five minutes and wouldn't ask, because it hurt so much to love him.

I slept fitfully and awoke to the cackle of bluejays and the rays of the sun, hot and bright on my face. I took a shower, dressed in my servant's whites, and went downstairs.

Nora was bent over bread dough. She looked at me as though nothing had happened and everything had happened. With a sickening lurch of my stomach, I pictured Bud's body on the sandy beach. "Not passed on," my counselor had said over and over, "not departed or late. Dead. D-e-a-d."

Murdered.

I walked past Nora and made myself a cup of tea.

"Am I late?" I asked.

"Heavens, honey, it's not even seven yet. You're the first up."

I stared into my teacup. "You heard about Bud?"

"Henry called last night and told me." She pounded the dough fiercely. "I've seen so many go."

"Yes, I know."

"It's terrible, getting old. Oh, not because you're nearer to dying. That never bothered me, my own death. It's just to watch people you love go. I can't get used to that." She brushed away a tear with a floury hand. "I'll miss that old man."

"So will I."

I found my way to the table and sat down. I drank my tea and listened to the intent flopping of the dough on the bread board.

"You should take the day off," Nora said. "There's nothing you have to do Jeff can't find someone else to do."

"I'm all right."

She turned to me with a vehemence I thought beyond her. "Well, you shouldn't be! Bud McCarty was your friend."

"I know, Nora. Please—"

"No one wants you here!" She held up her hands, full of

flour and dough and outrage. "Even Mr. Harrison, only he thinks he owes you because your folks got killed on his land. Well, I was here that day just like I've been here every day for forty-six years, and there weren't nothing Mr. Harrison or anybody else could've done to save your Daddy. Marty was so fired up about something that day he couldn't even talk never mind see to drive."

"Nora—"

She didn't even hear me. "I don't know what got him so excited, but it don't matter. Nothing matters except he's dead, and now Bud's dead, and you shouldn't be here. That's one thing your ma always said. She didn't mind working hard, so long as you didn't have to do what she and Marty had to. If you ever loved them—and, honey, I know you did—then you'll go on and get out of here."

"I can't do that, Nora," I said quietly. "Not yet. I—I owe it to Mr. Harrison to stay through the weekend at least."

She turned back to her bread dough. "You're a stronger woman than I'll ever be."

It was a bitter statement, but an olive branch nonetheless. I accepted it and made another cup of tea. I smiled at Nora and took my tea into the herb garden. I sat in the damp grass next to a clump of chives and placed my hand palm-down. An ant crawled across my fingers, then disappeared into the grass.

If I hadn't found the white lady slipper, Bud would be alive today. I don't know how I knew this for certain, but I knew.

I plucked a chive and sucked on it. The onion taste was a shock, as I knew it would be. I couldn't indulge in self-pity or guilt or even sorrow. Bud was dead. There was no changing that simple fact. But the lady slipper had caused his death—I looked up when a shadow fell on top of me. I recognized the Saratoga police sergeant who had listened to my story of harassment. The man at his elbow was tall, handsome in the way one expects men approaching fifty to be handsome: dark, clipped hair, gray at the temples; a downturned firm mouth; a cleft chin; and a trim body dressed in conservative golf clothes. I had seen him among the crowd last night.

"Michael Davis," he said, extending his hand, which I took as I stood up. "Harrison family lawyer. Jack and Todd

Hall spoke to me last night. You know Sergeant Warner, I understand."

Warner wiped his red brow. It promised to be a hot day. It never rains on Camelot, I thought. "Mr. Davis here told me what you all have been thinking, but it just doesn't check out. We caught those fellas who were pestering you the other night. They were hooplaing it up and down Broadway last night in that BMW of theirs."

"But—"

Davis interrupted. "Their names are John Vanheyden, Peter Smith, and Albert Hayner. The BMW belongs to Hayner. Do you know any of them?"

"Yes—no. Not personally. Smith and Vanheyden work in the fields, don't they?"

"Every summer for the last fifteen years," Warner said. "Hayner does, too, but this is his first summer. They've admitted everything."

"Mr. Hall's—er, theory was correct," Davis put in. "Vanheyden, Smith, and Hayner thought you had returned to Rosewood to locate Patrice Harrison's missing jewels. They, like Jack and Mr. Hall, suspected that your father had killed Mrs. Harrison and hidden the jewels and you knew where they were."

"They got real suspicious when they saw you on that back road the other night." Warner gave me a dark, unfriendly look. "You didn't tell me about that."

"I'm sorry," I said inadequately.

"Well, it doesn't matter now. They figured you were up to no good and followed you home and then on to the airport. These boys aren't too bright, if you ask me. They had heard all the talk about you and Mr. Harrison—young Mr. Harrison, that is—so they wrote that note to get you out of the airport, only you weren't in the airport, your friend was." He repeated his dark, unfriendly look. "You lied to me about her, too."

"I was afraid for her."

His wrinkled lips registered his disbelief. "We took a look around that old cabin, just to be sure. There's nothing there. Some signs of digging, but I expect that was our boys trying to find the jewels."

"Did you find the white lady slipper?"

"Wouldn't know it if I did and there's no reason to look,

so far as I can see, but you all can go and take a look if you want."

"What about Bud?"

Davis said, "There was evidence of a massive heart attack. Apparently he fell out of his boat—"

"Drowned before he could die of the heart attack," Warner interrupted. "But if he'd been home in his living room last night, he'd be just as dead today."

Davis glowered at Warner. "Sergeant, Mr. McCarty and Miss Pendleton were very close."

"Oh, sorry."

"It's all right," I said absently, then smiled in a way that I hoped showed how stupid I felt. "We've been grasping at straws, haven't we?"

Warner waved a hand. "Just a misunderstanding all the way around."

"In their own warped way, Vanheyden, Smith, and Hayner were trying to be heroes," Davis said.

"They beat up Holly, broke into my apartment, chased me up a tree—"

"We're not saying they're angels," Warner broke in. "From the looks of them, I'd say they'd keep a fortune in jewels if they got half the chance. But they claim they were just hoping for a reward, and you can't go and charge a man because of what he looks like he'd do. You can press charges of breaking and entering, and if Miss Dearborn wants to come back from Iowa she can get them for assault."

"They will ask for leniency," Davis said. "It's their first offense, and they can always say they were trying to prevent you from leaving town with Patrice Harrison's jewels—and proof that your father murdered her."

"All this would come out in the trial, wouldn't it?" I asked. "Oh, to hell with them, then."

I walked past Davis and Warner. Neither stopped me, and, without looking back, I went into the kitchen.

It wasn't Vanheyden, Smith, and Hayner I was worried about, anyway.

It was the fourth man.

The man with the cool, literate voice who had called his three goons off Holly. The man I hadn't wanted to mention to the police.

I hadn't thought much about him. I had assumed that if the police found the other three, they would find the fourth as well. But they hadn't. Now, for some reason that gnawed inexplicably at me, I wanted to keep to myself the fact that there had been four men in the BMW.

I got a big pair of utility scissors from my workroom and went into the conservatory. People went in and out most of the morning, but I ignored them and they ignored me. It was easier that way. Thinking of an appropriate remark to someone grieving the death of a friend was difficult. Answering one was even more difficult.

When Todd Hall strolled into the conservatory shortly before noon with Emily on his arm, I channeled my irritation with him into my scissors. I snapped off another stem of the four-foot umbrella plant I was pruning and tossed it aside.

"But what a horrible way to start the weekend," Emily was moaning. She looked tired and depressed, but her red sun dress and cheeks lit up the room, which is saying something since it was already bright. "Everyone got roaring drunk last night. They all have hangovers this morning—those that have bothered to get up. God knows about the rest. And what will they tell the other guests when they begin to arrive? It'll be nothing but death, death, death all weekend."

My scissors snapped together.

"It wasn't a very pretty sight," Todd said, "but no one will dwell on it unless you do."

I glanced around just in time to see Emily's hopeful Madonna look. "Do you think so?"

"Of course. You're the hostess."

"I'm not. Mother is, and she's an absolute wreck. She had to be given a sedative!"

"What's so unusual about that? Look, Emily, people are coming here because they expect to have a good time. How many of them even knew Bud? A few of Richard's old friends, maybe. No one's going to want to mope around all weekend—unless you force them to."

I pretended my next stem was Todd Hall's neck.

"What was that?" Emily's head shot around the room. "What—oh, Artemis. Hello."

I assembled my stems into a neat four-foot bouquet. "Hello."

"I—I'm sorry about Bud," she said quickly. "We all are."

"Sure. He was nice and loyal and I'm sure you'll bury his favorite bone with him." I stood up and went over to them. I thrust a stem at Emily. "Here, dump it upside down in a glass of water, and in a week or so you'll have a baby umbrella plant. Excuse me."

Emily's mouth hung open. "Artemis."

I had hurt her feelings. I was going to apologize, but Todd spoke before I could. "You'll have to excuse Artie, Emily. She had a little too much to drink last night herself."

The little glint in his eye reminded me of his parting gesture a few hours ago, and I felt guilty and stupid because I knew I was acting out of hurt and exhaustion. Emily smiled weakly. "It's—it's all right."

Todd turned to her. "Would you mind waiting for me in the terrace?" he asked. "I can see Artie is about to fling a thousand and one insults at me. I'll be with you in a minute."

Emily gave Todd a trusting smile and, without looking at me, left. She still had her umbrella plant stem in her hand. I wondered what she would do with it.

"Don't attack me with your shears, for heaven's sake. What have I done now?"

"I sat up in my room all night waiting for someone to tell me what was going on."

Todd fingered the yellowed foliage of one of the umbrella plant stems in my hand. He said coolly, "I don't recall locking your door."

"You—oh, never mind." Wallowing in self-pity never had gotten me anywhere. "I suppose you know all about Vanheyden, Smith, and Hayner?"

"Yes, and I can't say I'm sorry it's ended this way. A lot of melodramatics for naught, wouldn't you say?" Todd smiled and let go of the stem. "Sergeant Warner said you decided not to press charges."

"Why bother? I don't feel like having every newspaper in the state report that my father was suspected of having killed Patrice Harrison. This whole thing was dumb from the very start," I said. I had already decided not to tell

Todd about the fourth man, either—at least not yet. When I had more information and knew I was on the right track, I would tell him. I was through looking stupid. "I'm just glad it's over. Does everyone know about it?"

"Nearly. Jack and I are the ones who look like fools, Artie. You're still the beautiful and vulnerable victim. You should see the looks I receive when people find out I threatened you with a gun. It doesn't do any good to tell them you aren't as helpless as you look."

"My curse," I said.

Todd smiled, but his eyes weren't on me when he asked, "What will you do now?"

"Go back to my apartment, I guess."

"Will you be staying on at Rosewood?"

I could hear a note of uncertainty—even vulnerability—in his voice. He did care. Oh, God. I almost threw my arms around him and told him about the fourth man, but I shook off the thought. "Through the weekend, anyway," I replied quietly.

"Well, I'll see you before you leave."

"Todd—"

But he was already on his way out the conservatory. Wrong again, Artemis. The man's "lark" was over and so was his fling with the gardener. Why couldn't I accept reality? Or was I simply being paranoid? Todd had given me an opening to bridge the social gap between us, and I had done nothing. I was in a surly mood, to be sure, but I was also tired, hurt, and confused. Couldn't Todd see that and make the first move? Perhaps it was too much trouble. Perhaps *I* was too much trouble. It didn't matter. Not now. I bit a yellowed tip of a leaf. I would find the fourth man myself.

But first—first I had to find the white lady slipper.

Chapter Seventeen

I wore jeans, a navy blue sweat shirt, and blue running shoes. I braided my hair tightly and wrapped it around my head nineteenth-century style. I made sure my flashlight had batteries and got a hand shovel off my porch. There had been no ostensible reason for me to continue to stay at Rosewood, so I had come back to my apartment, and I was glad. No more Todd Hall, no more Jack Harrison. I was on my own.

I didn't expect the empty feeling that permeated every part of my body and spirit, but I told myself it would go away in time. I was used to being alone. And wasn't it better this way? If I shoved Todd Hall out of my life, I wouldn't have to compromise and put up with his demands and worries.

If I shoved him out of my life, I would never have to lose him.

And besides, I told myself boldly and cheerfully, if he and Jack knew what I was up to they'd tie me to the nearest tree. Maybe what it all came down to was that I was determined to do exactly as I pleased—as I nearly always had—without anyone trying to stop me.

I tried to call Holly one more time before leaving. She and Hans hadn't been home all evening. They still weren't. Hans's brother introduced himself—his name was David—and said he would tell Holly I was all right. He also said I was a nitwit and should take the first plane out of there for Iowa. I said I quite agreed and hung up.

A parting glance in the mirror convinced me I looked more like a Russian spy than a scared and confused twenty-five-year-old gardener. "Good," I said, and gave myself a feeble smile.

I took the back way into Rosewood and parked my Falcon among the trees on the downslope of the hill with the panoramic view of the estate. Then I walked down to the lake. It was the first night of the full moon, but even so, the going was rough. I decided to walk along the shoreline, where it was lighter and, I hoped, safer than either the path or the dirt road that encircled the lake.

I came to a thick, impossible tangle of brambles. There was no easy way of getting around them, except detouring into the lake. The water was cool and soothing on my ankles. I crouched down and tried not to slosh as I took a few more steps away from shore to avoid an overhang of the brambles.

I went in up to my neck. The shock sent my flashlight and hand shovel straight to the bottom of the lake.

"Damn!"

Even the whispered curse seemed like a gunshot in the still night.

I had to go on. The moon was bright enough, and I could use my hands and a stick to dig.

I took off my shoes and tied them together with their laces. My socks I let float away. Then I swam farther out into the lake. It would be quicker this way—or so I rationalized.

I did a quiet sidestroke past the pine grove and the narrow point, into the inlet. The ledge was a black mass, twenty feet high, impregnable. I swam into shore just north of the ledge; the bank here was still steep and rocky but, I thought hopefully, manageable. I climbed onto a boulder and caught my breath. Despite the clear, starry sky and the gleaming full moon, the woods above me seemed dark and threatening. I closed my eyes briefly, trying to dispel my mounting fears. I wished I hadn't lost my flashlight and shovel. I wished I had brought Todd Hall's gun. I wished I didn't know about the fourth man.

I wished I weren't here alone.

I put on my shoes, crawled off the boulder, and began my ascent. The bank was badly eroded. The first level consisted of piled-up sand and stones and wasn't as steep as the latter half, which consisted of exposed subsoil, dry, bare roots, and an occasional diminutive choke cherry. I walked erect part of the way, then gave up and climbed up gorilla-fashion.

I tripped on a root and fell hard. My knee banged on a sharp stone, and I felt the skin tear where my wrist scraped against the root. I continued climbing but on my hands and knees and splayfooted. The last few yards were very steep and so eroded that I could find nothing to hold onto but dirt. My left foot located another root, and I put all my weight on it as I groped for something above me to grab.

The root gave way. I slid down about a yard. My sweat shirt rode up to my armpits, and my bare stomach reaped all the rewards of stones, roots, and sand it met on the way down.

The air went in for a proper yell, but my mouth clamped shut and the air stayed in my lungs until I dared to let it out, slowly, through my nose.

There was a voice above me, toward the cabin. A man's voice, nervous and low. "Did you hear that?"

"Hear what?"

"I don't know. Something. Maybe we should take a look."

"Oh, for Christ's sake," came the skeptical response. "I didn't hear anything."

"I'm sure—"

"Go take a look, then. I don't plan to stay out here all goddamn night. You know what'll happen if we get caught?"

"Yeah, yeah."

"It was probably just a raccoon. Any idea what a white lady slipper looks like?"

I went even flatter against the dirt.

"I say we go get the girl and make her show us where it is."

"Oh, that'd be real good. We're lucky as it is we're not in jail. We touch that girl and the police'd nail us but good—or that son of a bitch would. Do you believe that crap about letting ourselves get caught? Didn't see *him* getting caught!"

"We've been over that, Smith."

The voice was impatient, but the scraping of the shovels

never stopped. I imagined them covering my body with the cool dirt, and shook off the thought.

"Yeah. Right. He's out to find the jewels himself and leave us high and dry."

"Not if we get them first. Keep digging, will you?"

"Think he found them the other night when he was out here?"

"His ass'd be on a plane out of here if he had, don't you think? Dig, for Christ's sake."

Then a third voice, from farther away, cut them off. "Quit yacking, will you? Get over here. There's nothing over there. And keep quiet!"

I didn't hear them move, but I knew they had. I lay still. My stomach shrieked with pain. Cramps had already begun in my splayed ankles and outstretched arms. My right cheek pressed hard against the pebbles. I was breathing dirt.

But I was thinking, and thinking clearly.

If I moved I was dead. John Vanheyden, Peter Smith, and Albert Hayner would drag me up the hill, drop me in front of my father's cabin, and make me show them the white lady slipper. And when I had, and they had dug up the jewels, they would kill me.

I didn't get the least bit of satisfaction from knowing that I had been right, that this affair was not as easily explained as the police had said, and not as Todd and Jack—and everyone else—had believed. Not the least bit of satisfaction at all. I wanted Todd Blakesly Hall, and I wanted him now.

He did not come.

My nose started to run. I let it. I also let the tears dribble across my nose and into my eyebrow. I sucked on my lips to keep them from opening up and emitting a frightened sob.

I could hear nothing. I had no idea if the men were still up there looking for the white lady slipper or if they had gone or even if they were standing at the top of my hill holding their sides and laughing at the prostrate body clinging to the dirt.

A clanking sound nearly shot me into the lake. My heart beat so hard it hurt. But then, slowly, I realized that the sound must have been a shovel hitting the ground. There was some low swearing. I couldn't make out all of it, but I got the general idea. They hadn't found the white lady slipper.

They decided to give up and go home.

Nothing signaled their departure other than words. There was no putter of an engine, no loud footsteps, no sudden darkness from flashlights extinguished, no little sign reading, "Artemis, go home. It's all over."

So I waited until I was sure. And even then I chose not to crawl the rest of the way up the hill and go find the white lady slipper myself. Instead I crept back down the hill and swam back to my car.

I drove like a maniac back to Saratoga, dragged my bleeding, sobbing self up to my apartment, and called Holly Dearborn. Hans's mother answered, and I could hear worry in her voice when she yelled for Holly.

"Artemis, is something wrong?"

I crumpled when I touched my hand to my stomach and it came up covered with blood.

"*Artemis!*"

My cut wasn't all that deep, but it had bled unchecked. I pressed my wet shirt against it. Now that I had survived, I was free to panic, but Holly was screaming at me from Iowa.

"I'm afraid I need more practice before I'd make a good Phillip Marlowe," I said lamely.

"What happened?"

I told her everything. Talking calmed me, but my eyes kept wandering to the door. Those men knew where I lived. I held a medium-size jade plant in my lap. It had a thick clay pot.

"Holly, I don't know what to do."

Before she could speak, Hans Erikson bellowed, "You put down this goddamn phone and call the Saratoga police!"

"Oh—Holly—I—"

"Hans is right, Artemis."

"We'll never catch the fourth man if I call in the police. He'll escape first."

"You goddamn nut!" Hans barked. "You want to live?"

"Hans," Holly said patiently, "let me talk to her."

The extension clicked, and she breathed a sigh of pure relief. "A sweatheart, isn't he?"

My laugh came out more a sob. I was alone, and I wanted Todd.

"Why don't you call in our he-man?"

"I can't."

"You won't."

"No, I would, but he'd kill me. Oh, Holly, I want to. I—"

"Artemis?"

There was no use pretending. "I'm in love with him, Holly." It felt so good saying it; much less frightening than I had expected.

"Ah."

"It's awful."

"But inevitable. I always knew you'd fall for some gorgeous rich hunk just as mule-headed as you are. He'd be the first person you'd call, but you're afraid of somehow alerting this fourth man that you're on to him. You think he's someone at Rosewood, right?"

"Yes! . . . I don't know! Holly, I can't call Rosewood or drive up there in the middle of the night without causing suspicion."

Holly inhaled deeply—on a cigarette, I imagined. "But I can."

"But Holly, Hans will be livid."

She scoffed. "All relationships are built upon arguments won, lost, and forgotten. I'll pretend I'm Leslie Hall and get your man on the phone. Then I'll tell him everything."

"Don't tell him I'm in love with him."

"Artemis, the man's an utter ass if he doesn't know he's the perfect match for you. You'll be all right, won't you? Oh, hell, Hans and David are packing their bags and loading their rifles. Leave everything to me. *Be careful!*"

She hung up.

Thirty minutes later, Todd burst in and nearly got a jade plant thrown at him, but I stopped myself just in time. He strode over to me, removed the plant from my lap, lifted me by the elbows, and looked at me with anger, worry, and incredulity mixed on his handsome face. Mostly anger, I thought. He was breathing hard.

"Holly reached you, I take it," I said, more hoarsely than I would have wished.

"Damn it, you're shivering."

That same mix of anger, worry, and incredulity was in his voice. He plucked me up and carried me to the bed, plopping me down unceremoniously. He snatched the hem of my wet turtleneck. I winced as he lifted it. He saw the blood and cursed. Carefully—even tenderly—he removed my shirt. Even with the pain, my nipples were standing out inside my wet, translucent bra, but he didn't seem to notice. His entire attention was directed at the bloody scrape on my stomach.

"It's nothing, really," I said. "Todd, did Holly tell you everything?"

His eyes, dots of flint, pierced through me. "Enough for me to know you're a damn fool."

I would have argued, but in several quick, lithe movements he disappeared into the bathroom, returning moments later with a damp cloth and a box of Band-Aids.

"Oh, the wound's clean. I swam in the lake afterward—"

His dark look shut me up, and I let him dab at the scrape with the cloth. He cursed the Band-Aids soundly, however, when none proved suitable to cover the cut. I pointed out that the bleeding had stopped and I would be fine. He scowled and made me hold the washcloth against it, anyway. I did so without a word.

Muttering about what a stubborn little nitwit I was, he reached around to my back and unhooked my bra. One arm at a time, careful not to let go of the cloth, I slipped out of it.

His gaze rested on the rosy tips of my breasts. I could feel myself responding just to his look.

"Artie, Artie," he grated, leaning toward me.

"I had to do it—"

He growled lowly, cutting me off with a stab of his tongue against my lips. Already the blood boiled in my veins. My lips parted, welcoming his kiss. His tongue shot in and forced all thought of pain and death and fear from my mind. There was only the taste and smell of him, the feel of him.

I shivered now not with cold, but with immediate, unshakable yearning. His thumbs struck out and kneaded my nipples. His tongue circled my mouth in the same slow, torturous rhythm. I clutched the washcloth with one hand, but the other grabbed his upper arm, still encased in an expensive cotton dress shirt. While I had been skulking about for thieves and murderers, he had been dining with the Harrisons.

Opening my mouth wider, I boldly met his hot, firm tongue and searched his mouth. The force of the ever-deepening erotic kiss pushed me down on the bed.

"Oh, Todd—"

His mouth was off mine; hot, wild flicks of his tongue tormented my chin and throat. Then they were on my breasts, hotter, wilder.

"Don't say a word, darling, not a word," he muttered.

He unsnapped and unzipped my jeans and tore them off with an intensity that further inflamed me. "Todd, I can't wait," I murmured breathlessly.

He stood up abruptly and pulled off his clothes quickly, recklessly, giving me no time at all to recover from his caressing tongue and lips. Just seeing him so perfectly naked made my body tremble and ache.

"Now, Todd," I cried, "please, *now!*"

"I won't hurt you?"

"No!"

He lay on his back on the bed and lifted me onto him, so that my knees straddled him. I had completely forgotten my superficial wound, even if he hadn't. He held my buttocks, and as he arched upward, I thrust onto him, driving that pulsing maleness deep, deep within me. He held me above him, kneading my breasts, teasing, never letting me collapse onto his chest and hurt myself. He drove into me over and over and over, responding willingly to the blinding pace I set.

"Oh—darling, darling . . ."

Then he was grimacing with pleasure, as my body drove and danced endlessly on him, and his filled me with strength and erotic delight. He held me lightly by the hips, not inhibiting my moves.

We burst together, breathing in great, ragged gulps of air, bound together in body and soul.

Afterward he handed me my white terry-cloth robe and dressed quickly, without a word. He put the kettle on to boil and dropped teabags into two mugs. We sat at the kitchen table. My hair had fallen out of its pins. My body felt warm and tingly and loved. Secure. I wanted to tell Todd so but didn't. I knew we had other matters to discuss.

"Holly said you didn't want to go to the police. Why not?"

"He hired Vanheyden and company and always seems to be one step ahead of us. The fourth man, I mean. He found out the police were only looking for three men, not four. Only I knew there were four men."

The kettle hissed steam. Todd filled the two mugs and brought them to the table. "You could be completely wrong, you know," he said soberly. "Your fourth man could be just another thug."

"I hope so, though Holly said he sounded too educated, too smooth."

"Will they find your white lady slipper?"

"Not where they were looking, no. It was a ways off into the woods, and as far as I could tell, they were digging near the cabin. And even if they did know where to look, lady slippers aren't blossoming now—and I sincerely doubt that particular lady slipper is still alive."

"But you remember where you found it?"

"Exactly."

Todd wrung out his teabag on his spoon. I usually used one teabag for two cups, but I didn't tell him that. "Look, Artemis, whoever's behind this may not *want* to come after you, but a few more nights skulking about the Harrison woods is hardly going to convince him of your innocence."

I dunked my teabag once more before borrowing Todd's spoon and squeezing it. Sharing a cup of tea with him seemed so natural, except that he preferred coffee and we were discussing robbers and murderers. "They didn't see me," I said, "and, in any case, if they're indeed after the white lady slipper I'm *not* innocent. I know where to find it."

"Damn it, all the more reason to go to the police!"

I shook my head. "I want that fourth man, Todd. He had Vanheyden, Smith, and Hayner get themselves caught so they could tell that cock-and-bull story to throw me—us—off the trail. But he was out there digging himself. Maybe Bud stumbled on him and—"

"But, Artie, you heard it yourself. He called off Vanheyden and company."

"That's because he doesn't want us to find the jewels—and he doesn't want his men to find them, either."

"Maybe those guys are right—he wants to keep them for himself."

"Maybe," I said. "But, either way, if the jewels *are* out there, they're a clue to what happened to Patrice Harrison."

"The police would have to reopen the case," Todd added slowly.

I nodded. "Right. But if we go running to them now—before we have anything more to go on—he'll get away, and we'll never know what happened to Jack's mother . . . or Bud McCarty."

"I know," Todd said reluctantly, sighing. "I know—and, unfortunately, so does Jack."

"Then you have talked to Jack?"

"Yes!" he hissed. "This isn't a goddamn lark anymore!"

"It never was for me. What exactly did Jack say?"

Todd took two sips of tea, wrinkled up his face, and shoved his mug aside. Then he looked at me gravely, but with a trust—even a confidence—that had never been there before, and one I felt I hadn't earned.

"All right," he said heavily. "Look, obviously we have to readjust our thinking. This thing *isn't* over yet. And God only knows how ugly it might get before it does end. I'd like nothing better than to ship you off to the south of France for a month, but Jack suggested you might be more amenable to coming back to Rosewood. Even if our fourth man is lurking about, you're safer there—and closer to the action, if you'd rather look at it that way."

"But I no longer have any plausible reason for being at Rosewood other than for my job."

"Yes you do: Jack. You know about the rumors circulating about you two."

"Yes, but they're completely false—"

"So? That's not the point. All you have to do is to capitalize on them and fake a budding romance between you and Jack. Accept his invitation to stay at Rosewood as a guest. People can fill in the gaps."

"He suggested this?"

Todd nodded solemnly, his eyes searching my face for something.

"Does he know about us?"

"What 'us,' Artie? We fight and make love better than any two people I know, but that's about it." My heart sank, but then he grinned to show he was teasing and reached across the table to run his fingertips over the top of my hand. "No, Jack doesn't know about us. No one does, otherwise I might have dragged you off to Rosewood myself by now and chained you to my bed. That might sound barbaric to you, but at least I'd know the next time you go off scaling cliffs."

"Todd, I won't have to stay in Jack's room?"

"Not unless you want to."

"No!"

"The huntress chaste and fair." He grinned. "Only not so chaste. Don't look so worried, Artie. Everyone knows—or thinks—Jack is half in love with you already."

"Do you?"

"I don't know," he replied, suddenly serious. "If he is, I may lose my best friend, because God knows I can't keep my hands off you."

"Then why go through with this?"

"Because it's the only way."

I shook my head. "No one will believe it."

"Everyone will believe it. R. W. practically treats you like you're already one of the family, and everyone's been waiting for you and Jack to get together, one way or another. I'll talk to him tonight, and he can come by for you in the morning. Will you be all right?"

"No reason I shouldn't be. I'll probably get the creeps—"

"Artie," he said irritably, "do you want me to stay?"

"No—yes." I sighed and said firmly, "Yes."

"Good. I'm glad I didn't pick another fight with Emily for nothing." He grinned, the dimple giving him an unexpected boyish look. "She was more than obliging. Anyway, it gives me an excuse for being out all night. Jack will call if I'm not back in another twenty minutes, and I'll tell him what's going on."

"And you say he doesn't know about us?"

He laughed. "Darling, when I left him, I'm sure the last thing he expected me to do was to make love to you within five minutes of walking in here."

"Oh."

"Yes. Now, if you don't mind, I want a blow-by-blow of your shenanigans tonight."

I obliged him with an unedited version. To his credit, he didn't yell once, just grunted and growled a few times. When I finished, he merely said, "Artie, you're losing your robe. Are you tired?"

I said no.

He looked at me, grinned, and said, "Good, let's go to bed."

We did, and sleep eluded us for a long time after that. We made love slowly, exquisitely, absorbing every detail of each other's bodies, pushing ourselves to the limits of ecstasy and beyond. Finally, cuddled together, we slept.

Chapter Eighteen

IN THE morning Todd left early and said he'd have breakfast at the track and be "seen," just in case anyone might get suspicious. I told him I felt like a fallen woman. He laughed and said only a fallen goddess. His car was parked on a side street a few blocks down. He gave me a lingering parting kiss and said, "Do me one favor, Artie: Don't fall in love with Jack Harrison."

"Don't worry," I said, grinning, "he's far too rich."

After he'd gone, I showered, got dressed, and made a pot of tea and a batch of blueberry muffins.

I was cleaning out Ralph's ears and getting impatient when Jack finally appeared in the doorway shortly before lunch.

"Sorry to keep you waiting," he said.

I tossed Ralph off the table. "Forget it."

Jack walked into my apartment. He looked out of place in his salmon-colored shirt and tan, wrinkleless pants. I sat there in a pair of old chinos and a madras shirt from my college days. I still had a gauze pad of dead ear mites in my hand.

No one will believe it, I thought.

"Ummm—Todd told me what happened last night," Jack said. "That was a crazy thing to do, Artemis."

I waved a hand. "Blame it on the full moon. I usually do. Can I get you a cup of coffee? No, I don't have any. Tea, then?"

"No thanks. Artemis—" He pulled out a chair at the table and sat next to me. "Artemis, I don't know how I could ever have suspected your father. I didn't want to. I—please forgive me."

The Venus Shoe

"Done."

He looked up at me. "And you. God, of all the people I know, you're absolutely the last one who would want a million dollars worth of anything. I've been an idiot."

I smiled. "I'm not getting too many points for brains either lately. Let's just forget it."

"All right." He pulled his hands apart and set them on his lap. "Artemis, you're the only one left alive who can find that white lady slipper—and therefore the jewels. That puts you in a very precarious position, to say the least. I agree with Todd that you can't stay here. Rosewood will be safer, but safest of all would be—"

"Iowa or Saudi Arabia or Nome, Alaska. I'm staying."

After a long, penetrating look, Jack accepted that. "Then let's get a few things straight," he said, taking on an imperious tone. "You're not to go off alone, ever. You're not to go anywhere near the lake, whether or not you're with someone. In fact, the more you stay inside, the better. You can go out on the terrace, to the pool and the tennis courts, and to the rose garden. That's all. Finally, you're to do as Todd and I say without arguing."

I crossed my arms. "Where do you get off making rules for me, Jack Harrison?"

"They make sense, Artemis," he said.

"I have to show you the white lady slipper."

"You can tell us where to find it."

"You two city boys?" I scoffed. "This is ridiculous. Those are Todd's rules, aren't they? Well, they're stupid!"

Jack wriggled in his chair. "Maybe so," he said, placating. "But if you don't agree to them, I'm putting you on a plane to Iowa."

"So, he bosses you around, too?"

Jack grinned. "Artemis, he bosses everybody around. He's not asking too much, is he? You're exhausted, you're hurt—don't you scowl at me, you are hurt. And you're beyond your emotional limits. Look, if I'd been the one hanging off that cliff—"

"Okay, okay. Damn you both. I'll agree to your dumb rules. No solos, no lake, no arguments."

But my heart wasn't in it. How could I be angry? Todd's rules meant nothing except that he cared and didn't want me underfoot. I had gone alone to my father's cabin, encountered unsavory characters, and returned alive. I had proved something to Todd Blakesly Hall—and to myself—but I had to admit the episode had taken some of the starch out of me.

Still, I preferred to make my own rules.

"Thanks." He seemed to relax. "Now, about this affair we're supposed to be having. I've put out a few feelers already, and I can tell you right now it's not going to be that easy on you."

"What is?"

"The gossip's been speculative up to now," Jack went on, ignoring my comment. "But now it will probably get malicious. Father thinks I should wait awhile before throwing myself at you. He's convinced it won't work and you'll be hurt. Adelia, on the other hand, thinks you're a conniving little fortune hunter. So does Emily. Marie—well, who knows what Marie thinks. You can pretty much divide up the guests along those lines. Father's friends will probably tend to agree with him, Adelia's friends with her, and Emily's with her."

"Most won't care," I said.

"Oh, they'll care," Jack said bitterly. "I'm the long-lost heir to Rosewood. Anything I do is subject to debate, and falling in love with a gardener whose father I suspected of having murdered my mother, I assure you, is not just anything."

"Does everyone know about that?"

"My erroneous suspicions? It's getting around."

I grimaced.

"Oh, and Artemis, there is one other thing I want to get straight." Jack licked his lips and looked at his palms. Then he looked at me. His eyes were soft but anxious. "I'm not in love with you. For a while I thought I might be, but—"

"You're not."

"That's all right?"

"Of course, it's all right." I smiled. "You've been listening to Todd again. He's a terrible judge of that sort of thing. You're not in love with me, and I'm not in love with you. We've both known that all along, when it comes right down to it. Well, I'm all packed and ready to go."

Jack winked and put his arm around my shoulder. We

were friends again. "Then let's get to it," he said. "We'll have lunch in town and head on over."

Etiquette called for Adelia Harrison to greet us at the door, but apparently it did not call for her to treat me like a welcome guest.

"Good of you to come, Artemis," she said icily. "I knew you would."

I gave her one of my goddess-of-the-hunt smiles.

"All the rooms on the main floors are taken." She glanced at Jack. I knew if he hadn't been standing there she would have made some comment about my sleeping in his room. "Of course, you would know that, wouldn't you?"

She waited for an answer. I could have been polite, but I opted for being cool. "Of course."

She cleared her throat. She hadn't expected that. I congratulated myself. "Well," she went on crisply, "Henry will take your things upstairs. You will be on the fourth floor again."

"How delightful," I said as if I meant it.

"Yes. I know you won't mind."

I had another remark all ready, but she was gliding back into her sitting room before I got off the first word. I muttered to Jack instead, "Charming welcome."

"I warned you. Why don't you settle in and meet me on the terrace in an hour or so?"

"Sure."

I brought my own "things" upstairs. The sheets and linens had been changed, and there was a bouquet of miniature Gold Coin roses, buttercup yellow, the buds just opening. Surely Adelia wouldn't have—

There was a card signed simply: Jack.

I felt a pang of loneliness and dismissed it with well-practiced firmness.

Then I dug Todd's Baretta out of my suitcase and slipped it under the mattress. I changed into an orchid sun dress and went downstairs to the terrace.

Jack and Todd were alone, drinking gin and tonics at a table next to the lawn. Jack offered me one.

"The woman only drinks Jack Daniel's neat," Todd told him cheerfully. "Or her blasted tea. Here, sit down, Artie."

I did so, trying to avoid Todd's eye. He was stunning: unruly tawny hair, laughing slate eyes, intriguing grin, marvelous body. A Boston playboy on vacation. I recalled what his father and sister had had to say about him. But then his eye caught mine and he winked. Last night tumbled back to me. Instead of Todd's crisp shirt and pants, I saw his trim, browned body, glorious and tempting in its nakedness. It would be a very long weekend.

I cleared my throat and turned to Jack. "So are you two going to sit around getting drunk all day, or are you going to root out this mur—"

"Artemis!" Jack hissed.

I crossed my arms, unperturbed. "If you two want to do all the sleuthing, then I suggest you sleuth. Otherwise I see no reason to keep my end of the bargain."

"All right," Todd said patiently. He leaned over the table. "We need you to tell us about your white lady slipper." He watched me as my eyes narrowed and, when I didn't say anything, he guessed what I wanted to hear. "We're going to the cabin this afternoon. Don't worry. Our story is that we're going to Saratoga, to a horse dealer. That should throw anybody off the scent."

That wasn't all I wanted to hear. "I should go with you."

"Artie—"

"It will look strange if Jack suddenly abandons me."

"He's not abandoning you. He's planning to buy you a damned horse. No one will think twice about it."

"And what am I supposed to do around here all afternoon?"

"Try to make a few friends, I would think," Todd said with an edge to his voice I didn't appreciate. "Just stay away from the lake."

"Don't go out alone, and don't talk to strangers," I said, mocking him. "I could find that white lady slipper in ten seconds."

"Good for you. Then you can describe it in sixty."

I sighed, unwillingly resigning myself to an afternoon of inaction—and worry. I preferred to be in the thick of things, no matter how terrifying, but I'd already lost that round. *"Cypripedium candidum,"* I said. *"Cypripedium* is from the Greek, meaning Venus's shoe. There are several varieties, all orchids, all temperamental, and all uncommon. The easiest to find is *Cypripedium acaule*—the pink lady slipper. It is purplish-pink, stemless, grows in dry pine forests. *Candidum* is very rare but perhaps the prettiest of all the lady slippers. It is generally know as the white lady slipper, sometimes the silver slipper orchid."

"Spare us the botany lesson, Artie," Todd said. "Where is the damn thing?"

I gave him a contemptuous look and continued. *"Candidum* has three or four light green, narrow, elliptical leaves. The flower itself is pouch-shaped—hence the nickname lady slipper—and very small, about three-quarters of an inch, white outside, purple-streaked inside. None of which matters because it's not blooming and almost certainly dead." Todd was glowering at me. I sighed. "I found it about thirty yards northwest of the cabin—more north than west. There's an underground spring that keeps the ground moist year-round and fairly sopping in the spring. The white lady slipper was growing above it, next to a rotted log. The log and the spring should still be there, anyway. There's a boulder—it must be six or seven feet high—a few yards to the east."

Todd couldn't help but grin.

"I hope you both get lost."

Jack smiled nervously. "We probably will."

"You want me to come, don't you?" I said to him. "You could just say I'm going to pick out the horse—that's ridiculous buying me a horse. They cost thousands of dollars—"

"Details," Jack said, suddenly amused. "It won't be a Triple Crown contender, anyway."

"Well, if I went with you—"

Todd exercised his assumed veto power. "No."

I gave up. "When are you going?"

"Right now." He downed the last of his gin and tonic. "Jack?"

"Coming." Jack kissed me perfunctorily on the lips and, with a wink and a pat on the arm, followed Todd off the terrace.

I got a piece of ice out of Jack's glass and sucked on it. There was nothing I could do. Jack and Todd were gone, and I was stuck here.

I could beat them to the lady slipper.

No, I admitted, I wasn't up to scaling any more cliffs or meeting Vanheyden and company—or even Todd Hall and Jack Harrison. I would just sit here and stare at the hanging baskets of petunias.

And wait.

Michael Davis slid into the chair next to me. Dressed casually but tastefully, he was, I thought, an exceedingly good-looking man. He smiled and said hello. My hello back was petulant, although I hadn't meant it to be. It didn't affect Davis's smile. "I can't understand how anyone could leave such a lovely lady," he said, making the trite phrase sound convincing. "Didn't I just see Jack leave?"

"Yes," I replied. "He and Todd are going to Saratoga."

"Oh?"

I offered coyly, "They won't tell me why."

"Oh, oh, I see," Davis said, laughing. "Well, you're the very kind of woman men love to spoil. Probably Jack plans to do just that."

I smiled innocently.

I was glad when Davis turned formal. "Artemis, if you're not busy right now, I would like to talk to you. It's about Bud McCarty. I know it's a difficult time for you—"

"What about Bud?"

"Mr. Harrison asked one of the housemaids—Nancy Lerner, I believe, is her name—to clean up Mr. McCarty's cottage, take out the garbage, food, that sort of thing. She found two items of interest and brought them to Mr. Harrison, who in turn brought them to me." Davis withdrew two envelopes from his sportcoat pocket. One was crumpled and lumpy, folded in half. The other was neat and crisp and white. "These were on the kitchen table."

I swallowed and watched wordlessly as Davis opened up the crumpled envelope, dumped out a set of keys strung together with forty-pound fishing line, and pushed them toward me. There was a note scrawled on the back of an order form for hardware supplies. It sounded almost ridiculous when Davis read it in his quiet, formal voice.

" 'Missy, I'm a sick old man. If anything happens to me, what I own is yours. There isn't much, but take what you want. Bud.' " Davis paused and gave me time to digest what he had just read. "It's not a classic will, Artemis, but I think it will do. The only problem I can foresee is transferring ownership of the truck and the boat to you. The rest of his things you might as well just take, if you want them. These are a second set of keys; they match exactly the ones Mr. McCarty had when—the ones he had."

I nodded and touched the keys with the tips of my fingers. If I looked at Davis, I knew I would cry, so I didn't look at him.

"And this," he went on, holding up the clean envelope, "is a copy of Mr. McCarty's insurance policy. It names you as the beneficiary. Very shortly, Artemis, you will be receiving a check for fifty thousand dollars."

I stared at Davis. "What?"

He smiled understandingly. "I know that must be hard for you to believe," he said. "But it's all here, paid up in full, and legal."

"But I—I don't want it!"

"Artemis—"

I clenched the keys tightly, trying to control myself, but the tears came. I jumped up. My chair tipped over, and I felt the panic sweeping over me. "I don't want it!"

Davis lifted a hand to me, but it just brushed my arm as I ran past him into the grass, toward the rose garden. I thought only of escape. Todd Hall's rules be damned. I needed to be alone. I didn't go into the rose garden but cut across the lawn between the elms and the maples, parallel to the lake but toward the duck pond. I wiped away my tears with my index fingers.

Jeffrey Chapman came up beside me. He had on work clothes and was sweating. Of course, I thought. Vanheyden, Smith, and Hayner had been fired, leaving Rosewood short of muscle. Jeff had to help put up the bandstand on the lawn above the pool. Under ordinary circumstances, I would have been amused.

"Are you all right?" he asked.

I nodded. "Just had a bit of a shock, that's all."

"This week's been full of them, hasn't it?" Jeff couldn't have known how much of an understatement that was. "Where are you going?"

"For a walk."

"I thought—"

"Jack's gone into Saratoga," I explained, and smiled, if

weakly. "I could kill him, but that's the way it goes. Is everything set for the party?"

"Just about. I hate to say it, but I kind of miss those three who got after you—their muscle, anyway. Why didn't you press charges?"

"They were just trying to be heroes."

"Maybe so," Jeff said, "but terrorizing you is no way to go about it. Listen, if you're all right—"

"I am. Thank you, Jeff."

He headed back up toward the house. I continued on my way, not sure where I would end up. At the duck pond I turned north, away from the flutter of the ducks in the shallow water and the weeping willows that flanked it, into a stand of poplars where the grass was high and the daisies were allowed to grow wild. I picked one, smelled it, and plucked off the petals, not muttering the ritual "He loves me, he loves me not" but just plucking. Then I dropped the stem and went on.

Just above the boat house, I came to the dirt road that encircled the lake and much of the estate. I walked along the pounded dirt and stones, observing the flickering shadows of the trees without fear or misgiving or thought.

I had only been inside Bud's cottage a few times. The last was eleven years ago. He had made hot chocolate and biscuits with honey for a friend and me after we'd gone ice-skating on the lake. I recalled being a very silly, pink-cheeked, pigtailed fourteen-year-old. I wondered how anybody could change so much in little more than a decade.

I found the key to the door on my fishing line and went inside. The tiny living room was even more ragged than I remembered. The faded beige wallpaper was peeling; it didn't go with the threadbare green rug or the floppy old burgundy couch. A table with a small television and a stack of Westerns on it stood under a window, next to a rocking chair. That was all there was in the room. Bud always claimed he had been a sailor too long to start collecting objects—that was the word he used, *objects*—now that he had settled down. That he had settled for thirty years seemed not to affect his seadog habits or prejudices.

I went into the bedroom, even smaller than the living room. The sun streamed in through the window, dirty and curtainless. The cot was stripped, revealing the lumpy horsehair mattress. But Bud's clothes—workpants, flannel shirts, a raincoat—still hung in the closet, and a pair of boots, mud still caked to the heels, stood in front of the ugly walnut-veneer bureau. I fingered the papers on top of the metal desk. An oil bill, Tuesday's newspaper, a purchase order—

I went through the desk drawers. Mostly they contained junk: screwdrivers, paper clips, old bolts, rulers, five kinds of tape, a sewing kit. I found an old picture of my parents and me at Christmas, and one of my graduation photos. I was touched; having no family of his own, Bud seemed to have adopted mine. There was a small iron box in the bottom drawer, but it was locked. Then I discovered I had the key to it on my fishing line.

I went through the contents of the box. Memorabilia: a list of the ships he had sailed on, the battles he had fought, faded pictures of him in port with various women, one picture of a woman alone, and a bulky packet of old letters tied together with a piece of dirty string and stuck in a larger envelope. I didn't consider it my business to read them. Bud McCarty hadn't met the Pendletons until he came to Rosewood. What he did during his war days was irrelevant.

Still, I took the iron box with me: it held his memories of his life—all that was left. I felt, somehow, it should be preserved. I would go back up to the house, apologize to Davis, and tell him to do as he saw fit with the rest of Bud's things. I had his little iron box. It meant more to me than his truck or his boat or his television.

Marie Harrison and Tom Avery caught me in the herb garden on their way up from the pool. They told me Jack was looking for me. I swore and went into the kitchen. Nora told me Jack was looking for me. I swore again and went upstairs.

Jack was in my room. He was swearing, too.

"Hello," I said cheerfully. "Did you find—"

"Artemis! Good God, where have you been? We thought something happened to you."

"Time got away from me, I guess. I'm sorry."

Jack stared at me, incredulous. "Where have you been?" he demanded.

"Out walking."

"Alone?"

I sat on the bed. "Well—yes."

He hit the wall. "Damn it, Artemis—"

"It's all right, Jack. I didn't do anything suspicious. I just went for a walk, for God's sake. I'm back now."

"This is the stupidest, most inconsiderate thing you've done yet."

I sighed. It wouldn't do any good to say I agreed with him, which I did. "I'm sorry, Jack. I thought I'd get back before you did so you wouldn't worry."

"You sound like a two-year-old. I was about to go and call the police." He yanked the door, even though it was open. "Get dressed for dinner and come downstairs. Todd may kill you—"

"Jack, I said I'm sorry. I have an excuse, sort of."

"No, you don't,"

"All right, I don't. Did you find the white—"

"No."

He slammed the door behind him.

Chapter Nineteen

I ARRIVED late for cocktails. Heads turned when I walked onto the terrace, as I knew they would. Holly Dearborn's declarations to the contrary, I was not naive about my looks. I used them when I had to, ignored them when I could. Right now I hoped they would disarm two men sitting alone at the table they had staked out on the edge of the terrace.

"What are you two, the ostracized lepers of Molokai?" I said coolly, smiling. "I expected you to be fending off my throngs of admirers."

Neither said a word. Jack stared while Todd slowly ran his index finger around the rim of his empty glass. I made a little shrug that I hoped was very feminine. "Aren't you going to ask me to sit down?"

Jack pulled out a chair, and I sat down gracefully. My eyes met Todd's; his were hard and angry. I added more dazzle to my smile. "I'm sorry if I worried you two," I said, meaning it. "If you want to shoot me or slap me or whatever, go ahead. I'm not in the mood to fight."

"That's a first," Jack said.

I kept on smiling. "All right, I've been a fool. What do I have to do to get you to forgive me?"

At last, Jack returned my smile. "That's a dangerous question, Artemis. Where did you ever find that dress?"

"It was my mother's."

It had been a gift from my father—her wedding dress. The classic lines and deep, dusty rose silk suited our similar looks. I was taller and thinner than my mother, and my hair was longer and blonder, but, I thought, she was more beautiful than I in every way. I had kept the dress in good shape and usually wore it with my hair tied into a chignon and my face very lightly made up.

"Well, I suppose I'll have to forgive you," Jack said. "You're very beautiful tonight."

"Thank you."

I glanced tentatively at Todd. At last he gave that languid grin of his. "I believe *ravishing* is the word you're looking for, Jack," Todd said. "Well, Artie, you've taken the wind right out of my sails. You knew you would."

"I didn't want to look out of place," I said.

"You didn't want me to drag you out into the fields and flog you," Todd muttered. "At least it's a change from your pigtails and servants' whites." He waved to Henry, who responded immediately. "Jack Daniel's neat for Miss New York here. I'll have another of these."

"A Manhattan, sir?"

"Whatever. What about you, Jack?"

"Yes, the same," he replied absently.

I tried not to frown, but I couldn't help it. When Henry had gone, I said, "Are you two getting drunk again?"

"The subtlest of delusions," Todd answered, indifferent to my sarcasm. "It's killing you to be pleasant, isn't it? Don't stick out that jaw. People are watching. Ah, Henry, bless you. Your bourbon, Artie. I suppose I should call you Artemis, dressed as you are, but I know that beneath that lovely exterior is a nosy little mind full of questions that will just have to wait. And don't think you won't have to answer for this afternoon. You will. Oh, you certainly will."

I couldn't prevent my smile from turning to ice. "I don't have to answer to you for anything, Todd Hall."

"Calm down," Jack urged. "You two can fight this out later. Right now Adelia and Father are headed this way."

Todd turned in his chair and spoke with the cheerful bravura of a man well on his way to intoxication. "Adelia, Adelia, don't you look exquisite tonight, as always. I've been looking all over for that daughter of yours, but I'm afraid she's scrapped me again. If only she had the grace and charm of her mother. Good evening, Richard."

"You mustn't take Emily too seriously," Adelia said sweetly, waving a hand heavy with diamonds. There were also diamonds at her ears, throat, and left wrist. Our jewel thief would have had a heyday at Rosewood this weekend, I thought. One diamond would have been a better complement to Adelia's white chiffon dress than her dozen or so, but that was only the gardener's opinion. I discovered I wasn't in a very delightful mood. Guilt, I supposed. Adelia smiled at Jack and Todd. "I hope you two have been enjoying yourselves. I've hardly seen you at all today."

"Oh, we've been here and there," Todd said.

"We're having a marvelous time," Jack assured his stepmother. "Father, won't you and Adelia have a drink with us?"

R. W. was staring at me in a way that made me want to hide. I know it made me blush. He recovered and looked at his son. "Thank you, Jack, but we have some guests we haven't greeted yet." R. W. turned back to me. "Artemis, you're exceedingly lovely tonight. Your dress is perfect."

Was that what was bothering him? "It was my mother's," I explained. "It was her wedding dress."

R. W. nodded and turned away. That was what was bothering him. It never would have occurred to him to tell me the dress looked familiar. That would have been gross and tactless, especially if I had to tell him I had bought it at one of my antique clothing stores.

"Jack," he said, "I wonder if I could drag you away from Artemis after dinner, just for a little while. I have some friends I would like you to meet."

"Some of your corporate hounds?"

"Yes, Jack, but they are friends first," R. W. said, hurt at his son's needlessly nasty remark. "I'm not trying to push you into anything."

Jack looked at me, and I came to R. W.'s defense. "Oh, go on, Jack. Indulge your father for once. Todd can amuse me for a while."

Todd took the cue, still displaying an easygoing, slow-witted charm. "I've been waiting for the chance."

I was watching Adelia. I could read her mind as she glanced at me sideways: Why waste two handsome, eligible, wealthy men on a gold-digging little hussy? She gave me a polite upturn of her lips when she caught my eyes on her.

"I'm sorry, Father," Jack said. "I'd be happy to see you after dinner."

R. W. grinned and clapped a hand on Jack's shoulder. Adelia coaxed him off to greet the other guests. I noticed that she had managed to say not a word to me.

"I thought finding out I was practically an heiress would change Adelia's opinion of me," I said lightly. "I guess I was wrong."

"Artie, what the hell are you talking about?" Todd asked, not particularly interested.

"My fortune."

He was amused. "Darling, your fortune is before us."

"Cad," I said. "My face isn't worth a nickel, and neither is this dress. I, Mr. Jack Harrison and Mr. Todd Hall, am a proper heiress. Bud McCarty wants me to have his entire estate, boat, television, truck, and all."

"Well, well, well," Todd said, grinning. "I'll drink to that. I don't mean to burst your balloon, Artie, but that's hardly a fortune."

"What, he has a wonderful old couch. I bet I could get thirty dollars for it at a flea market." I was enjoying myself now. The bourbon on an empty stomach helped. "And his steel-toed boots—do you know how much those things cost?"

Jack had Henry bring me another bourbon. He liked me tipsy and sociable.

"I'll probably lose my scholarships," I said, sighing.

Todd laughed. "Oh, I'm sure."

"But I suppose I can pay my own way with fifty thousand dollars."

"Fifty—" Todd sat up straight. "Artie, what's this all about?"

Suddenly tears welled up in my eyes and my lips trembled. Jack's hand met mine. "I'm all right," I said, and collected myself. "Bud named me beneficiary of his life insurance policy."

"I see," Jack said. "You went to his cottage this afternoon."

I nodded.

Todd gave me an unsympathetic look. "Cheer up, Artie. Having a little money of your own isn't the worst thing that can happen to you."

"I don't want the damn money! Don't you see? Bud left me a set of keys and a copy of the insurance policy on his kitchen table. He knew he was going to die. And I killed him. I—"

"Artemis, that's enough," Jack said, his tone sharp and commanding. "You had nothing to do with Bud's death, do you hear? Nothing."

"But *I* found the—"

Todd cut me off. "Here comes Emily. Can we postpone this little discussion? Thank you—well, hello, Emily."

She was dressed in black, perfectly made up, holding a champagne glass in one hand and caressing Todd's shoulder with the other. "Mother said I'd hurt your feelings," she cooed. "I'm sure that's wishful thinking on her part, but here I am to save you from a boring evening."

"You're too good to your mother," Todd said.

"Oh, Todd, don't be mean. I'm trying to make peace."

"At Adelia's insistence, I'm sure," Todd replied, unruffled. "She's my greatest champion—has no idea what a didactic son of a bitch I am. Here, sit down and have a drink with us. I haven't seen you all day."

Emily remained standing. "That's not my fault."

"I never said it was."

"Where were you?"

"In Saratoga with Jack. And don't pretend you missed me, Emily. You spent the entire afternoon at the pool with some musician or another. That's up to you, so let's not argue. Are you staying or leaving?"

To my surprise—and disappointment—Emily smiled. I was hoping she'd give Todd Hall some of his own arrogant medicine. "I'm asking you to come in to dinner with me," she said. "Would you?"

"Of course."

They departed, Todd in his best playboy swagger, Emily clinging to him.

"Strange pair," I muttered to Jack.

He laughed. "I'd hardly call them a pair. Emily likes her freedom, and Todd's not about to get dotty over any woman—except you, perhaps, though you'll have a hard time getting him to admit it. Dinner?"

I smiled so he wouldn't notice the flush that was hot in my cheeks. "I'm as ready as I'll ever be," I said. "I studied up on my Emily Post—"

"All you have to do is keep smiling, and no one will notice that you eat with your fingers," he said good-naturedly and offered me his arm.

"This," I said, "should be fun."

The dinner was anything but fun, but at least I was one of the first back out to the terrace. Todd was lingering over almond torte and Emily. He managed, however, to give me an admonishing glance as I left.

Pierre Lecouvreur pulled out a chair for me. He had designed clothes for Harrisons for three decades and was a fixture at all their parties. "Thank you, Monsieur," I said, smiling.

"Your dress," he said in his French accent, sitting down with his champagne. "Where did you get it?"

He did not, I observed, have Richard Harrison's tactfulness, but he had such an inoffensive manner that I answered his question without any sneers.

"Your mother? Oh, yes, yes, I see now." He touched the bodice, then frowned. "No, I do not see. This dress I design for Mrs. Harrison—the first Mrs. Harrison, you understand. I think first your mother must copy it, but no, this is impossible. See, the finest silk, the most expensive buttons. I chose them myself. Exclusives, you understand."

"No, I don't understand. I always thought my father gave this dress to my mother for their wedding."

Lecouvreur shrugged philosophically. "Maybe so, maybe so, but I design the dress and Mrs. Harrison pays me for it."

"But Father couldn't afford a Lecouvreur original!"

"No matter." He waved his long fingers. "Beautiful dresses are for beautiful women. When you marry Jack Harrison, I design a dress for you that makes everybody speechless. Yes, speechless."

"We're not talking wedding yet, Monsieur!" I said, laughing, forgetting about the dress and my father, feeling a little garrulous. I had another glass of Jack Daniel's in front of me. "We—oh, hello Todd. You know Pierre Lecouvreur, don't you? He tells me this dress is one of his originals. I'll have to treat it with more respect. I've been known to wear it as a Halloween costume. Oh, but, Monsieur, I wore it on my first dinner date as well. It was with an older man. My grandparents nearly had a fit! He was twenty-four, and I was nineteen. Of course, I ruined the whole effect by wearing a turban and lavender eye shadow. I've become much less gauche in my mature years. Poor Paul didn't know what to make of me that night."

"You are a beautiful woman, and it is the curse of beautiful women that men do not understand them," Lecouvreur said with great chivalry. "Excuse me, please."

"Yes, of course," I said.

When he had gone, Todd sat down next to me. "Overdoes it a bit, doesn't he?"

"You didn't hear half of it. You could learn a few pointers on charm from him."

"I'm sure." Todd stretched out his legs, not interested, preoccupied with something else.

"Is something wrong?" I asked.

"What?" He shook off whatever he was thinking and sat up straight. "No, no, nothing's wrong."

"What were you just thinking about?"

He pretended not to hear me. "Nice night, isn't it? Romantic." He gave me a leering grin.

I lowered my voice. "Did you and Jack see anything out at the lake this afternoon?"

"Dinner was excellent, wasn't it?"

"Todd, damn it!"

"No, Artemis," he said through clenched teeth, his voice steady and uncompromising. "You put me through hell this afternoon. I thought finally I could trust you—I thought you'd show a little sense. Obviously I was wrong, so what the devil makes you think I'm going to tell you another damn thing?"

I stared at him. "You can't do this to me!"

"I can," he said calmly, "and I am."

By now, anger and hurt had brought me to my feet. It was all starting again! I was being shut out, even though I was the one principally concerned. My eyes met Todd's, but there was nothing in his—nothing that indicated that he would change his mind, or was even sorry. Without a word, I turned on my heel and stalked into the conservatory, not stopping until I reached the liquor pantry in the kitchen where I grabbed a half-full bottle of Jack Daniel's and slipped out the back door.

The rose garden was at the end of its season, but still beautiful. It was enclosed by tall hedges with climbing polyantha thick and rampant on the arched wooden gate. Martin Pendleton's masterpiece. Patrice Harrison had helped design it, insisting on the formal geometric pattern and the statue of Apollo in the middle. I had been in it once as a child—with my mother. She was making a point. Any man who could create this, I remember her saying, hardly deserved to be called a dumb gardener by anyone. I had looked around me and agreed. I never called my father a dumb gardener again.

I lay down on my stomach next to a Percy Thrower. It was quite dark, and the ground was cool. A giggle floated from the terrace, then a guffaw. I sighed and pulled up a handful of grass.

Todd was being callous, heartless, and unfair, getting his revenge for my disappearance that afternoon. Going to Bud's had been thoughtless. I knew it. But I wasn't used to having people worry about me.

"I have a right to know what's going on," I muttered. I threw the handful of grass up into the air and watched it fall onto the sleeves of my expensive silk dress. "Oh, damn, Todd. Oh, damn."

Moments later, a woman's flirtatious laugh at the garden gate told me I was no longer alone. I made a move to acknowledge myself but changed my mind when I heard Emily Harrison's voice. "Oh, love, it's such a beautiful night!"

The response was little more than a grunt, but I had heard Todd Hall's entire repertoire of grunts.

They were on the other side of Apollo. My helpful twin, I thought wryly.

"You are having a good time after all, aren't you, Todd?" Emily went on. "I hope all that—that nonsense about Patrice Harrison's jewels and murderers and—well, you know. I hope it hasn't ruined your weekend."

"It hasn't, Emily, not at all."

I thought I heard a wistfulness in his tone, but couldn't be sure. Maybe it was simply the echo of my own wistfulness. When would I walk through a rose garden with Todd Blakesly Hall? I should have acknowledged myself then, if not before, but I didn't. I just closed my eyes and pretended that I was asleep.

"Do you think Artemis is satisfied that this whole thing is over and done with?" Emily asked.

"Of course," Todd answered sharply, any hint of wistfulness gone now that my name had popped up. "Why shouldn't she be?"

"I don't know. I thought—well, she still seems very agitated. Why?"

"That, Emily dearest, is none of your business."

He sounded exactly like his father. It occurred to me Todd's mood was about as delightful as mine.

"You needn't get nasty," she said huffily. "There's no hope for us, is there, Todd? I suppose there never was. I'll be on the terrace."

My eyes had sprung open, but now I closed them again. I wrapped my fingers around the neck of the bottle of Jack Daniel's, laid across my chest for security.

I could sense Todd standing above me. "All right, damn you," he said. "Get up."

I knew I never could pull it off. I opened up one eye, then the other, then grinned. " 'Evening, Mr. Hall."

"What the hell are you doing out here?"

"Escaping."

"Well, I suppose you enjoyed listening to that little scene?"

"So plebeian of me to eavesdrop, I know." I sat up and spit a blade of grass out of my mouth.

Todd took me by the elbow. "Come on, get up. We might as well get back to the house. Oh, for Christ's sake, you've grass all over you. What—" Then he spied the Jack Daniel's, now nowhere near half full. "How much did you drink?"

"Not enough."

"Brush yourself off, for God's sake. Look, your hair's coming down all over the place. How much *did* you drink?"

"I want to know what's going on," I said sulkily.

"Of course, you do. Oh, hell, Artie—"

Then I was in Todd's arms and he was kissing me hungrily, holding me hard against him, a desperation in the way his tongue circled mine, probing, tasting, perhaps even forgetting.

"I'm sorry, darling," he whispered, "so very sorry."

I clutched his upper arms and tried to seize any bits of

anger still floating in my consciousness, but I could grasp nothing but my own desire and love for Todd. "Me, too. I didn't stop to think this afternoon—I was so preoccupied with Bud."

"I understand, darling. But Artie, Artie, I was so damned afraid something had happened to you. I'm not used to dealing with a woman like you . . . feeling the way I do about you."

The Jack Daniel's had dulled my senses, but not so much I wasn't aware of how much I wanted this man. I slipped my arms around his broad shoulders and tried to breathe as he kissed my neck.

"It's all right," I said, gulping for air, "I'm not used to dealing with a man like you, either . . . and God knows I'm not used to feeling about someone the way I feel about you."

"We're a pair, Artie," he said, laughing, and held me at arm's length. "It wouldn't do to be discovered necking in the rose garden, would it?"

I laughed. "Adelia would hardly approve."

"You can handle her abuse, can't you?" he asked seriously.

"Of course! If I can handle you, Todd, my love, I can handle just about anyone."

We left it at that and went back to the house. If anyone suspected what we'd been doing in the rose garden, no one said.

Chapter Twenty

Todd left me on the terrace with a cup of black coffee and went to find Jack. Fifteen minutes passed, and neither Jack nor Todd had showed up. I hadn't drunk any of the coffee, my head was spinning from the bourbon, and people kept staring at me, waiting for a reaction. Well, I gave them one. I stretched out my legs, crossed my arms, and blew at the loose hairs on my forehead. That must have been Emily's cue. She eased down into the chair next to me.

"Well, Artemis," she said, "I'm afraid tonight isn't turning out any better for you than it is for me. I saw Todd a little while ago. He was—er, taking Jack upstairs."

I straightened up. "Why? What's wrong?"

She smiled sympathetically. "Why, nothing's wrong, exactly. Jack's drunk—throwing up drunk, to be precise. He really is ill. I gather the meeting with Richard didn't go too well. Anyway, Todd, good friend that he is"—she wasn't hiding the sarcasm—"is putting poor Jack to bed. I think they're both through for the evening, frankly."

"Oh, wonderful."

"I can introduce you to some of my friends, if you like."

She was being the polite hostess. Emily did not want to have me stuck to her side all evening, and I didn't blame her, but I appreciated the offer and told her so. "I've had a little more than my share to drink as well," I added. "I think I'll look in on Jack—"

"Todd said not to bother."

I frowned. "That far gone?"

"Oh, yes, indeed."

"Well, then, I'll just go on up to bed."

For form's sake, Emily put up an argument. "But, Artemis, it's barely ten o'clock—"

"I have a book to read. Thank you, Emily."

I summoned what dignity I could—it manifested itself in a smile instead of a growl and a saunter instead of a stomp—and headed upstairs.

But I did not go to bed or read a book. Granted, I had an appreciable amount of Tennessee bourbon floating in my system, but I think if I had been as sober as a judge, I'd have done the same thing.

I tore off my dress, threw on some dark clothes, and got Todd's Baretta out from under the mattress. I stuck it in my pants pocket and ignored the bulge.

Jack Harrison was not drunk, and Todd Hall was not putting him to bed.

They both had gone out to find the white lady slipper.

They'd never do it, not in the dark. So I'd just mosey on out there myself, take them to one *Cypripedium candidum,* and get this whole damned mess over with.

And, I hoped, keep them from getting killed.

I met no one on the brick path to the boat house. The night was cool and clear, light enough that I didn't regret not bringing a flashlight. I lifted a lightweight aluminum canoe off the rack and slid it into the water. The lake mirrored the starlit sky; the canoe seemed to slip across it as if on glass. My strokes were deep and strong but noiseless.

I began to sweat but not from the exertion. The night air and my solitude on the lake were sobering me up quickly. I knew what I was doing was idiotic.

But I also knew I could not turn back.

I beached the canoe at Todd Hall's pine grove and hid it—not very well—behind a boulder. I moved cautiously inland, where it was dark among the pines, and found the path that led to my father's old cabin.

I tripped over a fallen branch and landed on my elbows and knees, but I went flat and held my breath, waiting for the rush of men through the woods. I listened. Nothing. I crawled to my feet and proceeded, frantic with fear now. It didn't seem to matter if I moved slowly or fast, if I tiptoed or walked flat-footed—I still made too much noise.

My front teeth dug into my chin as I slunk up behind a tree at the edge of the clearing. The moonlight caught the cabin so that I could see the sagging roof and the collapsing walls that cast a long shadow across the grass and junipers, to the ledge. But that was all I could see. There was not a sign of Todd and Jack. I took a step forward and whispered their names.

A breeze answered.

With a retch I realized I was alone. Alone.

Idiot!

I closed my eyes, but the fear did not dissipate in the darkness. But perhaps I was mistaken. Perhaps Todd and Jack had found the underground spring—or had heard my approach and were stopped as dead and still as I was, listening.

I stayed in the shadow of the trees and walked around the perimeter of the clearing, behind the cabin. When the trees were no longer the thick, old pines but younger oak and poplar and birch, I went back into the woods.

I found the boulder first, a dark, ominous blot on my right. I turned and headed left—west—deeper into the woods, and, I hoped, toward the white lady slipper. And Jack and Todd. The stars and moon overhead pointed out the trees for me, but the ground remained a mystery, a black rug without detail. I stepped on rocks and leaves and undergrowth—probably a *Cypripedium acaule* or two—but I kept walking.

My sandal-clad feet sank. I felt mud ooze between my toes. The underground spring! I forgot about Todd and Jack and my fear and instead got down on my hands and knees and crawled around, feeling for the rotted log.

I found it. My hands groped along the sodden wood till I came to the end of the log. The west end of the log, wasn't that it? Wasn't that where I had found the white lady slipper? I dropped my hands to the wet leaves.

There was no hole, no indication at all that the ground had been disturbed recently. But there was no white lady slipper, either. I was not, however, surprised at that.

I started pushing the rich wet humus away with my hands; then, as the soil became dense, I used a rock and a stick. I couldn't see what I was doing, but I could feel, and nothing that I sifted through my fingers felt like a million dollars worth of jewels.

They simply weren't there.

I sat back on my heels and tried to think. The white lady slipper had been here. Right here. Patrice Harrison wouldn't have buried the jewels directly under the flower, not if she expected someone to locate it. *Cypripedium candidum* is fragile and fussy. She knew that. But I had dug practically a square yard all the way around where the flower had grown—

Of course! On the other side of the log. I leaped over it and began to dig.

I uncovered another square yard. Still nothing. Finally I stood up, wet and muddy, defeated.

I went back to the clearing. I was thinking of ways I could tell Todd Hall not to bother looking for the white lady slipper without telling him why. I wasn't watching where I was going but just put one foot in front of the other instinctively.

So when I passed the cabin I didn't even see the silhouette standing in the door—not until it stepped out into the moonlight and spoke to me.

"Hello, Artemis."

Jeffrey Chapman did not have on one of his three-piece suits. He had on a black turtleneck and black pants, and the gun he pointed at me, I was sure, was black. I pretended not to see it. "Oh, Jeff, good God, you scared me," I said. "What're you doing out here?"

"Where are the jewels, Artemis?"

"What?"

"You found the white lady slipper, didn't you? The jewels. Where are they?" He waved the gun around. "Come on, talk!"

I didn't answer at once. I took a moment to swallow and think of a plan. "Jeff," I said, "listen to me. There are no jewels. There never were. My father didn't kill Patrice Harrison or steal her jewels. The white lady slipper—it was just a memorial for her, Jeff. The jewels aren't there. Go see for yourself."

"Then what are you doing out here?"

"I had to be sure, Jeff. Don't you see? People still think my father was a murderer. Oh, they won't admit it, but that's what they think. That's why you're out here, isn't it? Because you think Patrice Harrison hid her jewels before my father could get them. And you think I'm after the jewels myself. That's why you keep pointing that silly gun at me."

He looked at me measuringly. A shadow blackened one side of his face. "It's not going to work, Artemis," he said, taking a step closer to me. "Nice try, but it just won't work."

"Jeff! Please—" He took another step toward me. "What are you going to do?"

I wished I hadn't asked. He told me. I won't use his words, but the gist of them were that he was going to render my apparent virginity a thing of the past. Then kill me, of course.

I did the only thing I could do. I screamed.

Jeff shoved a hand over my mouth and wrestled me to the ground. I thrashed and kicked, but I might as well have saved the energy. I tried biting his hand, but all I got was a mouthful of dirt and salty-tasting skin that didn't seem to object to teeth marks. I didn't give up on the kicking, thrashing, or biting—only on the hope that they would succeed. Jeff maneuvered himself on top of me.

Then he was off. I gulped in air, tried to sit up, wondering what had happened, what he was going to do next—

There was the smacking sound of bone meeting bone. Jeff reeled to the ground, next to me, swore, and got up again. Only halfway up, actually. A dark figure pounced on him and hit him once more.

That was all there was to the fight. Todd won, hands down, with only two punches.

I was hysterical. "What the hell took you so long?"

He gave me an encouraging smile and a full dose of his Brahmin breeding. "My dear girl, I am not one to jump out in front of a gun. Where is the thing, anyway?" He looked around, then saw it lying next to my feet and picked it up. "Looks as though it could kill a walrus, doesn't it? Well, are you all right?"

I nodded.

"Nora said she saw you creeping out the back door. You're lucky I came down for a pot of coffee when I did."

"You mean Jack—"

"Drunk as a skunk. Didn't Emily tell you?"

"I—oh, dear."

"You didn't believe her," Todd said. "Damn it, Artie, if I couldn't find your goddamn *Cypripedium candidum* in broad daylight, do you think I'd attempt to look for it at night? I suppose you'll blame your bottle of bourbon or the full moon. . . . Did you tell Jeff the truth? You didn't find the jewels?"

"No," I said. "No jewels."

"But he's our fourth man."

"He must be."

"Well, we've another mess to sort out, haven't we? Here, stand next to me, will you, I think he's coming around." Todd helped me up, his arm going around me as he pointed Jeff's gun at him. I remembered—belatedly—the Baretta in my pants pocket and fished it out. "Artie, really, I think this walrus-killer will do. Fairly useless little thing, isn't it? Belongs to Father. Keeps it in the foyer—oops, I see an eye open. There, there, Mr. Chapman, I have no intention of wounding you further. Artie here tells me you were the fourth man in that BMW the other night. Were you?"

Jeff glared at Todd, his hostile look unlike the head gardener I knew. "I don't have to tell you anything."

"Quite true. Did you kill Patrice Harrison?"

"No!" Jeff made a move to sit up, but Todd shoved him back down with his heel. I thought he was enjoying himself. Jeff looked frightened now. "I didn't kill anyone, I tell you!"

"Someone killed her."

"Yeah, but don't ask me who. It—it's all a mistake. Artemis was right. I thought her father killed Patrice and she knew where the jewels were. I followed her out here. I was —I was just trying to scare her."

"I believe you succeeded. Congratulations, you're probably the first. Nevertheless, I did hear you threaten to kill her."

"That's your word against mine."

"Yes," Todd said, "and whose word do you think the police would believe? Perhaps I can forget what I heard if you tell me who killed Patrice Harrison."

"I tell you I don't know!"

Todd couldn't get him to change his story. Finally he had to send me back to Rosewood to call the police.

"Can you make it?" he asked. "You're not too far gone, are you?"

"No, I'm fine. Will you be all right?"

"As long as I remain the one with the gun. We make a great team, Miss Pendleton. Here, off you go."

Chapter Twenty-one

THE party had moved inside to the conservatory. Muddy and wild-eyed, I ran right through the middle of it. I found R. W. drinking alone and had him call the police. Henry got Jack out of bed, and soon Michael Davis and Adelia Harrison joined us in the study. The men decided to go out to the lake and meet the police. I was to stay at the house. Arguing would only waste time, so I sank into a leather chair and told them I would be there when they got back.

Adelia was choking down a martini and crying. "What a horrible, horrible, horrible night," she murmured. "This—this can't be happening! Jeff—Jeffrey Chapman. Oh, dear God, no!"

I was moved by the depth of her shock. "Don't worry, Mrs. Harrison." I winced at my platitude. "I'm sure Jeff will stick to his story that he thought my father had blackmailed Patrice Harrison and was just doing his civic duty in keeping me from finding the jewels, and the police will believe it. Unless of course, they *do* find the jewels—"

"You don't really think he killed Patrice, do you?" she sobbed. "Thirteen years ago he didn't even know Rosewood existed."

That, I thought, was a very good point. "I don't know anything, Mrs. Harrison."

"But—"

"Let's just wait and see what happens, okay?"

White-faced but calmer, she settled back onto the couch. I could see what she was thinking. She was praying the police wouldn't find the jewels. Her party could go on if the head gardener had merely attacked the little gold-digger upstart hussy of a gardener, but it could not go on if the murderer of the former mistress of Rosewood had just been discovered.

God must have been listening to her.

My friend, Sergeant Dick Warner, came back with the menfolk—Todd Hall included—and told us, first of all, that he had come in through the kitchen so he wouldn't worry any of the guests, and, second of all, that Jeffrey Chapman was sticking to his story. Warner added that he happened to believe it.

He asked me some questions. Every one of them gave me the idea that he thought if I had really wanted Jeff to spend some time in jail, I should have made sure I had received some spectacular cuts and bruises. Getting scared half to death didn't seem to count. Imminent rape and murder, he implied, would not impress a jury as much as a five-stitch cut on the forehead.

I informed Warner that Jeff wasn't trying to bruise me, he was trying to kill me. Warner replied that if I didn't learn to behave myself the next time, I might get killed. I told him there damn well better not be a next time, but all that did was prompt him to ask me why I hadn't told him about the fourth man in the first place. I gave him my reasons. He asked me to repeat them, so I did. He still couldn't quite believe me, but R. W. kept us from going over the whole thing again by putting a glass of Scotch in Warner's hand.

Jack told me they hadn't found the jewels. Warner grumbled something I couldn't quite make out, but I know it attested to his doubt that such a thing as a *Cypripedium candidum* existed. He drank his Scotch in two swallows, told the room he'd be in touch, and went back to Saratoga.

Before I could even think of my next question, Jack was telling me to go on up to bed, that I was exhausted. I looked at Todd, but he was blowing on his raw knuckles. Michael Davis was concurring heartily with Jack. Adelia was crying on R. W.'s shoulder.

I gave a general scowl and, leaving a trail of mud behind me, headed upstairs. This was not the ending I had in mind.

It was later—much later—when I sensed that someone was in my room. I lay still as death, my eyes shut, my breathing as normal as I could keep it.

The Venus Shoe

"Artemis." The whisper was hoarse and male, not unfriendly. My bed went down under his weight as he sat next to me. "Artemis, it's Jack."

I opened my eyes and let out a breath of relief. "Jack, for God's sake!"

"I'm sorry if I scared you, Artemis."

"Scared me? Men always sneak into my room in the middle of the night—what is it?"

He was wearing a bathrobe, his face still a little pale. "I . . ." He hesitated. "Artemis, what are you going to do now that Jeff's been caught?"

"I don't know. I hadn't thought about it," I said truthfully. "Go back to my apartment, I guess."

"I thought as much. That's why I sneaked up here. I want to ask you a favor, Artemis. You don't have to agree to it. God knows you've been through enough—"

"It's all right. In fact, it's about time someone asked me a favor."

"Always ready to do battle, aren't you? I've always admired your strength, Artemis. Your parents were strong, independent people as well. That's one reason why I don't understand my father."

I didn't follow his logic and told him so.

"Tonight my father made a strange request. He hasn't been himself all night, Artemis. He demanded I break off my romance with you. He threatened to do whatever he had to, to break us up if I didn't end the relationship myself."

"What? Why didn't you just tell him it was all nonsense, anyway—"

"This isn't like Father," Jack said quickly, his voice still low. "He never interferes like this."

"When's the last time you went out with a gardener?" I asked dryly, trying to dispel the sudden eerie feeling that was sweeping over me. "Look, Jack, we've got our four guys now. Why not just explain the charade and get your father off your back? This thing is finally over—"

"I'm not so sure," he said, half under his breath. He looked at me and smiled as if he realized he'd said too much, but his face was gaunt, and there was something in his eyes that made me shudder. "Maybe my father *is* just being a snob, but I have to know. Artemis, I'd like you to stay on at Rosewood and continue posing as my latest romantic interest."

I stared at Jack and tried to fight the terrible thoughts I was having. But I could sense his horror and knew he was thinking the same thing.

"Artemis, yes or no. It's just a favor. If you don't want to go through with it, I'll understand."

"No, I'll do it, but I know you're not telling me something."

"I'm telling you everything that concerns you," he said, not harshly, but conclusively: He wasn't answering questions. "It'll just be through the weekend."

"Does Todd know?"

"He knows what my father said. I'll explain the rest when I get the chance. I really do appreciate this, Artemis." He paused and added belatedly, "It's no big deal, you know."

"Right. No big deal."

Jack got off the bed. He thanked me again, tried a lighthearted smile that didn't quite make it, and said good night.

"No big deal," I muttered to myself, and rolled over.

Well, that was a lie. It was a very big deal indeed if Jack Harrison suspected his father was a murderer.

I couldn't go back to sleep. R. W. a murderer? I tried to put all the pieces of the puzzle together, but the result was still a mess. There were pieces that didn't fit where they were supposed to fit, pieces that seemed to go to a different puzzle, pieces that were missing altogether. And so I put the jumble away and wished that Todd Hall would sneak up to my room.

It was dark and quiet at Rosewood. The fourth man was caught. All was well. The little bit of intrigue among the gardeners was over. Jack Harrison, of course, was still having his fling with the pretty blond-haired gardener, but that would end quickly. Yes, I thought, Rosewood was just giddy with relief.

But I wasn't and neither was Jack and neither, I suspected, was my Boston publisher.

I slipped out of bed and glanced out the window. Nice night. Quiet. I could go for a walk. I headed out of the room and down the attic stairs, but I knew I had had enough

The Venus Shoe

fresh air for one day. I also knew I never had any intention of going for a walk. I stopped at the door to the room beneath mine. Ever so casually, but without knocking, I turned the knob, pushed open the door, and tiptoed in.

"Todd?"

He didn't scream. He merely sat up in bed and asked calmly, "Haven't you had enough excitement for one night, Artie?"

"Todd, I've just talked to Jack. You know he wants me to continue posing as his girl friend?"

"Umm."

"Do you know why?"

"I've guessed—and I gather you have, too."

"And you're not worried?"

"Not at the moment."

I didn't know if he was leveling with me, but obviously he'd said all he was going to say on the matter. He lifted the covers for me and I slipped in beside him, noticing that Todd Blakesly Hall of Hall and Son Publishers was sleeping in the raw. "I'm all wound up," I added boldly, and lay down on the extra pillow with my head on my folded hands. My right elbow was almost in his armpit. "Want to help me unwind?"

"I ought to flog you for putting me through what you did today," he informed me, but he nestled close to me as he leaned on his crooked elbow and held his head up with one hand. "Perhaps I should take to watching old Errol Flynn movies."

"I don't know," I said. "You looked pretty rough and tough to me. Have you ever thought about giving up publishing and becoming a cowboy? Or maybe joining the CIA?"

"Artie," he said, his voice low and threatening, belied by the big grin on his handsome face.

"Just a thought," I replied lightly, unapologetic.

He moved toward me and wound the tie of my nightgown around his index finger. "Tell me, Artie, exactly where are you tense?"

"Oh," I said, "everywhere."

He laughed and rolled the tie off his finger and ran his hand through my hair. "Here?"

"Not so bad there."

His lips grazed my forehead, then my eyelids, then lingered on my mouth. I lay very still. "Better?" he asked, his mouth not an inch from mine.

"Getting there," I replied, but before I had closed my mouth again he covered it with his.

The kiss was long and deep and awakened every millimeter of my flesh. I tingled all over with the anticipation of his touch, knowing what it would be like, wanting it. I wrapped my arms around his hard, naked body and curled up against him.

"I should be too tired for this," I murmured, running my hands up his sides.

He chuckled. "That'll be the day."

"Why you—" I tried to shove him away, playfully, but he curled those iron arms around the small of my back and held me to him. I laughed. "You've been playing Batman too long."

He rolled me from my side onto my back and, with his knees on either side of my hips, pinned me beneath him. Deftly, he whisked my nightgown over my head. I lay still in the moonlit room.

"I've been lying awake wondering if you'd come." His voice was deep, a half-whisper, intense. "I hoped you would."

I smiled and traced his taut abdomen with my fingertips. "How could I resist?"

He inhaled deeply, with a soft moan.

"It's you, Todd," I whispered, suddenly serious. "I've never wanted anyone like this before. I haven't been able to get you out of my mind since that morning on the island."

"I know how you feel, darling," he breathed. "Believe me!"

He placed his hands lightly on my throat and leisurely, lovingly moved them down my shoulders and arms, across my stomach, and back up, covering my breasts. Very gently, almost languidly, he explored their softness. My nipples stood against his palms like two pearl buttons.

"You feel so good," he rasped.

I dug my fingers into the hard flesh of his hips and felt

The Venus Shoe 209

his restraint, his tension, as he kept his hands so relaxed and incredibly gentle.

His hands again descended across my belly, avoiding the healing scab of my cut, and quickly, expertly darted lower, filling me before I realized what was happening. There was no denying the feverish passion that boiled within me. I knew he could feel the moist heat in his hands.

My body cried out with the need to be joined with his, my mind cried out with love and desire, *I love you, Todd . . . I love you!*

Sensing my urgency, responding to his own, he held me firmly by the hips. I arched instinctively. For an instant he was suspended above me, dark and unmoving, not breathing. And then he drove downward, entering me with a force that left me breathless.

"Artemis, Artemis, if you only knew . . ."

His voice trailed off into a low growl of lust. He pressed his hands into the bed alongside my shoulders and held himself above me. Quick, decisive thrusts plunged into me. In the moonlight I could see the man I loved: tensed, sweat dripping off his temples, passion twisting his features. Our eyes locked. We were still for a moment. Without words I told him I loved him.

Then I moved against him, danced, thrashed with frank abandon, and surrendered my thoughts, my consciousness, to the all-consuming ache in my body. My body rocked with volcanic explosions. Again and again they burst inside of me. Todd's pace never abated. When I was spent and satiated, he continued to thrust deep inside me. I arched against him, wanting him to explode with such force as I had, but suddenly, unexpectedly, the feverish passion boiled up again in my veins.

"Todd!" I cried out, panicked.

"It's all right, darling. It's all right! Just let yourself go with it . . ."

The desire was there, burning inside of me. I had no choice but to go with it. Todd lowered himself onto me, and I grabbed him, wrapped my arms around his back, pressing him deeper into me.

Endless minutes later we lay together, clinging, satisfied and joyous, cooling ourselves in the night air. We might have been lovers alone on an island, at peace.

A long time after that, Todd rolled off me and smiled. "Unwound, sweetheart?" he asked quietly.

I smiled back and touched his cheek. "Unwound."

At dawn I left him sleeping alone in his room and crept back to the attic. I never felt so completely alone in my life.

Chapter Twenty-two

I HAD the rest of the night and a good part of the morning to think of the several dozen questions I should have asked Jack when I had the chance. I went downstairs shortly before noon, intending to pull my alleged lover aside and begin with the first one on my list: Was R. W.'s request the reason you got stinking drunk last night? But Nora told me Jack was waiting for me at the pool. I turned around and went back upstairs to the attic—my body rebelled every step of the way, but I made it—and changed into a bright blue racing swimsuit. I threw a white oxford shirt over it, tied my hair into two pigtails, and told my reflection in the mirror that Jack Harrison was avoiding me.

The sun had settled high and hot in the sky over Rosewood. Most of the younger guests—a noticeable exception was Todd Hall—had already gathered around the Olympic-size pool. I spied Jack lying on a lounge. He smiled up at me, and I smiled down at him. People were watching. I wondered how many of them knew about Jeffrey Chapman.

I took off my shirt, tossed it on Jack's lap, and dived into the water. It was lukewarm and soothing, but, with two dozen onlookers and all the chlorine, not as pleasant as the lake. I surfaced, realized I was the only one swimming, and went back under.

I did several laps before swimming to the edge of the pool to rest. I noticed that Todd had made an appearance, with Emily at his side. I expected Jack to come over to me, but he just lay there on his lounge staring at his toes. Emily came over instead. She sat down next to me and dangled her feet in the water.

"Hello, Artemis," she said, toying with the strap of her black bikini. "You look tired, not that I blame you. Todd"—she nodded to him, mixing two gin and tonics in the shade—"told me about last night. You're lucky he was right there, weren't you? I never thought Jeff—"

"Emily—"

"I know, bad subject, I'm sorry. There is one thing I ought to tell you about Todd, though. He's a Brahmin right down to his toenails. He thinks *I'm* a snob, but—well, you'll find out."

I gave her a bored look. "Emily, what are you talking about?"

"Why, you and Todd, of course," she said irritably. "Oh, for heaven's sake, you're not still playing dumb, are you? It was Todd who rescued you, wasn't it? Jack wasn't there—"

"He was sick."

"He was drunk. Oh, forget it, Artemis. You can have Todd. I don't care. Just quit pretending that this affair with Jack is real. You three cooked it up so you'd have a good excuse to stay at Rosewood and look for your fictitious murderer."

My bored look turned sharp. But I didn't say anything. I didn't know where Emily got her dose of perceptiveness but it was clear to me that she wasn't speaking out of jealousy or compassion or anything I could think of but bitchiness.

"Jack Harrison isn't in love with you."

I sighed, embarrassed. "Emily—"

She pulled her feet out of the water and shook them off daintily, like a well-trained poodle. "And everyone's going to know it in an hour," she said. "Leslie Hall's on her way."

I let her words sink in, and when they still made no sense, I said, "So?"

She stood up and quite literally looked down her nose at me. I said, "So what if Leslie Hall is on her way?"

That shook her. "You mean you don't know?" She gestured vaguely in Jack's direction at the other end of the pool. "He didn't tell you?"

"Tell me what?"

"Why, that son of a bitch!" she exclaimed, hands on

hips. "Artemis, Leslie Hall is engaged to Jack. I assumed you knew. Well, I guess I've stepped into a hornet's nest. You didn't know anything about Leslie?" Emily let her mouth hang open for a second or two, then snapped it shut. "I'll help you castrate the son of a bitch if you want."

I jumped out of the pool and, dripping, stood next to Emily. Her contempt for me didn't even approach her contempt for men who were dishonest, cheats, and liars. I almost agreed to her plans of castration. But instead I said conclusively but unconvincingly, "Oh, yes, Leslie Hall. Of course."

I paid no attention to her "Oh, come on, Artemis" and marched over to Jack Harrison. My shirt was still in his lap. I snatched it up, rousing him from his daze. "Your fiancée is on her way," I said.

That jerked him back to reality—and all the way up to his feet. "What?"

I repeated my news, even less patiently.

"Leslie?" he said dumbly. "Here?"

"Yes." I stood toe-to-toe with him, furious. "Why didn't you tell me?"

"Because I—Artemis, she's not supposed to be coming here. I told her—"

"Why didn't you tell me you had a fiancée before I agreed to this? Now she's coming, and—and that's why your father disapproves of our relationship. Of course he'd rather his son married a damned Boston Brahmin than a gardener! I could—" I didn't finish with that thought. I just summed up all my anger with a solid, "Damn!"

"Artemis—Artemis, where are you going?"

I was two steps away from him already, and I was sure anyone who wanted to could hear my answer, but I said it, anyway. "Back to the house. I'd like to be dressed for my public humiliation—and packed."

"Artemis . . ."

This time I didn't turn around. I was playing this one my way; the Harrisons, the Halls, and all of Rosewood be damned. I was going to be Artemis Pendleton, the impressionable young gardener inexperienced with the two-faced ways of rich older men. If Jack still wanted to maintain that our affair had actually occurred, that was fine with me. But he was the one who was going to be the snake, not me.

That's not the way it turned out, of course.

When I came downstairs, Leslie Hall was standing in the hall outside the study hugging Jack. He had thrown on a pair of pants and didn't even look at me, but that was all right because I wasn't looking at him. I was looking at Howard Perry Hall. He was shaking hands with his son and telling a smiling Adelia Harrison he was charmed to be here.

I swore, not very loudly, but Leslie heard me. She pulled herself out of Jack's arms and glared at me. I knew I was going to have a hard time playing the impressionable gardener, but I said a friendly hello, anyway. She ignored me altogether.

I gathered that at some point Jack and Todd decided that if one of us had to be a snake, it might as well not be either of them.

Adelia quickly offered us the use of the study. She didn't say we were making a spectacle of ourselves, but we were. I went in first and sat next to the fireplace, and the three Halls and Jack Harrison took seats opposite me, like a firing squad. It was all just a game, I told myself. Jack would explain that the affair was just an expedient, and I would take my bows for a job well done and go home.

But it was not all just a game.

Howard Hall began. "This is all rather sordid," he said, wrinkling his lips as though he'd just had a sip of rancid wine. "I came here to meet my daughter's fiancé and to find out what had happened to my son's fiancée. What do I discover? Leslie's fiancé is now seeing Todd's fiancée. That alone is distressing enough, of course, but I also must confront the news that my son's one-time fiancée is not a scholar of Latvian and Bulgarian poets as she led me to believe, but a gardener. My, my."

If Howard Perry Hall was distressed, he didn't show it. I told him so.

"Young lady, if I were you, I should keep my judgments to myself."

Todd threw one leg over the other and grinned at his father. "But she is pretty, isn't she, Father? You said yourself she isn't the usual sort of tramp I bring home."

"No, she is a different sort entirely."

Todd laughed. "Take it easy, Father. I would have warned you about all of this if I had known you were coming. It isn't like you just to drop in on a party—"

"I did not 'drop in,'" Howard Perry pointed out. "I received an invitation a month ago, and I responded in the affirmative. I wanted to meet this fellow's family." He nodded contemptuously to Jack, then turned back to Todd. "If you had not been so busy chasing women you might have been informed of my plans. Now, young man, I would appreciate it very much if you told me what the devil is going on around here."

Todd told his father nearly everything, succinctly and more or less accurately. He didn't mention Bud McCarty's death, and he downplayed the dangerous parts.

He did not explain my alleged affair with Jack, and he did not for a moment suggest that the Latvian-and-Bulgarian-poetic-scholar-turned-gardener was actually in love with a Boston publisher. Which I was. Wholeheartedly. So much so I was willing to trust him and believe that this was all part of a scheme he and Jack had worked out and hadn't had a chance to explain to me. They had—at last—granted me the good sense to know to follow their lead. I sat up straight and paid attention to every word said.

Howard Hall pursed his lips, mollified, when his son had finished speaking. "Well, well."

"All right," Leslie said, definitely not mollified, "so you've been playing cowboys and Indians while I've been sitting around in Boston all week worrying about you idiots. I suppose I can accept that. But"—she gestured to me as she would to a bug—"what about her?"

I went to start my abused-innocent act, but Jack intervened before I could even get the right expression on my face. Obviously I'd picked the wrong role to play. He snuggled up closer to Leslie on the couch. "I'm sorry, sweetheart," he said to her. "The whole week has been so strange—"

"Did she know you were engaged?"

"Yes, of course." I managed to stay seated. He went on, "But, Leslie, look at what she's been through. I couldn't—Leslie how could I hurt her? You understand—"

"No, I don't understand! First you tell me you think her father killed your mother and she's after her jewels. Then she turns up in Boston, and Todd tells me he's in love with her and means to marry her. Then she tells some stupid story to Father about majoring in Latvian and Bulgarian poets, so I figure out this is the infamous Artemis you've been talking about for weeks. I get even more worried and she scares the life out of me, but does anyone tell me what's going on? No. So I sit and wait and worry some more, and now—finally—I come to Rosewood myself only to discover that you're sleeping with the woman you thought was going to steal your mother's jewels. And you expect me to understand! Damn it, Jack Harrison."

"Leslie—"

"If you ask me, you and Todd both have fallen for quite an act. I think little Miss Artemis here knows how to take care of herself."

I was going to say bravo to that and tell Leslie Hall a thing or two, but a flicker of warning in Todd's eyes kept me silent.

Surprisingly enough, Howard Perry Hall came to my defense. "Now, Leslie, it takes two to tango, as the saying goes," he said. "If there is a grain of truth to what Todd says, then I suspect the girl has suffered more this past week than any of us."

"Oh, horse—"

"Leslie!" Howard snapped, adding a sharp look that shut up his daughter. He smiled at me as a lord to a peasant, then turned to his son. "Young man, I can quite believe you forgot my plans to stay in Boston and sent this girl to plague me with her Latvian and Bulgarian poets—never mind that it was for her own good. What I cannot believe is that you forgot Hall and Son. Luckily, I looked after your affairs for you."

Todd grinned at his father. "Thanks, but believe it or not, I had everything under control."

"Under control! Do you realize—"

"Later, Father," Todd said patiently. "We shouldn't keep our hosts waiting. Well, who's going out on whose arm?"

Jack stretched his over Leslie's shoulder and apologized. She smiled up at him and patted his knee. All was forgiven. Todd held the door for them and his father. I assumed I was supposed to slither out on my belly, but I waved Todd on with a jerk of my fingers and stayed where I was. He hesitated but then closed the door behind him.

I took two minutes to collect myself. My head ached with confusion and not enough sleep, but I just sat there in the comfortable leather chair and decided that the next move a woman in my position must take was simple and understandable enough: She would retreat. I was the deposed princess, the gold-digging hussy—

The snake.

Jack and Todd had picked a charming role for me. I stood up and, head high and pigtails dangling down my front, went to face my humiliation.

I was headed to the terrace, but I didn't get four steps beyond the study door. Adelia caught me and asked me to step into her sitting room. I shrugged and followed her in. I had a feeling she was going to help me with my retreat. She closed the door behind her and leaned against it. I noticed how haggard and old she looked. The events of the past week had taken their toll on her as well, but she wasn't blaming it all on fate and bad luck. She was blaming it all on Artemis Pendleton.

"I understand that Leslie Hall is my stepson's fiancée," she said coldly, holding tightly onto the doorknob. "Am I to assume your relationship has been terminated?"

"I guess so," I said.

"You do know, of course, that the only reason I agreed to have you here at Rosewood as a guest was due to your relationship with Jack. I understand that you have had a trying week, Artemis, but so have we all. And we are your employers, not your family and friends. I think you should find comfort with them, not with us. I don't mean to be cruel, Artemis, but I think you would be happier if you just went home."

"I see."

Adelia looked me straight in the eye. "I hope you do see."

"Sure. You're throwing me out."

"Under the circumstances, I don't see what choice I have. This is an awkward situation for all of us."

"Does Jack want me to leave?" I asked.

"Yes, I'm sure—"

"Did he say so?"

"No." She paused long enough for a gleam of satisfaction to settle in her eyes. "Todd Hall did. He suggested that both he and Jack would be more comfortable with you out of Rosewood."

That was a switch, but also confirmation that I was going along with their plans. "Oh."

"You understand."

Yes, I certainly did. I was Artemis the snake, the crawling, little, totally harmless but nonetheless offensive snake. Well, I thought, I can play a snake as well as anyone. I drew myself up as haughtily as I could and started toward the door. What were Jack and Todd up to? Adelia moved aside—even pulled the door open for me—and let me pass.

I was glad I had packed and left my suitcase at the kitchen door, because now all I had to do was pick it up and walk out of Richard Winthrop Harrison's house.

I dumped my suitcase in the trunk. Then, with my usual cursing, kicking, and pleading, I got the Falcon to start.

If those two had manipulated me just to get me out of Rosewood . . . No, I wouldn't believe that, but it *was* possible. R. W. could simply have wanted his son to marry a Hall rather than a Pendleton, and that was all there was to it. Yet Jack and Todd had risked further inciting the wrath of Leslie Hall when all they had to do was tell her the affair was a fake.

So they *did* have a plan, and they knew I was perfectly capable of managing to leave Rosewood in disgrace.

Exit Artie the fire-eater.

My car rolled onto the driveway. They'd probably decided my apartment was safer for me than Rosewood at this point and were protecting me again. Curse their souls.

I coasted around the first of the driveway's notorious curves. I touched my brake pedal as the car approached the second curve. Nothing happened. I swore, blaming it on the many vicissitudes of my Falcon, and hit the brake harder.

Still nothing happened.

I sped around the curve and, approaching the third of the treacherous series, I slammed down the brake pedal.

I made it around the curve, but the driveway was getting steeper now, and I knew it would get steeper still before bending into a hairpin turn around a ravine and then, finally, flattening out into a long, innocuous slope.

My father hadn't made it around the hairpin turn with brakes. How was I going to do it without?

I peeled a white, frozen hand off the steering wheel and placed it on the door latch. Then I abandoned the wheel altogether and threw the Falcon into park.

There was a horrendous noise as the car jerked up, then veered onto a groomed bank lined with stately English oaks. I normally don't catapult myself out of moving vehicles, but mine was headed for a steep, tree-covered hill, so I did. I landed in a heap at the trunk of one of the oaks.

I uncurled my body with a groan. Some yards below me came the thud of my Falcon going dead against a tree. I lay there groaning at the sky until my lungs were again operating adequately and the pain in my chest had subsided enough to convince me that it was not because of broken ribs or myocardial infarction.

I crawled to my feet and stumbled to the edge of the hill. About fifteen yards down, my Falcon was bent around a very diseased, but nonetheless intrepid, elm. I allowed myself a single nostalgic sigh before racing down to it.

Then the shock began to wear off, and I knew that however many times my Falcon had betrayed me before, it hadn't this time.

This time someone else had.

I had left Rosewood ostensibly humiliated, and many would easily believe, ripe for suicide. What better, more symbolic way to end my miserable life than by plunging into the ravine as my parents had?

Someone, I thought grimly, had emptied the brake fluid from my car.

I paused at the open front door and felt a hard ugliness come into my face as the past suddenly boiled up before me.

My father had grabbed my mother and left Rosewood excited, ripe for an accident.

But there hadn't been an accident. Someone had emptied the brake fluid from my parents' car.

Someone had killed Martin and Nellie Pendleton.

I shuddered. Was the murderer on his way down here now to inspect his handiwork?

I found a scrap of paper and a stub of pencil in the glove compartment. I scrawled a note: "On my way to Iowa. Pay the towing charges yourself. Your driveway's a menace. A. P."

Then I crawled back up the hill and headed not for Iowa, but for the duck pond and then the lake.

I had a million dollars' worth of jewels to find.

Chapter Twenty-three

Bud McCarty's boat was tied up at the dock just as if he were up at the boat house muttering over purchase orders and figures. It was at least twenty years old, with three metal bench seats, a fifteen horsepower outboard motor, and all the charm of its owner, which meant it was piled with tool chests, greasy tools, and ragged life jackets. And I, the sole heir to Mr. Bud McCarty, had the key to it on my fishing line.

I like to think it was caution and not cowardice that made me head for my blueberry island. I reasoned that someone—meaning the murderer—could spot Bud's boat if I left it bobbing in the water below my father's cabin and would correctly infer that I hadn't died in the car wreck as planned and was now snooping around. Certainly, I reasoned, I couldn't haul the boat up the steep bank near the pine grove. So I decided that I would be safest dragging the boat onto the small, rocky shore of the island, hiding it among the blueberry bushes and staghorn sumacs, then swimming over to the cabin.

But that was all rationalizing, because, in fact, the shock and anger were wearing off, and I was beginning to realize that what I should do now—what I should have done in the first place—was to go screaming up to the house and call in the Saratoga police and whoever else I could get to take over for me.

I dragged the boat onto the clearing and collapsed under a birch to think of one—just one—acceptable reason for me to dive into the water right now and swim to the cabin.

There wasn't one. Someone had murdered Patrice Harrison, Bud McCarty, Martin Pendleton, and Nellie Pendle-

220

The Venus Shoe

ton, and it wasn't John Vanheyden, Peter Smith, Albert Hayner, or Jeffrey Chapman.

And that same somebody had just tried to murder me.

Todd and Jack knew something like that might happen and had craftily arranged my exit from Rosewood.

But the murderer, as usual, had been one step ahead of them.

The sparrows danced in the brush and trilled. *Madge, Madge, put on your tea kettle* . . . I could feel my father and mother near me, see the tiny wild blueberries between my father's calloused fingers, smell the muffins baking in the oven.

Murdered, murdered, murdered . . .

I wanted vengeance. But I sighed deeply, knowing I could never swim across the lake to the cabin. I was exhausted, angry, terrified. My head was pounding, my chest ached. Like it or not, Artemis Pendleton, I thought, it's back to Rosewood with you.

But then, as I moved to stand up, I saw the spade. It was lying in the grass, just a regular old garden spade. And near it, half-hidden under a tangle of choke cherries, was something long and thin that had been carefully wrapped in a black tarp and tied at two ends with rope. The tarp and rope looked new. But the body—the body, I thought grimly, that they shrouded was not new. It was thirteen years old. It was all that was left of Patrice Harrison. It—

I turned away and vomited in the blueberry bushes.

I don't remember running back to the clearing or dragging the boat into the water or starting the motor or even much about the ride across the lake. I remember the tears, the nearly overwhelming exhaustion, the impatience to get this over with, the clenched fist and the gritted teeth that were somehow supposed to make the boat move faster, somehow make me stronger, somehow make the picture in my mind of the new tarp and rope disappear. . . .

Somehow make it not true that Richard Winthrop Harrison had killed his wife and buried the jewels with her to make it look like robbery.

Had my father guessed? Was there something to the white lady slipper after all? Had Richard Harrison, in a stroke of sentimentality, buried his wife under a *Cypripedium candidum* and my father somehow guessed? Was that why he was killed? And Bud—what had he known, what had he surmised?

But what about me? I had known nothing, guessed nothing! Why kill me? But I knew the answer: Sooner or later, I would have located the site of the lady slipper . . . and the jewels . . . and Patrice, who must have been buried nearby.

I docked sloppily at the boat house. My whole body was shaking now, and I was getting dangerously light-headed. I ran onto the brick walkway that led to the house. I knew I was hyperventilating. I told myself to breathe more slowly, hold the breaths, let them out easily, don't gulp in more air, and keep running. Above all, keep running!

It was nearing cocktail hour. If I ran straight into the crowd of guests on the terrace, R. W. would never be able to hurt me.

But that didn't mean John Vanheyden couldn't, long before I got to the terrace.

I was halfway up the slope, wheezing badly, black spots in front of my eyes, when I ran headlong into him. It was like running into a brick wall, literally. I fell back, but he grabbed me by the elbows and lifted me up to his face so his beard could laugh at me.

"Found the jewels, didn't you, Pendleton?" he said.

I swallowed but didn't say anything.

"Well, well, let's just go and have a look."

He tossed me over his shoulder caveman style, but when I screamed he jerked me back down, cupped a hand over my mouth, and carried me under his arm like a dog. I kicked and thrashed, but he didn't even break stride. He walked back down the slope and all the way to the end of the dock. He dumped me in Bud's boat.

"There," he said. "Get the jewels."

I stared at him. "There aren't any jewels here," I said truthfully.

I got to my feet and tried to step out of the boat, but Vanheyden, standing on the dock, thumped a finger on my chest and knocked me back down. "Find them, Pendleton."

"Look," I said, hoping reason would prevail, "there are no jewels. I can't find them if they don't exist."

"They're here in the boat. Find them."

The Venus Shoe

I was going to tell him that they weren't here in the boat, they were over there on the island tied up in a nice new tarp with Patrice Harrison. But I didn't tell him anything. He had pulled out a gun almost as massive as his hand, so I swallowed my comment. John Vanheyden thought the jewels were in Bud's boat. Fine, I would look for the jewels in Bud's boat.

I sucked in a breath and held it as long as I could, but I was still dizzy. "Where should I start?" I asked.

He waved the gun impatiently, so I started with the toolboxes. I held up every wrench, every chisel, every kind of hammer, nail, saw, nut, and bolt, so Vanheyden could see that none of them was a diamond or a ruby. Then I went through the life jackets. I tore them open with my hands and spread out the stuffing for Vanheyden to inspect. When I had finished, he climbed into the boat himself and felt around for any secret hiding places.

Then he grabbed my neck and pulled me close to him. "All right, Pendleton, what'd you do with them?"

"I didn't do anything with them, damn it!" I yelled. "I don't know where they are. Jeff—"

"Oh, what the hell did Chapman know?" Vanheyden said with a sneer, but he released me and kicked a toolbox into the water. "Damn!"

"John," I said, suddenly aware that he knew little more about what was going on than I did. "John, who tried to kill me?"

He stared at me, baffled.

"My car is out on the driveway, totaled," I explained quietly, hoping he would listen—and talk. "Someone drained the brake fluid out of it. Do you know who? It wasn't you—"

"No way. No way. You shut up, Pendleton, d'you hear?" He took a step toward me, a hand raised. "What'd you do with the jewels?"

I sighed and tried one more time, slowly. "John, I don't know where the jewels are."

"But you got McCarty's keys! You been through his house," he said as though that explained his reasoning. "His truck! Maybe they're in his truck."

"What makes you so sure Bud had them?"

But Vanheyden wasn't listening. I don't know why I

thought he would. He tossed me out of the boat by my elbow, followed me onto the dock, picked me up by a pigtail, and dragged me to the boat house. I tried to scream, but he shut it off the same way he had the first, with a hand over my mouth.

Then, somewhere beyond the sweaty, dirty skin that covered my face, came Todd Hall's voice, low and insistent. "Drop her, Vanheyden."

The arm clamped around me let go, and I went sprawling face first to the ground. I looked up just in time to see Vanheyden leap forward and kick the gun from Todd's hand. Todd stared at his empty hand—he was acutely aware, as I was, that Vanheyden badly outmatched him in size—but recovered in time to dodge the next kick. The dodge sent him into Vanheyden's fist, and the blow to Todd's jaw stunned him. Vanheyden was about to follow it with a chop on the back of Todd's neck, but I, at last, came to life. I leaped upon Vanheyden, but he merely picked me off like a piece of lint and backhanded me to the canoe rack.

But I had given Todd the respite he needed to go for his gun.

It was lying in the grass a few yards to his left, but Vanheyden pounced before Todd could reach it. Todd managed to roll over and land both feet in Vanheyden's stomach, straightening him up for a moment.

I sprang to my feet, looking for Vanheyden's gun. Then I saw it, bulging out of his belt on his right side. There was no telling when he would remember he had it, but I wasn't going to remind him by trying to get it from him. Instead I let them wrestle—Todd was holding his own—and crept alongside them, toward Todd's gun.

When I was a yard from it, I dove, grabbed it, and spun around, pointing it in the direction of the two men. "All right," I said. "That's enough."

Todd heard me and paused, but Vanheyden didn't. He jumped at Todd and put his hands around Todd's neck. I screamed my instructions this time. "Stop it, damn it! I swear to God—"

Vanheyden heard me. He looked at me, then the gun. Then he dropped his hands.

"Todd, there's a gun in his belt. Get—"

The Venus Shoe

There was no need to go on. Todd grabbed Vanheyden's gun before John realized what was happening.

"Always the little fire-eater," Todd said, grinning at me through the blood on his mouth and coming around next to me, in front of Vanheyen. "Are you hurt?"

I shook my head, unable to talk. The heavy gun dangled from my hand. I was willing to let Todd Hall handle this one. Vanheyden was wheezing and moaning that he hadn't killed anybody, wouldn't kill anybody, and, when it came right down to it, hadn't even hurt anybody. Todd pointed to his bloody mouth. "That, Mr. Vanheyden, hurts," he said, then added, without looking at me, "Artie, Father's calling the police. They should be along any minute."

"The—" I blinked at my dizziness. "What?"

"Darling, we've all had quite an afternoon. I'll explain in time, but at the moment I would like to concentrate on Mr. Vanheyden. Are you sure he didn't hurt you? You're shaking all over. Why don't we all sit down? You first, Vanheyden. Artie, next to me."

Vanheyden and I both did as Todd said. Vanheyden had quit complaining, but he sat opposite us with his hands on his feet, sulking. Someone had used his greed—and his dubious intelligence—to keep an eye on me. But why now, when I was supposed to be dead?

"Todd—"

"Artie, I said I'd explain later, and I will," Todd said, brushing the sleeve of his white shirt across his mouth. The shirt was filthy, but the cuffs were still neatly held together with silver cuff links. Always the proper Brahmin. He smiled at me, but I could see the effort hurt.

"Todd, someone tried to kill me."

He sighed. "Yes, I know."

"You do? Damn it, you're the one who had Adelia throw me out—"

"I know that, too," he said dryly. "No doubt you'll have me doing penance for that for years to come. Where the devil is Father with the police?"

"He's not—Todd, you didn't leave him with Richard Harrison, did you? He—"

"Darling, please don't worry. Jack is watching Richard, just in case, but I don't think—"

"But I found Patrice's body! I—"

"*You what?*"

"It's on the island. It's wrapped up in a new tarp and—"

"You needn't describe the thing. Why the hell didn't you come back to the house after you ran your car over the hill?"

"My parents," I said dully. "They were murdered."

Todd didn't respond at once, but I knew he had heard me. At length, he simply said, "I see."

I was going to say that I thought he did, but Vanheyden, turning white, started to protest. "Murdered? Body—what are you two talking about? I don't know anything—"

"Yes, I'm sure," Todd interrupted. "Just shut up, will you? You'll have your chance to explain."

"Look, I don't know anything about any goddamn—"

But he stopped in mid-sentence when Michael Davis and Howard Hall came up beside him. I leaped up and started jabbering about the police, but I stopped dead in my tracks, between Todd and Vanheyden, when I saw that Davis had a gun pointed at Howard Perry Hall's temple.

"Todd," Davis said quietly but with authority, "give the guns to Vanheyden."

I wasn't looking at Todd, but I knew he hesitated. Davis's gun inched closer to Howard's temple. Vanheyden stood up, pushed me to one side, and held out his hand to Todd. Todd placed the guns in it. His went into Vanheyden's belt, and the other remained in his hand, pointed at me.

But then, quite unexpectedly, Vanheyden moved the barrel of the gun away from my solar plexus to Davis's. "You killed Patrice Harrison," Vanheyden said to Davis. "Chapman lied to me, Davis. There aren't any jewels. There—"

"John, give me the guns." Davis's voice was sharp and derisive, but there was no mistaking the undertone of fear. "I don't know what anyone has told you—"

"You killed her and you want me to cover for you. No way, I tell you. No way."

Then three things happened, very quickly, almost simultaneously. Todd knocked my feet out from under me and clamped me to his chest, Vanheyden fired his gun, and

The Venus Shoe

Davis fired his. I couldn't see, but I could hear Vanheyden's scream. We had lost—

Suddenly I was lying flat in the grass. There was another shot, then the cracking of fist meeting jaw. I couldn't look up. I couldn't bear to know what had happened.

"Artemis, it's all right. Good gracious, girl, your hands are nothing but grease." But Howard Perry Hall didn't really care. He pulled me close to him and let me sob and put my greasy hands around his conservative gray suit. "There, there," he said. "The shot missed entirely. Todd is quite all right. He is rather—durable."

"What about Vanheyden? He's not—"

"Writhing but alive," Howard said.

I pulled my head off the older man's chest. Vanheyden indeed was alive, but he had his eyes shut tightly and held onto his thigh with both hands. Blood oozed between his fingers. Todd was standing over an unconscious Davis with a gun—I had lost track of whom it belonged to—pointed at the lawyer's head.

"I saw him sneak out the back door after you left to look for your girl here," Howard was explaining to his son. "I had no other recourse, so I followed him. I suppose I should have armed myself."

Todd caught his breath. "That wasn't a very bright thing to do, Father. You could have been killed."

Howard shrugged, unperturbed.

"Did you call the police?"

"I left that to Henry."

"Good. What about Jack?"

"Still on the terrace appeasing Leslie and, of course, watching his father. I think he will be pleased to know Richard did not murder his own wife. Here, Mr. Vanheyden, take my handkerchief." Howard handed over a white handkerchief, neatly folded and pressed. "I owe you my life, young man. I shall see to it you receive capable legal counsel."

Vanheyden opened his eyes and blinked gratefully.

At that moment, the police arrived.

Chapter Twenty-four

Michael Davis was charged with a variety of crimes, including attempted murder. The police invited him to explain a few things—Patrice Harrison's body, for one—but he declined. Everyone, except me, thought John Vanheyden would be of some help. It turned out, not surprisingly, that his original story to the police was not all that inaccurate. Davis, the respectable Harrison family lawyer, apparently had Jeffrey Chapman talk to some of his hired hands and insinuate that Martin Pendleton had killed Patrice Harrison and that I had come back for her jewels. Vanheyden didn't mind terrorizing me, the daughter of a murderer, and beating me to the jewels; but he did mind being part of a murder.

Jeffrey Chapman declined another invitation for him to talk as well. The police decided he had acted as the mastermind of the four in the BMW, but they thought he knew more than he was letting on.

Peter Smith meanwhile had made his exit from Saratoga and probably, the police guessed, New York State. Albert Hayner they found lying unconscious in a pile of dirt in my apartment.

I asked about that later when we—Leslie, Jack, Todd, and myself—had gathered at our table on the terrace and drunk ourselves calm.

Todd grinned. He was on his fourth Scotch. "Well, Artie, I had to persuade him to tell me what the devil he was doing in your apartment. Your clay pots were the most effective means of persuasion at hand. I got him good with the jade—"

"Watch it, Todd," Jack said, "she's turning pale."

"Maybe if I go home now I can rescue it," I said, thinking out loud. "All it needs—"

"Artie, I'm afraid you'll need a backhoe and a dump truck to clean up the mess we made."

I sat back and frowned. "What the hell was Hayner doing there, anyway? What were *you* doing there?"

"Looking for you, on both accounts," Todd said. "I assumed that when I asked Adelia to toss you out of her royal palace here, you would go home and sulk, drink your tea, tend to your greenery, and try to figure out what was going on. I had no idea Davis had arranged a neat little suicide for you. I raced right past your car, I'm afraid. Hayner told me all about it."

"Did he?" I asked dryly.

"Of course, he swore up and down he had nothing to do with arranging the accident and he wasn't going to finish you off, but he was armed to the teeth with guns and knives and every other sort of weapon."

"But what made you want to get me out of Rosewood?" I asked. "You never suspected Davis."

"No, but we more or less suspected Richard, and Davis is Richard's attorney," Todd said. Jack winced at that, but Todd went on, "But that's not the point, really. The real reason I wanted you out of Rosewood was simply because of your father, Bud, and the white lady slipper. We had our suspicions about Richard, but we didn't want to believe them. So we kept playing around with the theory that Patrice was being blackmailed—"

"And that she told my father that if anything happened to her, he should look for a white lady slipper," I finished.

"Exactly. And when, after seven years, you found it— Bud was with you."

I nodded, remembering. "When Dad went out to the lake the next morning, he and Bud could have dug up the jewels—or Bud could have dug them up the afternoon before and shown them to Father—"

"And Bud could have been holding on to them ever since!" This was from Leslie, who was in a better temper now that I had nearly been killed and she knew that the affair with Jack was just a ruse.

Jack sipped his Scotch. "Obviously, Davis didn't want anyone to find the jewels because the police would have to reopen the case—and you can bet if they thought my mother was buried on the property, there wouldn't be a square inch of Rosewood left untouched. So he had Chapman move my mother's body and call off his goons just so we would all quit nosing around. But Vanheyden, Smith, and Hayner had suspicions of their own." He was quiet for a moment. Then, "I just can't understand what Davis knew about her that was worth a million dollars."

"Or why?" I asked, feeling the terrible waste of it all. "Why would Michael Davis risk everything for a scheme like that? He has plenty of money."

"The naiveté of the poor," Todd said wryly. "Economics 101, Artie: You can satiate needs, but you cannot satiate wants. Besides, thirteen years ago Davis was not as wealthy as he is today. He was just starting out in the Harrison empire. His first coup was getting to handle Patrice's half of the Emerson estate when her parents died. About a year after that, I believe, Patrice disappeared."

"He also killed my parents," I said. "He must have thought Father had found Patrice's body when he actually had found the jewels. But I don't recall Davis being at Rosewood then. He would have had to act quickly—"

"Artie, it's entirely possible Davis didn't drain the brake fluid from your parents' car the way he did from yours," Todd said gently. "Your father could have driven into that ravine on his own."

I shook my head. "He knew that driveway as well as anyone, and with my mother in the car he never would drive like a nut, even if he had just found a million dollars' worth of stinking jewels." I swallowed and began to sip my cup of tea, a concoction of herbs Nora had found for me. It was lukewarm and soothing. "I still can't believe they were murdered. That's going to take some getting used to."

"Did you think they had been murdered?" Jack asked tentatively. "Is that why you came back here?"

"Good God, no. I told you: I came back a little because of the job. I needed to get away from my grandparents for a while and a certain conifer pathologist—and—"

"What?" Todd sat up and grinned. "A conifer pathologist? What the hell is that?"

I smiled. "Another Actaeon in my life."

Jack and Leslie had no idea what I was talking about, but Todd did. He laughed. It occurred to me that I liked his laugh, but I shoved the thought aside. Later, I thought. I would call Holly Dearborn and tell her I was completely and hopelessly in love with my arrogant, rich Boston publisher. She would talk me out of it. I could trust Holly for that much sense. But, of course, she was marrying a beekeeper. . . .

"I'm still not sure what led you to Davis," I said. "Just the fact that he was Patrice's lawyer?"

"That and Emily," Todd replied.

"Emily?"

"She was doing some spying on us for him. He told her he wanted to help us if he could, but we wouldn't cooperate, so if she could just find out what it was we were up to—"

"But why Emily?"

Jack laughed this time. I was glad to see him laugh. So, obviously, was Leslie. "Leave it to Artemis Pendleton not to know," Jack said. "Davis was Emily's husband. The marriage didn't last a year, but she is—or was, by now—a bit under his spell still."

"Rich, handsome, older man, lawyer, father figure—all that." Todd grinned. "I suppose that's why she went for me. At any rate, I kept after her and finally got it out of her."

"You didn't have to throw a jade plant at her, though, did you?" I asked dryly.

"What? Oh—" Then Todd laughed and finished off his Scotch. "Artie, I do believe you're jealous."

"Don't flatter yourself," I said, but couldn't hold back a smile. "Well, I suppose it's over, isn't it? Even if we don't have the jewels. Maybe they're in Bud's truck. I'll look in the morning. Right now I just want to go home and sleep."

"Home?" Jack said.

Leslie touched my elbow. "Artemis, you can't be serious. Adelia understands about—about this afternoon. She's awfully embarrassed."

"Leslie," Todd interrupted, "you can't be subtle with this woman. You must be direct. Artie, you can't go home. For one thing, you don't have a car. For another, you're in no condition to clean up your bed. I believe a mound of rather pathetic plants awaits you, along with a mug or two and several of your tomes."

"You didn't throw Ralph around as well, did you?"

"Of course not. Though the beast *was* on Hayner's side." Todd smiled at me. "Artie, another day among the upper classes won't kill you."

I grinned at him. "I suppose I'll survive."

Chapter Twenty-five

By noon nearly all two hundred and fifty guests had arrived for the party. They immediately started buzzing about Michael Davis but forgot about him as soon as they found a drink and a spot in the sun. Over and over again R. W. was congratulated for his dignity, fortitude, and good taste in having the annual fete despite the arrest of his lawyer, the discovery of his first wife's body, and the attempted murder of his gardener. They didn't know that his own son had suspected him of murder, or they probably would have applauded him for weathering that as well.

The clock on my nightstand read ten-fifteen when I awoke. I could already hear the chatter of people three stories below, but my body informed me that it didn't intend to hurry. It took me fifteen minutes to get out of bed and thirty to soak in a scalding hot tub so I could stand up straight. I thought about putting my hair in braids or pinning it up, but I could hardly raise my arms, so I left it hanging. Holly Dearborn said it drove men wild that way, but I presumed I would need a suitable face to go with it. Mine was not at all suitable this morning. A bruise, not as spectacular as Holly's nor, I was sure, as the ones Todd would have, had turned up above my right eye. I had no idea when or how I had gotten it. Leaping out of my car? I didn't know, and I didn't care. It was there, purple and two shades of yellow. I thought it went well with the dark circles under my eyes and the all-around gaunt look. I experimented with a smile, but it just made me look even more gaunt.

So much for the dazzling Artemis Pendleton.

I put on a pair of jeans and a red cotton shirt and went

downstairs, groaning every step of the way. Nora had heard me coming and had a pot of tea waiting. I started to lower myself to a chair, but she shooed me out to the terrace where she said I belonged.

There were only a hundred or so people scattered about the lawn and lined up at the luncheon buffet. The other hundred and fifty, I assumed, were at the pool, tennis courts, stables, duck pond, or, if they were the hearty sort or simply hadn't heard, the lake.

I didn't know anyone personally except Todd, Leslie, and Jack, and they were gathered at their table, so I sat down.

"Well, it still stands," Leslie said to her brother after a perfunctory wave to me, "that Father and I have been running your company most of the summer."

Todd wrinkled his face at her, but I could see that required as much effort as picking her up and throwing her across the terrace. There was a cut on one side of his forehead and a bruised bump on the other, a swelling along his jawline, a puffiness at the corner of his mouth and a droop to his eyelids. "You and Father just think you have been running the company," Todd said.

"Ha!"

"Oh, I suppose you have taken care of a few boring details, but—"

"Sure, Todd, like whether or not we can pay the damn secretaries."

But she couldn't get to him. Todd grinned at her. "As I said, details. I provide the ingenious ideas on how to keep the company solvent, and you carry them out."

"Ingenious ideas, my ass. I still say we should sell to the Harrisons—"

That almost got Todd. "Never," he said in that way that meant he would entertain no arguments. "That's why Father made me president, you little traitor. Where is he, anyway? I thought he never slept past eight—"

"How would you know?" Leslie cut in. "In case you haven't noticed, Todd, Father is getting old."

"Father? He'll outlive us all. But he did have a hellish day yesterday. I think I'll look in on him."

"He does care," Leslie said, looking pleased.

I grabbed my empty pot of tea and trailed after Todd. He

smiled and slipped his arm around my shoulders, hugging me close.

"Can't stand to be away from me for a minute, can you, Artie?"

I couldn't stop smiling, no matter how much my face hurt. "Just refilling my pot of tea, Mr. Hall."

"Make one for Father, too, won't you, darling?" He kissed me on the top of the head, and we parted at the front stairs.

I went into the kitchen and put on a kettle to boil, despite Nora's glare. I grinned at her, and she came over and pulled me against her ample bosom. Tears glistened in her eyes, and I remembered Bud and my parents. . . . Upstairs in Bud's iron box were pictures that could help us—and maybe even Jack—smile at our memories. Dear, good Bud.

I kissed Nora on the cheek. "Watch my water for a minute, will you?" I took the back stairs, and suddenly Adelia Harrison was in front of me. We were on the landing at the third floor, she on her way down from the attic. I stared at her and uttered a surprised syllable.

She had Bud McCarty's iron box in one hand and a twenty-five caliber Baretta, silver and ugly, in the other. I thought I was getting good at recognizing guns. Too good.

She lifted her little gun toward me. "Artemis," she said, "you're always in the wrong place at the wrong time."

"I guess I am," I answered stupidly. "Look—"

"I think we should go back upstairs. Artemis, you really ought to do as I say. I will shoot you, you know."

I just looked at her and twisted my fingers together. "What's the difference if you shoot me here or upstairs?"

"I don't necessarily intend to shoot you. We—we might be able to work out a deal." She nodded to the iron box. "There's a million dollars' worth of jewels in there, Artemis. I should think they would come in very handy."

"Spare me, Adelia," I said, not bothering to hide my disgust. "You killed my parents. Do you think I'd make a deal with you?"

Her face went red with anger. There was nothing artificial and unreal about Adelia Harrison now. She waved the gun at me. "Let's go upstairs. Now, Artemis, or I will shoot you. Don't think I'm bluffing. I have nothing to lose, nothing at all."

She was right about that. Without another word, I walked past her and led the way upstairs. Had the woman's greed and demand for money and all it could buy led her to this?

Somehow, I was not afraid.

We went into my room where Adelia told me to sit on the bed with my hands palms down in my lap and my feet flat on the floor. I obeyed. She stood about a yard in front of me, her back to the door, her gun pointed at my head. I doubted she was a very good shot, but I wasn't ready to test her skill.

"I could make your death look like a suicide, I suppose," she said in her chirpy, patrician voice. We might have been discussing new fall fashions. "There must be a paper and pencil around here somewhere. . . ."

She glanced around the room, and I knew this was my chance to rush her. The gun hadn't moved a single degree, but still I put weight on my feet and started slowly to lift myself off the bed.

Then Howard Hall was in the doorway. I sat back down and bowed my head as though I were looking at my knees, but in reality I was watching every move he made as he cautiously, quietly, stepped into the room.

"Artemis," Adelia said impatiently, "I need a paper and pencil. Where—"

"In my suitcase," I said, gesturing to the closet on the wall at the foot of the bed.

"Get it."

Howard was perhaps three steps behind Adelia. I rose slowly, watching the gun as it rose with me, still pointed at my head. There was a slight tremble to Adelia's hand. I licked my lips. "No one will believe I committed suicide," I said. "You'll be caught, Adelia. Right now we can't prove you've killed anyone. If you just let me go—"

"Get the paper and pencil, Artemis."

She was beginning to panic. I didn't know if that was to Howard's and my advantage or not. I shrugged and turned toward the closet, away from Adelia and the white-haired man behind her.

Then I spun around and, I hoped without any warning at all, dove at Adelia's ankles. I missed and landed hard on the floor. The gun went off. I expected a sudden, searing pain—or death—but what I got was Adelia Harrison's petite, squirming body on top of mine. I tried to roll over under her and push her off, but she seemed impossibly heavy. Then I realized that Howard Perry was on top of us both, reaching for the gun that was still in Adelia's outstretched hand.

"Give me the gun, woman," Howard Hall said, the first to do something besides grunt. "You cannot possibly hope to win."

I wasn't so sure I agreed with him. All she needed was one shot—

But she wasn't going to get it, not with Todd Hall and Jack Harrison descending upon her. Todd yanked his father off Adelia, grabbed her wrist so hard that she screamed and dropped the gun on my head, and, finally, tossed her to Jack. Then he picked me up by my shoulders and told me I was an idiot and so was his father.

"You're supposed to be making a pot of tea, damn it!" he went on before turning to his father. "And you, I told you to stay the hell out of this."

Howard Perry shrugged, completely unruffled by his son or the fact that he had just nearly been killed. "Not all of us do everything you say, young man," he said, and pointed to the iron box that Adelia had set on my nightstand. "I believe you will find your so-called mythical jewels in there."

Todd stared at his father. "What?"

"This morning when I arose—"

"At eight?"

Howard frowned. "Ten. Yesterday was not one of my finer days. Will you please not interrupt when I am speaking? When I arose, I decided to breakfast in my room. When I finally emerged, I saw a rather unusual sight— Mrs. Harrison, rather stealthily creeping up the back staircase with a gun in her hand."

"You followed me!" Adelia cried from Jack's obviously harsh grip. "Damn it, you followed me."

"Yes, of course, I did. That is, I managed to linger in the hallway by pretending to want something from that young housemaid who was cleaning the third-floor rooms." He paused, proud of himself, but Todd just scowled at him. "I was talking to the young lady when Adelia came down from the fourth floor—presumably Artemis' room—carrying this iron box. I followed her a short way, but, of course, she ran headlong into Artemis."

Todd shot me a fierce look.

"Yes," Howard said, "what would have been a simple project of following Adelia until a propitious moment to confront her with her folly became rather an unnerving project of rescue."

Todd looked from his father, to me, and back to his father again. "You're lucky she didn't kill you both," he said. "Artie, you carry the iron box. Father, you aren't going to have a heart attack or anything, are you?"

Howard looked insulted. "Young man, every morning in Maine I chop a load of wood in preparation for winter. I am not going to die from wrestling with a woman."

With that, Howard led the way downstairs, with me after him carrying the iron box, and Todd and Jack with Adelia.

Chapter Twenty-six

I THOUGHT the jewels were the least interesting item in Bud McCarty's iron box. They were scattered on top of the other contents, but apparently Adelia had found them tucked in among the letters I had considered none of my business to read. Laid out on the coffee table in the study, the jewels didn't look like all that much to me—certainly not worth four lives. There was a heavy gold choker, an emerald necklace, three diamond rings set among some other precious stones—rubies and whatnot—and a pair of diamond earrings.

But it was the letters, not the jewels, that told the real story of Patrice Harrison.

Todd said I should be allowed to read them all first, privately, but I said no and made him read them to us aloud, even the one addressed to me. We were gathered in the study—Todd, Jack, Leslie, R. W., Emily, Marie, Howard and myself. Adelia had been taken away by the police in an unmarked car. The guests were laughing and hollering and having a great time outside, completely oblivious to the grim story that was unfolding inside.

It took a while, but eventually we were able to separate reality from fiction, assumption from truth, things we wanted to believe from things that were.

The story began shortly before World War II when Patrice Emerson, a pretty debutante well-schooled in vulnerability, joined her aunt on a summer tour of the British Isles. They toured England first, uneventfully, then went on to Edinburgh, where Patrice fell in love with the romantic sublimity of Scotland.

One evening, the aunt left her niece to her own devices

while she wooed an archaeology professor at the University of Edinburgh. Instead of staying in her hotel room and attending a concert as her aunt expected, Patrice went out on her own to experience Edinburgh nightlife. She passed a bar bursting with Scottish brogue and laughter, and, intrigued, she went in. There she met a sailor, who saw that the young American girl was out of place. He took her aside, fetched her some hot tea, and made polite conversation. He was in his mid-twenties, handsome in a thoroughly Scottish way, unmarried, charming. Patrice fell in love instantly.

And so did Bud McCarty.

The affair lasted two weeks. It ended when the aunt decided she had played her final trump with the archaeology professor and made plans to go to Wales. Patrice begged her lover to do something—anything—so that they could be together. He refused. She was too young, too wealthy, too American. She must go back home and marry a man her social and intellectual equal. And forget him.

Patrice had no choice. After Wales, it was Ireland. By the time she and her aunt had seen the last of Dublin, Patrice knew she was pregnant. She went back to Long Island in disgrace. Her parents sent her to an aunt who lived in Northampton, Massachusetts, and let people think Patrice was at Smith College. The following spring, Patrice delivered a baby girl. A childless couple who ran a dairy farm—friends of the aunt—arranged to adopt the baby. Patrice enrolled at Vassar the following autumn . . . and tried to forget.

Patrice's Scottish lover meanwhile fought for Great Britain in World War II and, when it was over, set sail for America. He had no intention of finding his love of eight summers ago.

But he did, by accident, after ten years in his new country. He had found work in Newport, Rhode Island, building and repairing boats of all kinds, including a yacht owned by Richard Winthrop Harrison of Saratoga Springs and New York City. The Scotsman did work for R. W. on and off for a year before he ever met Harrison's wife, and even then he did not recognize her. Eighteen years had changed them both. But she knew him at once. She almost left without telling him, but the pain and humiliation of having

The Venus Shoe

given birth to an illegitimate child and then putting her up for adoption were too much for her.

She told Bud he had a daughter. He was furious. Why hadn't she told him? He would have married her. He would have gone to America at once. He would have given the child a name, a father. How could she give away her own baby?

He demanded to see the child. Patrice had to arrange it, he said, or he would tell her husband everything. Patrice argued. The child was happy. She had parents who loved her, a home, a good life that he would ruin. But then Bud explained that all he wanted to do was see the child, his daughter. He would never tell her who he was, never. He only wanted to see her.

Patrice understood. Bud McCarty was a lonely man. He lived alone, he worked alone, he had no family and very few friends. Seeing his daughter meant everything to him.

She told him to be at Rosewood in a month. She would have Nellie Bradley, their daughter, there for him to see.

Patrice went to her gardener and close friend Martin Pendleton for help. She trusted him to go to the Bradleys and persuade them to bring Nellie to a party given on behalf of her old aunt. He was candid with them. He told them about Bud and his threat—and added that if they didn't let him see the child this once, he could easily ruin her life, not to mention Patrice's.

Reluctantly, the Bradleys agreed.

But then two things happened that no one expected. First, Martin and Nellie fell in love. Second, Richard Harrison offered Bud a job at Rosewood. At first Bud refused, but when he saw that his daughter intended to marry the head gardener, he changed his mind. He had his family.

Yet, through it all, Nellie Bradley Pendleton never knew that her biological parents were her employer's wife and her husband's best friend.

Todd folded the last letter—the one to me—and sighed, as we all did, and rubbed his chin. "Well," he said, "I guess now we know why Patrice was being blackmailed."

I sat cross-legged on the floor next to the coffee table. "She was my grandmother."

Todd smiled. "Bud was your grandfather."

"And I," Jack said, changing positions on the couch, "am your uncle."

"Noble blood does run through her veins after all. Now, Artie, don't go pale and start to cry. We all know you're a Pendleton before all else."

I swallowed a sob and stiffened my lower lip. Then I turned to R. W., who was sitting next to Emily and holding her hand tightly. She seemed strangely untouched by anything we said. Occasionally she would reach over and pat Marie on the back as she cried, freely and quietly, on the floor, but that was the only sign she gave that she was even aware of what was going on. Yet I knew she was, and I knew she would be all right. I had said it before: Emily Harrison was a survivor.

"Mr. Harrison," I said, "you knew I—about Bud and Patrice."

"I didn't know about Bud," he replied. His voice was hoarse and hollow, but steady. "But I knew Patrice had to be in your family tree somewhere when I saw you in that dress with your hair done up the way Patrice did at your age. I—Artemis, you look so much like her."

"I see," I said. "That's why you asked Jack and me to break off our romance."

"Your romance that never was." R. W. glanced at his son. "I wish you had told me about that, Jack."

"Father, at that point I was wrestling with the whole idea that you had killed Mother. I didn't honestly believe it, I'm sorry."

Richard Winthrop Harrison grunted, the apology accepted, the matter forgotten.

"Well," Todd said, sitting forward with his hands folded on his knees, "what I would like to know is how the hell Michael Davis and Adelia found out about all this."

"It's very simple, really," R. W. said, taking on a businesslike attitude, which I supposed would help carry him through the rest of this ordeal. "When Michael was working on Patrice's inheritance, she asked him to set aside a trust fund of five hundred thousand dollars of her own money for Artemis."

Todd whistled. "Welcome to the upper classes, Artie."

I thought he wasn't taking this very seriously and told him so.

The Venus Shoe 243

"Todd rarely takes money seriously," his father answered dryly. "Please, Mr. Harrison, excuse my son's rudeness."

R. W. smiled weakly, but at least it was a start. "The trust fund was set up as Patrice requested, Artemis. The money is yours."

"That's what set Davis off, isn't it? Oh, God. First it's me and the white lady slipper, now it's me and a damn trust fund."

Suddenly, Emily Harrison cleared her throat. "Don't blame yourself, Artemis. You didn't kill anyone. I wish you had—God, I wish you had—but you didn't. My mother did, and my ex-husband. I wish I could hate them for it, but I can't. And what good would it do, anyway?" She pulled her hand out of her stepfather's and said to him, "Should I tell them, or will you?"

"Emily—"

"It's all right, Richard," she said, then turned to us. "My mother and Michael were having an affair thirteen years ago. Michael told me about it when he was drunk one night. I divorced him immediately. I assume they cooked up this idea to blackmail Patrice together."

Richard nodded. "She told me most of it on the way to the police station. I'm not sure why she did. I think Adelia's a very sick woman. She has been for a long time. I was too selfish and busy with my own work—and suffering—ever to pay too much attention to her problems. I wish I had. Bud certainly would be alive today, perhaps even Martin and Nellie—"

"Father, please," Jack pleaded. "All the guilt in the world isn't going to change a thing."

"You're right, of course. I know that. Well, Emily is telling the truth. Michael and Adelia had an affair. I knew about it but thought it was over by the time we married. Of course, I couldn't imagine that they were the ones who had murdered my wife." He exhaled a long breath, rubbed his hands over his mouth and then up through his hair, and inhaled again. Then he continued, "Michael had asked Patrice why she wanted to set up a trust fund for the eleven-year-old daughter of two employees at Rosewood. She refused to tell him. I gather he told Adelia all about this, because she claims she got him to look into the Pendletons' background. It wasn't too difficult to find out that Nellie had been adopted and Patrice's year at Smith—the same year Nellie was born—was a farce. Michael brought the information back to Adelia, and what started out as a joke quickly became a plan."

"But I don't understand!" I interrupted. "Neither of them needed any money. Why risk their lives—everything—when they were already rich? And, no, Todd, I don't buy your Economics 101 explanation. There has to be more."

"Not much more, I'm afraid," Emily said. "My father died bankrupt. Mother didn't expect that at all. You know her. You know she can't live without money. She has to have her dinners and dresses and trips abroad and weeks in health spas. Well, when Father died she had nothing. Her affair with Michael was just to fill the time between rich husbands. Then this business about Mrs. Pendleton came up, and she saw a way to get rich fast and still have her handsome man. I know Michael is plenty rich for you, Artemis, but even now he would have a hard time supporting a woman like my mother, and then—well, he was just starting out, really. He didn't even own a house."

Richard took Emily's hand again, but he looked at me. "Michael and Adelia contacted Patrice—anonymously, of course—demanding she pay them with her most expensive jewels, just this one time, in return for their silence," R. W. said. "She was to have made the whole thing look like robbery. All she had to do was plead a headache at the last minute and stay home from a dinner party. Then she would bring the jewels to the cabin on the lake—her choice—and leave them there for the blackmailers to find."

"Michael and Adelia couldn't risk being seen near the main grounds," Jack said.

"That's right," R. W. said. "Well, apparently she did everything as planned, except instead of leaving the real jewels in the cabin, she left copies; and instead of going back to the house, she stayed in the woods."

"Like grandmother, like granddaughter," Jack muttered. "Poor Mom. Davis recognized the jewels as the copies, didn't he?"

"Yes. He and Adelia probably would have just left well enough alone and given up, but I gather Patrice came bounding out of the woods like a wild banshee to find out who had the audacity to try to blackmail her."

"So they killed her," Jack said.

"Michael did. He shot her before she could tell him what she had done with the real jewels."

I blew the hair up off my forehead. "The *Cypripedium candidum.*"

"What?"

"The white lady slipper, Father," Jack explained.

"Oh, yes. I never did understand what Martin was up to. The morning after Patrice disappeared, he came to me and told me that the day before, when he and Patrice were working in the rose garden, she had mentioned that her favorite flower was the white lady slipper and asked him always to remember that in case anything ever happened to her. He thought it was a little strange, but I told him—damn it, I told him it probably didn't mean a thing."

"It was her clue to him," I said. "Of course, he knew that Mother was Patrice's daughter. He must have guessed that she had been blackmailed."

"So he began his all-out search for a white lady slipper," R. W. said. He hesitated, grinding his teeth together in thought. Then he went on, "Michael and Adelia didn't know anything about it, of course. They knew the real jewels were missing, but they had no idea where to begin to look. And, besides, Patrice's death had torn their relationship apart. I was free then, so Adelia decided to hook me and reel me in. She paid no attention whatsoever to Martin's mutterings about white lady slippers, until the morning he came back from the lake so agitated. She thought he had found Patrice's body and was going to the police, so she drained the brake fluid out of his car and hoped he would die in a wreck."

"But he had found the jewels," I said quietly. I was just listening, trying to sort out everything, hoping I would finally understand why and how my parents and my grandparents had been murdered. "He gave them to Bud—or Bud came back for them, but, anyway, they ended up in his iron box. Why the hell didn't he turn them in?"

"He didn't want to drag you through the mud," Jack suggested. "Can you imagine what it would have done to you, Artemis, to find out that your parents had been murdered? That Patrice was your grandmother and that she had been murdered? That he was your grandfather? He was thinking of you, Artemis."

"Oh, come on—"

"Wait, Artie," Todd interrupted. He had been digging in the iron box again, and now he held up a scrap of paper. "It says so right here. I didn't read this before, but it looks like a recent postscript to Bud's letter to you. Shall I read it aloud or would you prefer to read it yourself—"

"Go on, go on. Read it."

"All right. It says he has the 'goddamn' jewels and plans to find out who blackmailed Patrice. 'Should have done it years ago, Missy, but you went through enough. No need giving you a harder time than you deserved. But now you've gone and stuck your nose where it doesn't belong. Think your own father did a murder! Well, you know now.'" Todd folded the letter back up and put it in the iron box. "This letter to you must have been a diary of sorts for him. I doubt he ever would have mailed it."

"Oh, Todd, I don't care. Who killed him? Davis?"

"No," R. W. said heavily. "Jeffrey Chapman. Adelia hired him. He's been her lover for—well, for years. She got him to look for the white lady slipper once she realized that Martin hadn't found Patrice's body. She wasn't sure, but she thought he must have found the real jewels. When the Dobermans were found out at the cabin, Adelia got Jeff to move the body and keep an eye on you, Artemis. And keep looking for the white lady slipper, of course. Adelia thought you had returned to Rosewood to claim the jewels. Then Jeff caught Bud prowling around the cabin. He had a heart attack, and Jeff just threw him in the water. He drowned. Or so Adelia tells me. By the time she got to Jeffrey's role in this ordeal, she was nearly raving. I—I'm sorry. All of you, I am very deeply sorry. None of this need never to have happened, but it has."

I could barely make out R. W.'s last words. He had talked enough. We all knew it, but it was Howard Perry Hall who announced it to him. Then, from his position next to the fireplace, Howard addressed Jack. "Young man," he said, "you will take over outside for your father. Leslie, you will assist. If anyone asks for Adelia or Richard, say they are upset over Michael Davis's arrest for attempted murder. That presents everyone with enough of a scandal while averting the major issue. Be firm: Say you will not discuss any details."

Jack nodded, his exhaustion obvious. Leslie smiled at him and patted his knee as she rose. He followed her out of the study.

"Emily," Howard went on, "I think you should see to your sister."

Emily didn't even look at Howard Perry Hall but calmly put her arms around Marie, still crying in that silent, painful way, and led her out. Emily told us all that they would be fine. I, for one, believed her.

Then Howard rose, went over to the liquor cupboard, and poured three glasses of Scotch. He handed one to Todd, put one in R. W.'s hand, and took the third for himself.

"Your Patrice must have been quite a woman," he said. "Quite a woman. We'll drink to her just as soon—Artemis, where do you think you are going?"

I was already to the door, but I stopped and turned to Howard Perry Hall. "Home to call Holly Dearborn."

"Yes, of course, your friend from Back Bay. I know her father. You should call her, of course, but—"

"Good," I said, interrupting. "Then I'll be going."

"And how do you expect to get there?" he asked, irritated. "I will not have a future daughter-in-law of mine thumbing on the streets like some damn—"

Todd nearly choked on his Scotch. "Father!"

Howard Perry Hall turned to his son. "Young man, I have known you to do a number of things of which I do not approve, but never to lie to your family. Did you or did you not—"

"Father, will you please let me handle this? Artie, into the hall, please."

Since I was practically there, anyway, and the prospect of discussing my relationship with Todd Blakesly Hall with his father was not at all appealing, I went into the hall. I caught Todd's grin at his father but, luckily for him, it disappeared when he closed the study door and looked at me.

"My father is an interfering, bossy old man," he said.

"Yes, I know," I said dryly. "Like father, like son."

"Artie—"

I looked at him seriously. "Wait, Todd, please. *Do* you lie to your family?"

"Never," he said, grinning, the dimple there.

"Then that message you left Leslie—"

"True. Every word of it. Don't look so goggle-eyed at me, Artemis. I've been in love with you for weeks, and now that I know Jack Harrison's your blasted uncle and we've got the crooks locked up, so to speak, there'll be no stopping me! I don't care if I do have money—"

"That never would have stopped me."

He looked at me, those slate eyes hard flints. "What do you mean?" he asked sharply.

"I mean I love you."

We were both serious now. I took a long, bold step and landed against his tall, lean body. Again his eyes reminded me of the ocean on a cloudy November day.

"My beautiful goddess," he murmured, folding his arms around me and holding me close. He breathed into my hair. "I love you, Artie. I love you, I love you, I love you."

I laughed, tears stinging my eyes, and tilted my chin up to meet his kiss. Our lips touched lightly, promising so much more than we could give there in the hall with our bodies still hurting and our minds still reeling from all that had happened.

"My parents would be proud," I said softly, "and Bud . . . and Patrice. Oh, Todd, I'm so happy! I love you so very, very much."

His eyes danced, telling me he shared my happiness . . . and welcomed my love. "Then would you care to explain to me why the hell you were leaving?"

"Oh—" It seemed so silly now. I smiled. "Your father poured only three glasses of Scotch."

"Only three—" Todd stopped and laughed. "Artie, that's because he knows all you'll drink is Jack Daniel's. Come on, I bet he has a glass waiting for you."

He did. No water, no ice.

VELVET GLOVE

An exciting series of contemporary novels of love with a dangerous stranger.

Starting in July

THE VENUS SHOE Carla Neggers 87999-9/$2.25
Working on an exclusive estate, Artemis Pendleton becomes embroiled in a thirteen-year-old murder, a million dollar jewel heist, and with a mysterious Boston publisher who ultimately claims her heart.

CAPTURED IMAGES Laurel Winslow 87700-7/$2.25
Successful photographer Carolyn Daniels moves to a quiet New England town to complete a new book of her work, but her peace is interrupted by mysterious threats and a handsome stranger who moves in next door.

LOVE'S SUSPECT Betty Henrichs 88013-X/$2.25
A secret long buried rises to threaten Whitney Wakefield who longs to put the past behind her. Only the man she loves has the power to save—or destroy her.

DANGEROUS ENCHANTMENT Jean Hager 88252-3/$2.25
When Rachel Drake moves to a small town in Florida, she falls in love with the town's most handsome bachelor. Then she discovers he'd been suspected of murder, and suddenly she's running scared when another body turns up on the beach.

THE WILDFIRE TRACE Cathy Gillen Thacker 88620-4/$2.25
Dr. Maggie Connelly and attorney Jeff Rawlins fall in love while involved in a struggle to help a ten-year-old boy regain his memory and discover the truth about his mother's death.

IN THE DEAD OF THE NIGHT Rachel Scott 88278-7/$2.25
When attorney Julia Leighton is assigned to investigate the alleged illegal importing of cattle from Mexico by a local rancher, the last thing she expects is to fall in love with him.

AVON PAPERBACKS

Buy these books at your local bookstore or use this coupon for ordering:

Avon Books, Dept BP, Box 767, Rte 2, Dresden, TN 38225
Please send me the book(s) I have checked above. I am enclosing $_____
(please add $1.00 to cover postage and handling for each book ordered to a maximum of three dollars). *Send check or money order*—no cash or C.O.D.'s please. Prices and numbers are subject to change without notice. Please allow six to eight weeks for delivery.

Name _____
Address _____
City _____ State/Zip _____

Velvet Glove 5-84